The Traitor & The Cursed

BY

Koel Alexander

Raven & Fire Series

Raven & Fire Series

Copyright 2024 Koel Alexander.

All rights reserved. This book or any portion thereof may not be reproduced or used in any manner whatsoever without the express written permission of the publisher except for the use of brief quotations in a book review.

ISBN 979-8-35099-199-4
ISBN eBook 979-8-35099-200-7

Printed by Bookbaby,

    7905 N. Crescent Blvd. Pennsauken, NJ 08110

Koel Alexander © 2024
Raven & Fire Series

DEDICATED TO

To my wife Carolyn who remains my biggest fan of me and the series.

To my book club for sticking with me even though life has changed for us all. We have less time to discuss our growing story, but the input is invaluable

I dedicate this to my beautiful son Andre who has changed my life completely since the first day I laid eyes on him. I strive to be a great role model for you and to show you that nothing is out of your reach. I love you son.

Finally, I dedicate this to the fans and to anyone else that has read or purchased any of my work.

Thank you all

K.A.

Table of Contents

1 — Awakening - Kare 1
2 — Baecation - Rollo 13
3 — Misery In Paradise - Kole 23
4 – The Answer Is Still No - Octavia 27
5 – Exit Plan - Kole 35
6 – Private Lessons - Kare 41
7 – The Party Never Ends - Kare 53
8 – Welcome to Ragnarsson - Rollo 66
9 – Worth Every Bite - Rollo 80
10 – Another One - Kole 91
11 – I Hate It Here - Octavia 100
12 – A Gift Worth Giving - Cassia 111
13 – Death's Kiss - Kare 116
14 – Fun While It Lasted - Rollo 124
15 – Romans Revenge - Octavia 135
16 – Peace Comes At A Price - Octavia 148
17 – Blood Ties & Northern Skies - Kare 155
18 – Is This A Rift? - Kole 164
19 – Your Only Daughter - Kare 173
20 – I'm Not Mad I'm Disappointed - Kole 182
21 – Monster A Monster - Rollo 194
22 – A Painful Existence - Kare 209
23 – Got That Dog In Em - Octavia 217
24 – A Plan Unfolds - Octavia 228
25 – Bruised Ego - Kole 235
26 – The Curse - Kare 242
27 - Layers Of The Flower - cassia 251

Koel Alexander © 2024
Raven & Fire Series

28 – Calm Before The Storm - Rollo 259

29 – Now It Begins - Octavia 268

30 – Middle Child - Kole... 276

31 - Family Feud - Octavia 285

32 - Beautiful Monster - Rollo 297

33 – Blood And Lust - Kare... 301

34 – We Still Don't Trust You - kole 307

35 – Did We Have A Moment? - cassia 317

36 - What About My Choice - Octavia 325

37 – Why Am I So Different? - Kare 333

38 – I'm Not Very Popular - Kole 340

39 – Old & Cold - Octavia 344

40 – Cursed Head - Kole.. 353

41 – What A Surprise - Rollo 359

42 – I Really Hate Your Brother - Octavia 364

43 – The Keeper - Kole.. 368

1 — Awakening - Kare

It was like I was experiencing life for the first time in its totality. Nothing was cut off from me, I could hear and feel almost everything. The vibrations coming from the moon, the sway of the wind as it bounced between the trees and even the light footsteps of the tiny animals in the forest. The ones that believed they were hiding from me, but my senses have never been better. Their movements were slow, but it didn't make them safe; rather, it tugged at the predatory nature building up in the back of my throat.

The pain from my transformation felt like a distant memory, but it was a night I would never forget. I was taken to the brink of death, saw the doors of the great hall for an instance, only to be snapped back to reality with a ravenous hunger burning from the core of my body. Gio was at my side when I woke up explaining to me how my life was going to change. I knew I was different, but to say I was prepared would be a miserable lie.

Another small rustle of the leaves came from the forest, stealing my attention from my thoughts. The instinct to hunt begging to take over and dominate my prey. I closed my eyes and slowed my breathing the way Gio taught me. The exercise was meant to center me and remind me that I was more than the hunger that ravaged my insides. I wasn't a killer, I wasn't a monster, I was Kare Alexsson, not the abomination my enemies wanted me to be.

I did the only thing I knew I could do to distract myself, because to be honest the breathing exercises were not working, and any minute now I was going to barrel into those woods and kill whatever I could find.

We had plenty of humans that lived in the caves to keep us from roaming around and hunting the unwilling as a part of the treaty with my brother. If I was going to kill something, at least I could bring back some food for them to eat, it was the least I could do for the service they provided us. I grabbed my bow and quiver of arrows and took off into the woods.

Being the former protégé of the huntress, there was no better teacher than Gio when it came to hunting. We would spend hours together working on my technique, hand placement, reading the terrain, and even the perfect spots to aim for a clean kill. The information was priceless and offered a welcoming distraction from the burning. I needed to get this under control before Kole and Octavia returned from their honeymoon. I want him to know that I am still his little sister, I am still his family, and we need each other.

Tav will come around soon, deep down I knew that, but I wanted to prove to her that I am better than the dark cloud that hangs over what I have become.

I relaxed my thoughts to focus on the hunt. Tracking my prey was so simple it was almost unfair. I tilted my head back and opened my senses to everything around me. The sound of steadily flowing water caught my attention, and if I listened carefully, I could hear an animal drinking slowly. I tilted my nose in that direction and picked up the scent. Whatever it was, it was big.

I wasn't as good as Gio yet, I was unable to tell what type of animal it was just based on the smell. A smile stretched across my face as I pushed off the ground and scrambled up the tree in front of me. My speed was so enhanced it was effortless for me to move from branch to branch without making a sound, another gift from the transformation.

I focused harder on the smell leading me directly to the tiny river just south of the cave where we set up camp. As I perched on a branch directly above the river, I spotted a giant buck leaning over the riverbank. His horns rested on the surface of the water as he drank.

I took a minute to admire the creature, who had no idea how much danger he was in. He looked so peaceful and majestic that it was going to be a shame to take him down, but his sacrifice would not be in vain.

"Aim right between the neck and the ribs," I could hear Gio's lingering words in the back of my head.

The buck was looking straight ahead. There was no way to get the shot from this angle, and moving might spook him and then all would be lost. The sun would be rising soon, and I didn't have a ton of time to get this done. I needed to improvise.

An idea popped into my head, but I would need to be fast and flawless to pull it off. I couldn't help but smile again. I'm a vampire, I'm nothing but fast and flawless. Loneliness struck right after that; both of my siblings would have enjoyed that joke. I grabbed a branch off the tree as quietly as I could, and the buck raised his head in caution just as I planned. With all my strength, I threw the branch into the woods causing the buck to turn his head, distracted by the noise he heard.

I had just enough time for me to draw my bow and deliver the arrow in the perfect spot, confident he didn't feel anything as he went down.

I was never happy to kill anything, but it felt good to get something right, and now the humans would have plenty to eat. I climbed down from the river and gathered the buck over my shoulders, he was as light as a feather, another marvelous gift from my transformation, and I made my way back to the caves.

Two vampires were waiting at the front of the cave as I returned. A young man, a recruit by the name of Jordan, stood tall on the left. He was skinny pale and almost had a baby face, he joined us shortly after the wedding once the vampires were allowed to live in freedom. He couldn't wait to receive the bite and, by the blessing of the gods, he completed the turn.

On the left was Veronica. From what I know she had been with Gio for some time before I was turned, at least. She was about the same height as me with long blonde hair. She held the usual blank look on her face. It was like nothing could make her happy, and even when she was being nice her expression never matched her words.

"Holy shit Kare, looks like the hunting lessons are paying off," Jordan smiled as I handed the buck to him.

"I wouldn't give him all the credit, the Norse aren't bad hunters after all," I said.

"Let's not pretend the super senses don't help," he responded.

"Okay, maybe you're right," I smiled as I tried to make my way inside the cave before Veronica stepped in my path.

"For some reason, Kare has become Gio's favorite, even though I don't know what about her is so special," she said in a flat tone.

"What is that supposed to mean, Veronica?" I asked.

"It means that I've been here longer than you but you're the only one who is allowed to roam the forest and get private hunting lessons, while I'm stuck on watch with the recruits," she said dismissively.

"Well, none of that is my choice now, is it? Maybe you should run down and ask Gio why you are here, it certainly has nothing to do with me. Don't place your blame on me, be a big girl and ask for what you want." I attempted to move around her, but she blocked my path once again.

"And there is my problem with you. He is our King, not just a man that you may refer to as whomever you like. But I suppose we all know you are only here because of this fragile peace with your brother." The mention of Kole's name stirred the predator I was fighting to keep at bay. Ever since the turn my emotions were haywire, as Gio explained would happen. I was protective over my brother when I was human, but now I would rip someone apart for him.

"Let's get one thing straight, Veronica." I made sure to pronounce every syllable in her name. "I didn't choose to be here but I am. Gio is King but so is my brother. I treat them with respect but I do not bow for anyone. Any day you want to hash that out let me know, but for now, I'm hungry so please continue your watch and move out of my way." She remained in my path for a brief moment before moving to the side to let me pass.

"I'll see you inside, Jordan." I looked back and smiled, ignoring the other jealous vampire. I thought being immortal would put me above such things, but I guess not.

The cave was lively tonight as it always was hours before the sun came up. The vampires partied almost like the Norse. Food and wine were passed around by the servants, and vampires carried goblets to hold their meals for the night.

A servant passed by me and handed me a cup, my attention immediately stolen by its contents. I forgot how hungry I was on the hunt. Even the altercation with Veronica added a distraction, but now with it right in front of me, I gave in to the hunger tossing back the cup. The blood was warm and revitalized me as it made its way into my body. I could try to explain what it felt like in words but there weren't any words to explain it. It was an energy, a sort of lifeforce, and it was a bridge that held that slumbering monster in check until it looked to be satiated again.

Gio promised the need would lessen over time, but I would never be rid of the feeling. Never was a long time especially when you were immortal. I dropped the cup from my mouth, basking in the bliss of settling the beast when another beast was in front of me in a blur.

"When I told your brother I would look after you, I didn't know that meant I would have to clean up after you," Gio stood before me in a dark black vest with nothing underneath, his chest and his arms exposed. I looked up at his face and his fangs curved on the edge of his smile as he reached up and wiped the excess blood from the corner of my mouth, sending a rush through me that I was not prepared for.

"I can clean up myself, you just caught me at a bad time," I said nervously trying to not look as awkward as I felt.

"I see you have been busy. Jordan walked in with a giant buck. You take care of the humans better than I ever could," he smiled.

"Well, if we want them to continue to work with us, they need to eat too. I won't have them starving for my benefit," I answered.

"And here I thought being amongst me was blessing enough," he said sarcastically.

"Don't flatter yourself, King Gio." I made sure to throw up my hands to stress my point. I walked over to the table in front of the throne as another servant brought me another goblet. I nodded in thanks to her and made myself comfortable.

"I want you all to make sure you thank Princess Kare for her kill," he announced to the crowd which I was not prepared for.

"I'm not a princess!" I yelled.

"Oh, but you are, my flower," he smiled sending another nervous jolt through me. I wish he would stop doing that. I would be lying if I said I didn't notice that he paid so much attention to me, but I had grown used to it. Ever since I had turned, he has been there, none of it seemed out of the ordinary to me.

Koel Alexander © 2024
Raven & Fire Series

We all thought he would have fallen into a murderous depression after Selene decided to let him go and be free, but we were wrong.

After the wedding his mood was so much improved, maybe he took Selene's advice and decided he was going to live the life he was gifted. The miserable monster at the end of the cave was replaced by this charismatic leader. He was still an arrogant ass, but it was a breath of fresh air compared to the man I met before.

Travelers in the forest stumbled onto the Delphi cave all the time and they were allowed to continue on their way. Even if they wanted to join us, they had to prove themselves before receiving the bite. Living in plain sight seemed way easier than hiding.

The peace was holding strong. Kole would be proud of what he managed to build. Yes, the warning from Selene was on all of our minds but it had been very quiet since that night.

Kole and Octavia had yet to return for Midselium. None of us expected them to be gone for this long but it must be one hell of a honeymoon. They deserved a break; with all they have been through for the sake of each other I could understand why they wouldn't rush back to the responsibility of ruling. It was not a cause for panic. Everything seemed to be falling into place. I wasn't in power, but I made sure that Gio kept me in the loop, not wanting any unnecessary surprises.

I was lost in my thoughts until Veronica appeared before me, giving me a death stare on the way to the big ugly throne that Gio sat on in the middle of the cave. I could hear the voices of some of the other members of the family, cursing me for having so much freedom unlike them but I paid them no mind.

Being a princess I was not a stranger to gossip, although Lundr was much more pleasant.

They were all hanging on the words of Veronica who for some reason had it out for me. I didn't understand what her problem was and why she thirsted so much for his affection. I am not the one to blame for his lack of attention toward her. Whatever she had planned for she wanted me to see it play out in the open as she leaned over to Gio's ear whispering something but never taking her eyes off me.

The King's eyes rolled up to meet mine taking in all of the alleged information that she was relaying to him. I wasn't afraid of what was being said but I was curious. I had done nothing wrong, and this was a fragile attempt to gain favor.
It was embarrassing honestly; I wondered how far she would go.

Once all the gossip was shared, Gio waved her off and she strolled away with a smile and some false sense of success. Gio rose from his throne and made his way over to me.

"So, I hear from a little birdy that you do not bow for any kings." He took a seat right next to me.

"Would this blonde birdy happen to have a bad attitude and one fang longer than the other?" I joked.

"Why must you poke at her? You know she has been having a hard time adjusting." He leaned back against the table.

"I have done nothing to make her feel that way, I do my part and look after the family, nothing more nothing less. Do her a favor and give her the attention she wants, it's clear that she wants to be at your side since Marcella is gone." I continued to drink.

Koel Alexander © 2024
Raven & Fire Series

"Ugh, I hate when they beg for attention. It takes all the fun out of the whole thing, besides she is not the one deserving of my attention," he smiled. I tried with all of my power to hide my smirk but I wouldn't give him the satisfaction.

"And who would that be?" I asked.

"Oh, my flower, that is a conversation for another day don't you think? Besides it's getting late." He quickly changed the subject.

"Have you heard anything from Marcella and Rollo? Are they okay?" I asked. He stood from his seat and stood directly in front of me, I honestly never noticed how fit he was, he always kept himself covered when we met. I assume this new mood has contributed to his new wardrobe.

"Marcella writes that they are still journeying to his home. The journey is long, but they are doing well I suppose. They seem to be growing very close." He sounded unimpressed.

"Assuming she does not end up killing him for talking too much," I laughed.

"That is still an option," he smiled.

"So does this mean you're not going punish me for not bowing to you as king?" I asked in jest.

"Of course. As I said when I turned you, you are a light in this world, not to be diminished under the heels of a king, you are the future." I looked at him in surprise because I did not have any words to respond to that. What made me so special? Not long ago I was just the sister of a Norse king. He was the future, not me. I am still trying to figure out where I fit in this world. Gio walked back to his throne and banged his cup to get everyone's attention.

"It has been brought to my attention that some of you have some concerns about your position in this family. I assure you there is no need to worry, but for the sake of making things official, we can stop the chatter. From now on, until the return of our dear Marcella, Princess Kare will be taking her place as my right hand, effective immediately. For those who object according to the rules of this family, you may issue a challenge at any time." Gio put his hands behind his back and waited, but no response came. "If there are no objections, I expect you to show her the same respect you show me, and Marcella before her. Now the night is late, I will be retiring for the day." He finished the rest of his cup and walked off the throne out of the room leaving me and the rest of the crowd in shock.

    I scanned my eyes over the crowd. Jordan was clapping and smiling but then my eyes fell to Veronica, her fangs extended, and the cruelest snarl was spread across her face. She stared right through me like she planned to rip me apart and pick her teeth with my bones. FUCK.

2 — Baecation - Rollo

It was right around midday when I was thrust out of my sleep. We managed to find a quick shelter to lay low for the night and used the furs to make ourselves comfortable. Now the thought of traveling in the night with Marcella sounded amazing at first, but maybe I underestimated a few things.

For one, I didn't anticipate how exhausted I would be. I was barely sleeping. I got a few hours here and there throughout the day, but it felt unnatural to sleep the entire day away. When nightfall came, we tried to cover as much ground as we could on our way to Ragnarsson. I never thought I would miss the daytime so much. Sometimes when Marcella was asleep, I would just sit and bask in the warmth.

Was this something that I would have to give up being with her? I hope she didn't see the uncertainty all over my face because honestly, even though I was having a hard time adjusting, I would have made the same choice a thousand times over. I glanced over to Marcella. She was in her usual unnatural deep sleep, and her hair was draped over her face as she lay motionless. She tried to warn me about it, but it's something that you have to see for yourself. I checked to see if she was still alive, which I do every night even though the answer is always the same. Even half dead and asleep, I was speechless. I had to just chuckle at the half-dead part.

I needed to stop staring so I took a walk outside of the cave for a minute, giving my mind some relief so that sleep would come. We were only a day or two away from Ragnarsson at this pace, but I was going to end up slowing us down if I didn't get some rest.

I sent word with my army to start building the dome on the land behind my father's longhouse, this way I could see Marcella whenever I wanted to and she wouldn't feel so contained.

I could not wait to get home. I've been away for too long, and I needed to give my mother and sister a break from ruling over my kingdom... not that I have been much of a king since my father died. I wrote a couple of letters back to Gio to keep in touch with him and Kare. Surely they would be the first to know when Kole and Octavia returned, but as of the last letter, there was still no word from them.

Seriously, how long could the two of them do it? I immediately regret asking that question considering the only thing that occupied my thoughts day and night was doing the same with Marcella.

We slept separately because I did not want to overstep, but it was painful to be near her and not be able to touch her. I didn't recognize myself. I have no idea who I have turned into. I was never one to take it slow, but something about her demanded my respect and my honor. She didn't have to worry because I was going to adhere to it.

"So much for clearing my head," I said to myself. I opened my fist and let the lightning dance across my palm. After my fight with Marcus, my powers continued to grow like a muscle that was building strength with every exercise.

My next goal was to be able to control an energy mass the same way Marcus did. He held so much power, and if that idiot could do it, it wouldn't take me long to master it. I closed my eyes and willed the power to my palms, funneling all the energy I could muster into one place. It sprang to life in my hands, initially unpredictable and volatile, but slowly I tamed and sculpted it. I was so close to perfecting it, I could feel it. I just needed to maintain my focus.

A branch snapped behind me, jolting me out of my concentration as a bunny scurried across the forest. The lightning ricocheted out of my hand, splintering the ground and all the trees around me.

"Damnit!" Another attempt failed. How was I ever supposed to use it in a fight if a tiny bunny caused me to lose control? I laid my head back against the tree and closed my eyes and to my surprise, I managed to drift off into some semblance of rest.

"Maybe you have met your match, young king," I could hear her beautiful voice before I saw her. "What did those poor trees do to you?" I blinked my eyes open, and she was standing in front of me. Her hair was neatly braided down her back and her eyes pierced mine followed by that devilish smile. The sun grazed the outline of the scar her cowardly father had given her. My beautiful monster. She was dressed in a black shirt with pants, her sword was strapped to her back obviously waiting for a reply from me.

"I must have dosed off out here," I said embarrassingly.

"You sure you weren't trying to keep your distance from me," she smiled.

"Now why would I ever want to be parted from you?" I rose to my feet.

"I mean I look dead when I sleep for one, but there are many other things you don't know that would make you run," she moved closer.

"I'm still waiting to hear about these other things because right now you couldn't get rid of me if you tried," I smiled. "Now let me gather our things so we can be on our way." I walked back to the cave only to find everything packed up and ready to go. "Seriously, how long was I asleep?" I turned to her.

"Not that long but I'm faster than you think. How about we get going? We can't be far from Ragnarsson now," she assured sounding confident.

"How can you tell?" I asked.

"I can feel the energy shift in the air like the power in this land just feels different. It's hard to explain," she looked up to the sky.

"Don't worry I know exactly what you mean. The closer I get to home the more connected I feel, we aren't far at all. I'll grab my hammer then we can go, it should be a smooth trip the rest of the way."

We made our way quickly through the woods. I tried to keep up with Marcella, but she was so fast most of the time I just struggled to keep pace with her. She moved so effortlessly like obstacles were never a problem, like she could see what was coming before it even crossed my vision.

This was getting ridiculous. Why is she so damn perfect? Not that I'm complaining, but seriously nothing about this woman could turn me away. All the other things I liked about her were completely occupying my thoughts, I didn't even realize that she had stopped running just ahead of me. I shifted my momentum to the side, so I didn't slam into her.

"If you're going to outrun me and stop in the middle of the path, you should give me some kind of signal. I almost trampled you," I joked.

"Shh," she put her hand up to shield me.

"What's wrong?" She didn't say anything, just tilted her head to the side and slowly crept forward.

The forest was silent. Whatever she heard was quiet enough to avoid my hearing.

"There is something out there," she whispered softly.

"I don't see anything," I tried to squint hoping that something would become visible to me. "How do you know something is out there?" I asked.

"I'm not sure, but I can feel it. Like a part of me is watching but at the same time it's sending a chill up my spine." She turned to me and moved me out of her way again.

"I'm not usually afraid of anything, but you're kind of freaking me out. We can outrun whatever it is. Let's try to put some distance between us and regroup when we aren't the ones being hunted." The way she was moving had me on edge, making it even harder for me to relax. I tried to grab her arm and steer her back toward the path. We were so close to home. Whatever she was hearing we could easily defend ourselves with more soldiers. "Come on Marcella, let's get moving," I urged.

"Shit! It's too late," she said. She reached back and grabbed her sword and pushed me out of the way with her other hand. I fell to the ground shocked by the force of her push. Before I could protest, a giant blur swept through the forest with unbelievable speed, scooping Marcella off her feet and carrying her into the brush of the trees. It was so fast I barely had time to react. The only thing I could do was head in the direction I think they went.

"What the fuck was that?" I grabbed my hammer and took off with everything that I had. The Gods could not be that cruel to bring this woman into my life and have her taken from me in an instant. The only thing I could hear was my feet slamming into the dirt and my heart pounding in my chest. The silence was crushing my spirit, but wherever she was I knew she was putting up a fight. Marcella was too stubborn to give in.

"Marcella!" I screamed at the top of my lungs as I kept running. "Marcella!" I heard a struggle coming from just over the hill followed by a deep feral growl. I changed directions quickly and ran as fast as I could.

What animal could have snuck up on both of us, especially Marcella? She was a protégé of one of the greatest hunters that was ever created. What the hell was fast enough to carry her this far that fast?

"Marcella!" I screamed one more time, my throat was getting hoarse from yelling so much.

"Can you stop yelling like a little girl and help me?!" I heard her voice just as I got over the hill. She was pinned under what looked like the biggest dog I have ever seen. She was using her sword to keep its jaws from closing on her face. Marcella was focused on the beast trying to avoid him ripping into her flesh, her fangs protruded from her mouth, and maybe I was losing my mind but I could swear that she was smiling. God, I love this woman.

"Are you going to stare all day or are you going to help me?" she yelled snapping out of my imagination. I grabbed my hammer and quelled the power from my center. I charged the beast with everything I had preparing to smash it to pieces.

The animal sensed me coming and released Marcella, quickly dodging the strike from my hammer, which should have been impossible for a normal animal. We stood face to face with the beast, his eyes were yellow and piercing as his lips peeled back to show rows of sharp teeth that led up to his hooked canines slicked with blood. His jaw looked strong enough to crush boulders.

"How the hell is that wolf so big? It's almost as big as Fenrir from the old stories my father used to tell me." I said holding my hammer as the wolf paced around us. I circled with it, holding Marcella behind me and maintaining our distance.

"I've never seen anything like this in all my years," she said her eyes never leaving the beast. She reached down and grabbed her leg, and I could see the blood that soaked her pants.

"You're hurt," I instinctively reached down taking my focus off the beast for half a second.

"Rollo focus!" she yelled as the beast took advantage of my lapse of attention and charged us both. I grabbed her as quickly as I could and rolled her under me to a safe distance. I rose to my feet in the same motion and fired a streak of lightning directly at his head. The beast unnaturally shuffled his feet to one side and dodged my attack, leaving me completely bewildered.

"How the hell is it able to move that way? It's like he knew what was coming next," I thought I spoke to myself until Marcella answered me.

"I don't know, but we need to either kill it or get out of here. Until we know what this thing is we are fighting blind. This is not an ordinary animal." She grabbed her injured leg.

"Well, I never run from a fight." I grabbed my hammer moving the element from my hand to the hilt.

"Neither do I," she smiled and picked up her sword. The beast howled to the moon and charged us again, it used its teeth and its long claws to force us to keep a distance, and every time I attacked it managed to predict my moves.

Marcella and I tried a series of different strategies, all of which failed. If she pressed her attack to distract him, the wolf always turned to intercept me before I could launch an attack. Nothing was working.

"Rollo, do you hear that?" she yelled to get my attention.

"No, I don't," damn her for having super hearing.

"Sounds like the cavalry is coming." That's right, we were so close to Ragnarsson that there is no way they hadn't heard the fighting, or at least heard the thunder from all my attacks.

"We need to fall back and buy some time for them to get here," she grabbed her sword and started to take steps back toward the sounds.

"I thought you never ran from a fight," I joked.

"I don't, but there is a first time for everything, like the first time I'm seeing a wolf that is bigger than a horse." I must admit she had a point.

The beast lunged for us one more time, but Marcella was expecting it, she slashed it right across his snout causing him to yelp and fall back. The slash did not seem to bother it much, all it did was piss the beast off. The beast lowered its head tracking our every move, fully aware that we were leading it toward reinforcements. It huffed in disgust and launched a bone-chilling howl directly at the moon before it disappeared into the forest.

The soldiers appeared seconds after, swords in hand as they discovered us covered in blood and dirt, completely confused by what just happened.

"My king?" the soldier slowly approached. I looked to Marcella and did the only thing I could do.

"Welcome to Ragnarsson!" I laughed.

Koel Alexander © 2024
Raven & Fire Series

3 — Misery In Paradise - Kole

Only I would believe that I could go toe-to-toe with the Gods and win. I had done everything the way they told me to. I returned home, I became king. I took Octavia home and helped her get rid of that psycho Marcus, and blended the two lands just as they asked. I married the woman of my dreams and gained the allies I needed. What else was I expected to do? How is this not enough to be done with this journey?

Was this a hero's story that was destined to end in tragedy? Octavia and I joked about the sentiment but now it was feeling all too familiar. I just wanted to go back to my wedding day, I wanted to go back right before I swore in front of the Gods that she would be mine. For one second, for just one measly second, I was happy. Happy to be in her arms, in her presence, and happy to leave the world behind and focus on what was important.

I draped my feet over the edge of the bed and looked back at the only decision that I have gotten right in my entire life, as she nestled herself under the furs to keep warm. Her hair hung over her face as she enjoyed her blissful sleep. I could only think about how beautiful she was without even trying. She needed the rest. We had no idea what manner of torture the spirit would bestow on us today. The first couple of days trapped here were complicated, to say the least.

    First, Delphi started messing with the magic in the villa. The rooms stopped cleaning themselves, food was not being replenished. It only took a couple of days for Octavia and I to work around that. While it was annoying, we still had each other to lean on.

    When that didn't work, she altered her approach to a more direct threat. Earthquakes, random fires, lightning storms, and floods would follow. Trying to sleep in a room with water up to your knees is not as easy as it sounds. It didn't necessarily set the mood either. After we survived the torture, she would reveal herself and offer us the same deal all over again. The whole thing was exhausting, but we did what we needed to do to survive.

    Neither of us could tell how long we had been in Midselium since there was no sunrise or sunset. The spirit infected this place, sucking whatever magic was left.

    Day after day the villa was going haywire, the conditions falling deeper into disarray. We had to succumb to rationing and saving what we had, not knowing if we would return to another meal.

    The portal remained the same, the magic water that could take you wherever you wanted to go bone dry. The initial punishment for denying her request. She must have known I would never give in to her demands, not after I had sacrificed so much to get here. I would do everything in my power to keep my word and honor. The only problem is she was equally as dedicated.

Delphi promised us motivation, and as much as I despise the vile spirit she did not hold back on her word. She continued to send something new every couple of days to shake our resolve. She wielded so much power here that it was clear she had help. Maybe all the ramblings about the other Gods were true.

"How am I supposed to sleep when I can hear you trying to think your way out of this?" A smile stretched across my face at the sound of her voice.

"I'm sorry, my love. I didn't mean to wake you. Sleep isn't something that brings pleasure these days." I pressed my forehead against hers.

"Has the witch decided to bless us with her presence today?" She leaned up and brushed her hands through her hair.

"No sign of her today, but I wouldn't count her out just yet. As soon as we think things are getting better, she swoops in to make everything worse," my blood boiled at the thought of her outsmarting me and trapping us here. A soft hand rubbed against my cheek and snapped me out of my anger.

"We will figure this out, my love, I promise we will." She pulled my face closer, and her soft lips closed over mine. Nothing could relax me like her touch, the heat from behind her hands bringing everything inside me to life.

"Don't start, Octavia," a sly grin placed on her face said that she was going to do just that.

Koel Alexander © 2024
Raven & Fire Series

"Don't start what?" she said deceivingly as her hands traced down my chest pausing over my stomach as she progressed toward my pants.

"You know what I'm talking about," I chuckled.

"Even though it is completely ruined, it is still my honeymoon, my love." She smiled planting kisses on my lips after every word. Her lips pressed against my neck as her hands continued to her goal. I was on the edge of being a gentleman for only a few more moments, but the Gods never intended for me to have any type of happiness.

A loud crash shook the room and sprung us out of this precious moment that we needed so badly.

"You have got to be kidding me!" My anger swelled right back to the surface as the darkness coated my limbs. Heat blazed right beside me as I saw Octavia half-covered in flames, we have been through this so often that we already knew what was coming next.

"I hate this bitch so much," she exhaled.

4 – THE ANSWER IS STILL NO - OCTAVIA

There was no need to rush outside, we already knew who it was. The mangled body of the little boy that greeted us at the omega when she first trapped us here stood before us right on schedule. The look of his decaying body made my skin crawl.

The green mist seeped from all the many openings in his body as he pranced around putting that diabolical laugh on display. Gods only know what she had in store for us this time. We were no closer to getting out and the spirit didn't give me the impression that she would relent. But we have been here for so long eventually something had to give. I had to get back to the real world. The others would be so worried when they didn't hear from us.

"If it isn't the stubborn king and queen," the little boy stopped in front of us.

"If it isn't the evil bitch that can't take a hint," I retorted.

"You would think you would be nicer to me, after all I am the one controlling your fate," the boy smiled and stretched what was left of his face. "This villa is looking a little rough around the edges, I'm not sure why you would want to keep staying here. This all could be over if you just agree to my terms." The same terms she repeated every time before she came back here to apply more pressure on us.

"Let me guess, you will let us out if we go back home to our respective lands and go back to hating and killing each other, does that cover it?" I made sure I didn't miss a detail.

"That would be correct, do that and I let you go home." The boy said seriously.

"Well, as amazing as that sounds, I'm afraid the answer is still no. Whatever you're going to throw at us next, just get on with it." Being impatient for torture had to be a new low for me.

"Tsk tsk," the boy paced back and forth, what was left of his brow furrowing in frustration. The spirit was angry and I'm not sure why she expected not to be. Kole and I were never going to give in.

"And here I thought I was being reasonable with my motivation, but I see now that the two of you don't care about yourselves. I mean how could you when everything you have done is to save the world? I have had some time to think about this, and now I believe extreme measures are warranted." Her tone grew more sinister which immediately caught our attention.

"What the hell does that mean?" I asked.

"Wouldn't you like to know?" the boy laughed.

"What the fuck did you do, you evil bitch?" I yelled.

"I see I've touched a nerve... now we are getting somewhere." I didn't know what to say next. All I wanted to do was cut off her head.

Believe it or not, I tried that the first couple of times. Somehow, she would reattach the head with magic and come right back, but usually it bought us a couple of days.

"You two are way too righteous to be moved by my antics in here. You're committed to living in pure squalor. So, I've sent the threat after something you care about way more," the boy bellowed a laugh deep from his stomach before we could even answer.

We both knew eventually she would take it up a notch, we just didn't know how. We could endure just about anything in here, but we couldn't do anything but speculate what was going on back home.

"You didn't," I said my eyes filled with disbelief.

"I told you that I would be coming back for my side of the deal you made, young king." The boy basked in what he already thought was a victory.

"I made that deal to save a friend and the people of Gracia!" Kole yelled.

"You made that deal to spite me, and now you will pay for your arrogance. I have no need to torture you here, the beast will run rampant through the country righting all of your wrongs." The boy's laugh was high-pitched and out of control as he mocked our inability to do anything about it. "The beast returns, my king. When your precious Odin told you to spare him, I wonder if this is what he had in mind." The boy yelled through the laughter.

"Ivar," I said under my breath.

The boy laughed harder, pointing and holding his stomach mocking us both. The anger outweighed all my reasoning. I grabbed Kole's axe and cut the boy's head off before I even knew what I was doing. The boy's head rolled to the side with ease, no blood just a decomposed body as the mist swirled away into the distance.

"We need to get out of here now!" I spoke frantically.

"Yeah, I know. At least this will buy us some time, she is going to need some time to possess the body again." He reached and grabbed his axe from me.

"I have an idea. I'm not sure if it will work but at this point, I'm incredibly desperate," Kole turned and looked out towards the omega.

"We need to try to get through to the Gods. There has to be a way to contact them or at least we can get a message out." I was uncomfortable with the idea. Every time we asked them for a favor, a deal needed to be made, and honestly, we weren't doing very well in that department.

"Are you sure we can trust them?" I asked already knowing how I felt about the answer.

"No, I don't trust them. It was Odin's stupid idea to leave Ivar alive in the first place, and we see how much good that has done. If you have a better idea, you should speak now." He sounded panicked.

"Fine, I don't like it, but let's do it." I let Kole lead the way.

The omega stood just the same as the last time I saw it. The pillars stretched over the clouds, the same as the villa. The structure didn't change, but everything was different. Delphi showed us just how much power an ancient spirit could have here. How has she managed to completely block any of the other Gods out? I approached the plateau and ran my hands across the stone, the symbols of our houses beneath my fingers. I tried to feel the tug of the flames just like I felt the first time I came here, but now it just felt cold and desolate.

"I can't feel anything." I placed both my hands over the spear searching for anything, any glimpse that the God of War was connected to this place.

"I can't feel anything, either," Kole's eyes were pitch black as he scanned the area.

"What are you looking for?" I asked.

"I can usually see auras with Odin's sight, I was looking to see if there were any remnants of the Gods left here." He walked the entire plateau laying his hands on every symbol. "Somehow Delphi managed to block all of their connections here, which couldn't have been easy. I wonder how long she has been working on this." He spoke as he continued to scan the omega.

"The plot gets thicker, while we were living it up, she was planning our downfall." The words seemed just as grim as I felt.

"Well, I'm sorry for trying to do something nice. How was I supposed to know that she was plotting revenge on us the entire time?" he said sarcastically.

"Oh, maybe the woman-sized warning at our wedding. Selene told us this would happen, but we didn't listen. We let our guard down and got sloppy," I snapped.

"You think I don't know that?!" Kole yelled causing me to take a step back from him. He had never raised his voice at me, and to be honest I was not a fan of it. I could feel the darkness pulsating off him. "I get it, Octavia. I made the wrong choice AGAIN! I made another stupid deal, AGAIN!" I could see all the stress, guilt, and pain in his eyes, but that still was not an excuse for him to speak to me that way.

"You need to calm yourself down. I know you are going through a lot, but if you didn't notice I'm here too," I yelled back, and the flames sprung to life without my control.

How dare he try to pass over the fact that I was stuck here too, that my family however small it is was in the real world in danger, as well. It was arrogant and selfish, and not like the man that I married.

"I suggest you calm down because the only thing you are doing is pissing me off." I walked up to his chest, my power pressing against his, fighting for position.

The omega started to shake underneath my feet responding to our struggle.

"I need to figure out how to get us out of here," he said softly but sternly, as he turned his back to me indicating the conversation was over.

"Why do you always have to fix everything yourself? I know Odin gave you those powers but trust me, Kole, you are not a God." He flinched as he walked away, my words stinging with a truth I never wanted to say. Kole turned back to me, attempting to maintain whatever composure he had left because evidently mine was out of the window.

"Me fixing everything has kept us alive up to this point, this is the first I'm hearing of these complaints." He was quick with his response.

"I was fully capable of taking care of myself before I met you, trust me," I snipped back.

"The shackles and the rolling box could have fooled me, my Queen," he spoke under his breath and turned his back to me again.

"You, asshole," I aimed to punch him right in his ribs for bringing back the memory of that stupid box, but he caught my fist.

"Were you really going to punch me, Octavia?" he seemed surprised.

"Yes Kole, because of the way you're acting, you deserved to be punched!" I groaned. He looked at me his eyes still pitch black from wielding the darkness and a low chuckle came from his throat. It seems he was looking to push every single button I had today.

"Exactly what is so funny?" My fist clenched waiting for his answer.

"Nothing, it's just our first fight as a married couple. I would like to take a moment and enjoy it," he laughed again. I didn't know if I was going to kill him or kiss him. He was acting like an ass, but he was so unbelievably charming. How could I even take a fight with him seriously?

He closed his hands around my wrist and pulled me closer to him, his other hand gliding across my cheek, each touch sending a shock down my spine. He pressed his lips onto mine lighting a completely different fire in my body, one that needed to be fed so badly. He was what I longed for night and day, every second, minute, and hour. I returned his kiss without a thought. I already forgot what we were fighting about. The only thing I wanted to do now was get to the part where we make up.

Kole picked me up and placed me on the plateau positioning himself between my legs. I did not resist as his hands ventured to every part of my body, the power spilling off him. It was intoxicating, drawing out the flames in me as we continued to get lost in each other. Kole planted kisses on my neck softly. I tilted my head back and closed my eyes to enjoy this moment of lust... but all I could see was flames, endless flames dancing through the skies. I couldn't tell if it was real or an illusion of my pleasure.

"Let it go!" The booming voice slammed into my mind severing the moment I was having with my husband.

"What's wrong?" He asked his eyes still leaking black smoke.

"This is going to sound strange, but I think I have an idea," I said.

"You came up with an idea in the middle of all of that," he asked.

"Not intentionally, but unfortunately that is not required for this plan to work," I pointed down to his pants and backed away slowly watching his excitement disappear.

5 – Exit Plan - Kole

The Gods really do hate me, there is no way to convince me otherwise. That disagreement was not ideal, but it took a very convincing turn halfway through. I had a feeling I was going to enjoy where it was headed. Time here was beginning to weigh on us both. But if Octavia had an idea to get us out of here then I was all ears.

Rollo has no idea what we know and what could be coming. If Ivar got to him first and hurts him, I'll be damned if the Gods save him again. I'm going to wipe him from existence. Delphi had somehow recruited him as an ally, but to what end? We didn't need to be reminded how much damage he could cause.

My thoughts went to my brother and the words he burned into my head the day I banished him. Would his hate for me run so deep that he would let that monster hurt our family? I liked to pretend I knew what he was capable of... but how could I know for sure?

Floria was proof that just because you are family that does not mean that envy and jealousy can't cloud your judgment. She felt buried underneath the shadow of her sister, the future queen, and Octavia didn't even notice. A mistake that I made, as well. How long was the envy for my future burning my brother's love for me?

"Hey, are you still with me?" Octavia looked at me with concern in her eyes. "I need you to focus, this won't work if we don't work together, and even then, it's not a guarantee," she warned.

"I'm good. I'm just thinking about Rollo. I sent him directly into that trap and he has no idea what is waiting for him." I put my head down.

"You did not force him to go, he volunteered, and he is more than capable of handling himself. Especially with Marcella by his side." She grabbed my hands attempting to console my nerves.

"Yeah, you're right. So, what's this plan of yours, my love?" I asked.

"Well, when you were," she stopped talking and tried to hide her smile. "I closed my eyes, and the flames covered my vision. While we were talking, I swear that I could hear Mars' voice faintly," she was recanting her vision.

"You heard Mars?" I questioned.

"Yes, I believe so," she answered.

"But why now after all this time? We haven't felt even a spec of their presence here." I turned and started to pace like I usually do when I'm trying to think. Octavia just stared at me in disbelief. "It's not that I don't believe you I just don't understand what could have sparked them back to life all of a sudden." The whole thing was puzzling.

"That's it," she yelled completely ignoring everything else I was saying. "This all started when you were being an asshole," she shrugged before she continued. "Both of us were upset and I could feel our powers pressing against each other fighting for position," she continued.

"Okay, but what does that have to do with the Gods?" I asked skeptically.

"I will tell you if you stop interrupting me." I threw up my hands in defeat and pressed my fingers against my lips to let her know I would speak no more. "The voice that I heard told me to let it go. What if that was Mars telling us to let our powers build up, and maybe that could somehow spark some life into the omega?" She turned to me with a smile on her face waiting for me to say something.

"Oh, I'm allowed to speak now," I joked.

"Yes, you are allowed to speak now. Tell me what you think." I could see how much she wanted this to work.

"I say fuck it. Nothing else has worked so let's give it a try. We need to hurry before that spirit decides to come back."

We knew there was no way to replicate the emotions from earlier, but we were both in control enough to build up enough energy on command. If this was our one shot, then I was going to put everything I could muster into making it work. Rollo, Kare, my family, the whole damn world was depending on us.

Koel Alexander © 2024
Raven & Fire Series

We ushered in this new world and we were determined not to leave it undefended. I could give a damn what that stupid spirit wanted. The longer I spent dealing with her it made sense why Gio wanted to kill her so badly. As soon as I found a way I swear I was going to wipe Delphi out myself.

"Kole, focus!" Octavia yelled forcing me out of my thoughts. I looked towards her and the flames burned furiously out of her eyes and sparked from her fingers, completely engulfing her arms seconds later.

I closed my eyes and dove into the deepest parts of myself. The darkness the All-father placed in me was patiently waiting for me. The ravens welcomed me as one of their own and spiraled around me, gifting me the powers of their master. My eyes snapped open, and the sight allowed me to see Octavia's aura and my own, pulsating and pressing inside the omega.

"Keep going!" she screamed. "We need to make sure we release enough energy to break through." I gave myself over to the darkness, same as I had done in the arena, but I feared if I dove any deeper than it would consume me. A shriek came spilling out of her mouth, a sign that the flames started to have a similar effect on her.

"Octavia, we need to do this now, we can't hold on any longer." She ignored me and summoned more. "Octavia, that's enough!" I screamed but again to no avail, she was completely entranced in power. "Octavia!" I pleaded.

She wasn't responding, her eyes burning. There was no life left inside of them. I was terrified. I had never stopped to consider if I could lose her to the flames.

All around her, they were growing larger and larger. The heat that usually did not affect me started to thin the air in the omega. The darkness clouded the sky all of it was pouring out of me. If I was going to make a move now was the time. I focused all my energy on a concentrated area and stretched the darkness to pierce the flames. The immediate intrusion of my power finally grabbed her attention, but when she looked at me it was not the eyes of my queen. A foreign gaze stared back at me.

"Octavia, its time, let it go!" I pressed my power harder against hers trying to suppress some of the fire, but it was too wild. "I'm sorry in advance, my love," her face twisted in confusion as I took everything I had and released it directly into her body.

The blow caught her off guard, but the impact to the ground seemed to snap her back into control as her frightened eyes finally made their way back.

"Let it go, now!" I yelled and on cue, she closed her eyes and expelled her power while I used mine to shield myself from the flames. As the flames purged through the omega, the air was being sucked into the sky like a vacuum. The power she unleashed pierced a hole in whatever seal Delphi had on the omega.

A giant spear peeled its way out of the clouds in the sky as the God of War squeezed his way through the opening. The God rose to his feet, grabbing his spear to wedge the opening wider. The vacuum of air ensued, pulling at everything around us. It took all my strength to keep Octavia and I planted to the ground.

Black smoke began to seep out of the opening as the All-Father came falling out of the void, his ripped and tattered black robe barely breaking his fall. He rose to his feet and raised his hands, his spear rumbling through the void after him. Mars reached up and pulled his spear from the opening, stopping the air from swallowing us into the void. If I can be honest neither one of the gods looked very good. I won't pretend to know where they have been this whole time. One thing was for sure, I could feel their enormous power. I would never admit it, but I was ecstatic that they were finally here.

"It's about fucking time," Odin said.

6 – Private Lessons - Kare

I removed myself from all the chaos in the cave ever since Gio forcefully promoted me to second in command. A position I neither asked for nor wanted, and in doing so he placed an even bigger target on my back.

Veronica has recruited tons of vampires to her side. It wasn't a secret, but she hasn't made a move yet. Her I understood, but how could the others hate me this much and not even know me? None of them blamed Gio, and he was the one who made the decision. I am the one who died for their leader in the arena, but all they can think about is all the perks the newcomer is getting.

All I wanted to do was be a part of this so-called new family. At least until my brother came back or I decided to be honest with my mother. I didn't even know anything about being a second in command. What would be expected of me? What was I responsible for? More importantly, how much power did I have? Gio really should have talked to me before doing this. I was completely in over my head, and I hadn't even done anything yet. What if he asks me to exile someone or worse what if he asks me to put someone to death? This was all too much too fast. I needed a distraction, so I decided to take a walk.

The forest was full of life tonight, or my senses are running wild at this point. I couldn't process the difference. I wish I could fast forward to the part where everything calmed down. The bloodlust, the heightened senses, and the unsettling urge that I have been pushing down since I turned.

When I first ventured into that cave with the others, they made Gio seem like an untrustworthy monster. In some ways I felt the same. He was nothing more than a means to an end, but there was something else about him, something that he liked to keep under the surface.

Whatever connected us was stronger than I would ever share with the others. He must have felt it too, or I doubt he would be so protective of me. Being able to recollect your own death was so strange but I found myself replaying it often. I'd like to think I would have jumped in front of that blade for anyone but maybe there was something else that influenced my decision. Now, he calls me his flower, sending a chill through me every time. Unfortunately, with all the twisted feelings tangled up in my transformation, I'm uncertain if it's my heart reacting to his words or my body yearning and burning for a new experience. Thor's beard, all of this is confusing.

I pushed through the forest far enough, knowing I should head back... even though I'm more frustrated than I was when I left. Stares and whispers are all that wait for me. Vampires weren't the type to hide how they feel either, mainly because we can hear everything. There was no need for anyone to be shy about how they feel.

The sound of branches breaking pried me from my thoughts, not much could sneak up on me nowadays. Whatever was coming barely touched the ground and had no scent, so it must be another vampire.

"No need to hide, I know you're there," I called out over my shoulder.

"Sorry Kare, I didn't mean to surprise you, just getting used to moving so fast." Jordan came stumbling out of the forest picking the leaves from his hair.

"No need to say sorry, Jordan. Like you I am still getting used to this." I continued walking as he fell into place right beside me.

"The good thing is that we don't have to do it alone. With everyone's help, we will get the hang of this vampire thing in no time." I sounded less than enthused I imagined.

"How do you do that?" Jordan asked.

"Do what?" I asked.

"Stay so positive even after all the things Veronica and the others say about you. I know you can hear them, we all can." I wanted to tell him that I wasn't positive, I wanted to tell him that I hated her for treating me this way. Every day it took all my resolve not to lose it and try to rip her apart. But I knew that wouldn't help me. I'd like to think I had my fill of violence after Alexandria.

"They are just words, Jordan. For some reason, she believes Gio favors me above all the others." I shrugged off the notion.

"I mean he does." I looked up at him in surprise that he would say it out loud.

"So, you agree with Veronica?" I asked him curious about his answer.

"Oh no, of course I don't agree with the things that she is saying, but to say that Gio doesn't show you favor above the rest just wouldn't be true," he shrugged playfully.

I know he was right, but it was way more complicated than that.

"Do you think that it is any fault of mine that Gio decided to show me the attention that the others crave?" I countered.

"No, of course not," Jordan said quickly. He realized that I was starting to take this personally.

"Do you think it is something that I sought out when I decided to come back here?" My words started to come out more aggressively than I would have liked.

"No," he shook his head.

"Then as you see, I am not at fault. Veronica is jealous, and instead of going to the source and losing even more favor, she thinks words and slander will scare me." I stopped walking and looked Jordan directly in his eyes. "But what they don't know is that I am still a Norse all the way down to my core, and just like my brothers I embrace fear, not run from it."

"Okay, okay no need to get all raging princess on me," he laughed.

"Let's hurry back. I need to make sure I'm in time for my training with Gio." I knew I shouldn't have said the words as soon as they passed my lips. Jordan just flashed a sly smirk and walked with me back to the cave.

Tonight was the same as every other. Vampires piled into the common area sitting at tables, laying on couches and enjoying the never-ending party. I walked in with Jordan. He spotted some of his friends and branched off to join them in the festivities.

The first couple of weeks I was here, I loved it. I danced and drank the night away, admiring the freedom of my transformation. For a moment, everything was perfect, my brother was happy, Rollo was ecstatic he was on his way back home, and I made it through the wedding without my mom finding out that I died and came back to life as something else. I was free to breathe and find out who I was supposed to be. But as free as I was, one thing would always have me in a chokehold.

The hunger.

It always returned. It always crippled any type of fun that I was trying to have, scratching at the back of my throat. It never wavered, causing my fangs to pulsate against my gums. I tried to fight it, but it was a losing battle every single time. My temper was short, my mood was erratic, and physically I felt sick whenever I tried to resist the pull.

While the others were watching me try to fight the hunger, Gio stepped in and continued to be my guide. The more he inserted himself in my progress, the more my feelings toward him became a blur. In my head it made sense to distance myself from those feelings, but I wasn't going to torture myself by avoiding him. He was the oldest and the strongest, anything I learned from him would go a long way. He took time out of his incredibly leisure day to give me personal lessons on honing my skills as a vampire.

First, it was controlling my emotions, which in turn curbed my hunger. He suggested distractions to hold off the hunger like hunting, fighting, drinking, and one more suggestion that I was way too embarrassed to speak even think about.

He showed me how to control my newfound strength and speed. It was awkward to try to walk across a room and end up sprinting into a wall, or patting someone on the back and almost breaking their shoulder. I practiced on the stone walls of the cave at first, and then when Gio trusted me enough he let me practice my punches on him. After a couple of broken ribs, he started to dodge the punches. Admittedly, I'm still working on the strength thing.

He informed me tonight we would be working on influence and compulsion, neither I was familiar with. I made my way through the cave passing Veronica and her crew of followers on my way to Gio's room. I tried not to listen but naturally, I focused on her voice to hear what the new gossip was.

"Gio's little pet is heading to our master to do her job." The group laughed as she continued. "There is only one reason he would make her his second. Why not make the king's sister a sex slave, as well? It's the perfect way to stay in favor with the Norse and get some pleasure out of it," their laughing continued.

My blood was on fire. I clenched my fist at my sides trying not to let her see the effect her words had on me. I was trying to keep my cool, but she was really pushing it. She was spreading poison and lies in order to do what? Her leader made that decision. I had no hand in it, but now to say that the only reason I was here was to be Gio's sex slave was the last straw. I would have words with him about what she was saying because I did not come here for this, and my peaceful nature only stretched so far.

What if this rumor got back to my brother or worse got back to my mother? What would Najora think about its princess being labeled as someone's pet?

"Fucking bitch," I said to myself as I tilted my head up high and made my way to Gio's room.

You had to pass through a series of curtains right behind his throne to get to his room. It was always the biggest space, depending on where we stayed. In the Delphi caves, it could have been an entirely separate cave altogether. Candles aligned the outside walls of the room, a couch over to the left next to a giant mirror trimmed in gold. I would have to ask him how he got that in here. I wonder why I never really noticed it in any of our other sessions. Come to think of it, how did he get any furniture? I lived here and I still didn't know how.

On the right side of the room was his giant bed covered in beige silk sheets and a giant black wool blanket. Vampires didn't get cold, so I assume the blanket was for comfort. The bed could easily fit three or four people. I refrained from thinking of the reason why he needed one that was so big.

Parchments were scattered all over the floor next to the bed. I walked over to pick up one of the pages. I still had no idea how to read Latin so I couldn't understand the words, but the symbols looked familiar. He must have been researching anything that was related to Delphi and what she had planned next.

It had become a very sore topic for him since the wedding. If you wanted to get him upset, you only had to bring up one name. Even though his mood was a thousand times better than before, that one name still ignited his anger very quickly. And not knowing what she had planned next had him even more on edge.

"I'm sure that snooping wasn't part of the plan for tonight's lesson," his low, calm voice startled me and made me drop the papers back onto the floor. Gio crept slowly from the shadows into the room, his hair released down over his shoulders. He usually kept it tied back in a ponytail, but he was much less formal these days. He wore a red shirt missing entirely too many buttons and a baggy pair of black pants.

"If you leave everything scattered on the floor then you weren't trying to hide it, so technically I am not snooping," I responded.

"This is my room. I feel no need to hide what I do in private," he moved closer to me.

"Well, you invited me into the room, so again it's not my fault when you leave things out. I am a curious girl, always have been." I took a step closer to him.

"If only you knew how curious I am about you," he teased, stepping closer and eliminating the space between us. I could smell the wine and blood mixed on his breath, and even though my body was on fire, I stood my ground. He didn't move an inch either, and something in me begged for him to reach out, but all he did was let out a low growl from the back of his throat before smiling and walking away. I was confused before but now I was unbelievably lost. I shook off all these useless feelings. Right now, I needed to learn as much as I could.

"If you're done fighting over the details of me reading your old papers, what are we working on today?" I asked.

"Oh, how quickly you dismiss our moment, my flower," he laughed while pouring us both cups. "And here I thought you would handle my heart with care."

"It was only recently that I realized you had a heart, Gio," I replied dryly.

"Another strike for the princess, you are on a killing spree," he laughed even harder this time.

"I am not a princess, Gio. The vampires already look at me like I'm weird. I don't need you convincing them that I'm better than anyone else."

"But you are better than everyone else," he handed me a cup. The scarlet liquid swirled around the bottom unclenching that hunger inside.

"Is that why you made me your second? Because you think I'm better than some of the vampires that have been with you for years?" I asked curiously.

"I made you my second because just like Marcella you are brave and strong, everything I need in a fellow leader," he answered before sitting down on the giant couch. "The others tell me what I want to hear and listen to me with a blind devotion, and that for lack of a better word is just so...boring," he smiled.

"Boring?" I repeated.

"Boring, but not you. Just like Marcella, you challenge me. You force me to see things differently and call me out when I'm wrong," he turned and looked into my eyes. "And that is why I made you my second, now tell me was that answer sufficient?" He waited for me to answer, but all I could do was shift my weight awkwardly to escape his gaze. Truth is I never considered that I made an impact on anything that he did. He had always projected a notion of control and self-assurance.

"That answer will be sufficient, but can you do me one more favor and tell that to your lapdog Veronica? She is spreading lies about me to everyone, and I'm trying to stay out of the conflict." I searched his face for any indication that he would help, but his dismissive body language made his answer clear.

"Helping you with that will do more damage than good. Vampires thrive on power, my flower. It is of the upmost important to us. Do you know why my word is not challenged?"

"No, great ancient one, why don't you tell me?" I questioned sarcastically.

"I display my power, and anyone that challenges me feels the weight of it." He got up and walked in front of the mirror. "Veronica is testing you to see how far she can push you before you give in."

Of course, she was testing me, that I already knew. But the question is: what is her end goal? She knew I wasn't going anywhere.

"You are the second. Your word is an extension of mine. Marcella knew that, and the people respected her as such. You already have the love of most of the vampires for what you did for me. Now you need to show the rest of them that you have what it takes to back up your word." He continued to admire himself in the mirror. "A show of force would do," he smiled finally tearing himself away from his reflection.

"A show of force?"

"Yes, something that shows you're in charge, something that shows you are not to be fucked with," his fangs peeked out with the curve of his smile.

"Great," I mutter under my breath.

"Yes, great. Now are you ready for the lesson, or do you want to keep talking about Veronica?" He came back to the couch and sat next to me.

"Yes, I am ready. What are we training on next?" My excitement at learning a new skill was practically seeping from my pores, and I could see Gio's own excitement curiously shine through his eyes. He snapped his fingers and two servants walked in and stood silently waiting for their next command. "What the hell is this about?" I asked furiously.

"This lesson requires volunteers," he laughed and sprinted over to them before I could react. "This is the best part, well second-best part about being a vampire."

7 – The Party Never Ends - Kare

Gio was so hard to understand sometimes. Usually, he spoke just like everyone else, but when it came to his vampire lessons you could tell he was over a hundred years old. Nothing was ever simple; it was like translating a thousand riddles. I know I should be appreciative of having the king of all vampires as my teacher, but it did not make it any less frustrating. The two servants stood completely still in the doorway waiting for Gio to instruct them on what to do next. The whole situation was getting awkward, so I decided to speak up.

"Are you going to tell me what they are here for?" I asked cautiously. Gio came back to the couch to sit down next to me and poured himself another glass.

"I have a question for you, and I want you to try to answer honestly," he spoke softly.

"Okay, ask away."

"When you first met me, how did you feel?" I leaned back from him with surprise. What kind of question is that, and what makes him think I could just answer that?

In my mind, I traversed over all the different feelings I had when I first encountered him. I knew he was dangerous because of what my brother told me, but from the minute I walked into that cave something about him drew me in. I couldn't possibly put that into words, nor did I want to.

"Before you try to answer, let me guess. You were drawn to me," he took a sip from his cup. Now I know I looked startled. How could he possibly know that? Or was he just that arrogant?

"What would make you think that I was drawn to you?" I deflected attempting to hide the fact that he spoke the truth.

"Besides my obvious appeal? There are plenty of reasons, but the main one being that vampires by design are built to be desired," he explained slowly and deliberately while lifting his face and looking me dead in the eyes.

"Why would we be built to be desired?" I asked bracing myself for the inappropriate comment that was surely coming my way.

"Remember what I told you about hunting. Scared and injured prey spoil the rest of the meat." I hated when he referred to people that way. I needed blood to live but that didn't make them animals for me to kill. "We were made to be desired so that our prey never suspects a thing before we strike. So, when we met for the first time, your mind was so wide open that you were susceptible to my influence without me even trying." He claims this so casually you would think he'd be describing something as mundane as the weather.

"You mean that I was drawn to you because of what you are, and I had no choice in the matter?" His body language changed, anticipating where my mind was going next. "And what about now? Do I still have no choice but to be drawn to you?" The question must have pleased him because his smirk reappeared.

"Your virtue is safe, princess. Once you are turned into a vampire, that influence no longer works," he sounded almost disappointed. "You all are still under my command as your master, but rarely do I have a need for that these days," he shrugged.

"What do you know of my virtue?" Immediate regret washed over me for even opening the door to this conversation. He leans over and gently runs his hand through my hair sending a chill down my right arm.

"I'll save that for a different day. If you are still drawn to me now, then that my flower is all you," his voice was sultry and seductive, and even though I wanted to pull away it just felt right. "I must admit few have been able to resist."

"Well, there is a first time for everything," I snarked. We laughed together.

"There is one more thing that can be used with your newfound vampire influence, one that is far better than just merely drawing people to you," he ditched the seductive tone for a more serious one.

"And what would that be besides the raging hunger and the now constant unwanted attention?" I smiled sarcastically.

"The art of compulsion," he divulges.

"Compulsion?" I repeated. He stood in front of the two servants and called me over. They remained still, about an arm's length apart as I waited for his next instruction.

Koel Alexander © 2024
Raven & Fire Series

"If the mind is open enough, you can compel humans to do whatever you want. They have not moved since I compelled them to enter. Did you not notice?"

"You mean I can control them just by thinking it?" The very thought alone seemed impossible... and somehow wrong.

"Technically yes, but humans that are strong mentally are able to resist the compulsion to an extent. As you get stronger, more minds will open up to you," he explained.

"Have you ever used that on my friends or my brother?" I asked really hoping that the answer was no.

"Your brother and your friends are royal blood making it much more difficult, but their trip to Midselium seems to have blocked any kind of influence at all. I assume because they share the spirit of their descendants." He took another sip from his cup.

"And what about me? I wasn't blessed like them in Midselium. Wouldn't you have been able to control me?" another question that I wasn't sure I wanted the answer to.

"Your mind was open to influence, but you had just enough royal blood to keep me somewhat at bay. Now that you are a vampire, compulsion would not work," he grins.

"What's so funny?" He was increasingly getting on my nerves.

"Do you really think I would ever try to compel you? To force you to stay here with me?" He never turned to me as he spoke.

"I'm not sure. This is all new to me, I didn't even know any of it was possible," concluded, even though I knew deep down that I was not compelled to be here.

"I turned you because I feel that someone like you will be the perfect vampire for the others to mold themselves after. You are kind, powerful, stubborn, and beautiful. Everything that we need in this dark, cruel world," his eyes burned with passion as he enunciated every word describing me.

"I don't know why my looks are important, but I appreciate the compliments," I quaver. We locked eyes without saying a word for what felt like an eternity. I fought the urge to let my eyes linger over him, to take in just how attractive he is, but I don't want to be the first to break the connection.

"Shall we move on to the next step?" he suggests, breaking our eye contact and finally allowing me to breathe. He walked me over to the servant waiting at the door. He was a tall muscular man that towered over the other servant who was a woman. He waited patiently for his king to tell him what to do. Instead, Gio walked me over and began to talk me through the art of compulsion.

"Find his heartbeat and my voice. Now isolate it from all the other sounds," the pounding of his heart spreading blood through his veins prompted my fangs to shoot out without me being aware, a response to the bloodlust. I covered my mouth trying to hide my lack of self-control. I feel Gio grab my hand quickly, squeeze, then drop it. "Don't worry, I got you. Look him directly in the eyes and find that small opening in his mind, that will be your way in." I followed his instructions poking at the outskirts of his mind until I find a tiny opening.

A crack so small I squeeze my way through like a slow leak. I expected to be confronted with fear, sadness, anything that would show me his state of mind, but inside it was empty, as if nothing mattered. I pulled back confused at what I had just felt.

"Why is his mind empty?" I asked Gio.

"That would be my fault. I may or may have not cleared the path for you," I turned to him completely annoyed and horrified.

"You did this to him? Why would you subject him to this?" I yelled.

"I wanted your first time to be easy to build your confidence. Invading someone's mind can be delicate and dangerous," he explains. "Prying around in there could have some serious consequences if you are not ready."

"Thanks for the vote of confidence," I sighed in disappointment.

"You can be mad at me later. Let's try giving him a command. Tell him to pick up the woman and carry her across the room, that should be easy enough and no one gets hurt," he directs with a sarcastic slight bow as I dove back into the man's empty mind.

It almost seemed natural to control his limbs like a puppet. His body responded to my commands as I instructed him to pick up the woman. There was no push back as he walked across the room before setting her down on the couch.

This feeling, this power over his will, was too natural and it felt wrong to wield something like this. I began to think how many people have fallen susceptible to this influence. Did the people here actually want to be here or did the vampires compel them to stay? Gio was going to have to answer these questions inevitably because there was no way I was going to join a cult where people were forced to stay against their will. I forced myself out of the man's mind and his shoulders relaxed. He turned to face his king.

"You two may go now," he dismissed the servants. I could not hide the disgusted expression on my face.

"You better undo whatever you did to that man to clear his mind!" I demanded.

"I will, don't worry. More importantly, how fun was that?" He was smiling, completely carefree as if we didn't just invade someone's mind. My next question was going to stir up some issues but I wouldn't forgive myself if I didn't ask.

"Are all the humans here compelled?" I asked him sternly and his body hunched over signaling I had ruined his happy moment.

"Is that you talking or Octavia?" he replied sarcastically.

"I'm serious Gio. Are the people here because they want to be, or are they compelled to stay?" I wanted a clear, definitive answer.

"I won't say that I haven't enjoyed the perks, but it has been a long time since I've had to resort to that type of control," he zipped over to me in a blink, my face level with his chest, his hand running through my curls. "I'm not the monster that I have been painted to be," he whispered in my ear as his lips grazed my cheek, sending that shiver all the way down my body.

"You couldn't tell me that from across the room," I looked up and my eyes focused on his lips.

"I could have, but this seems like it is exactly where I need to be," he smirks. Damn him and that alluring smile of his.

Koel Alexander © 2024
Raven & Fire Series

"Some of the others may compel humans, and if that is the case you have my permission as my number two to abolish it, but I feel I should warn you. If you think the others challenged you before, they will come for you even more if you try to change their way of life." He moved even closer eliminating the space between us.

"Their way of life is barbaric," I hissed out the words.

"And what if we like bar-baric?" he spaced out every letter in the word, his lips drawing closer to mine making my body started to lean up in response.

A loud crash jolted us apart as a vampire came running into the doorway.

"My king, sorry to interrupt, but we have a situation in the throne room." He didn't wait for a response as he ran back out. A deep growl came from Gio's throat, agitated with how this lesson ended, and honestly, so was I.

I followed him out directly into the mayhem. I rarely paid attention to all of the noise coming from the throne room. The vampires rarely partied quietly, and I needed to drown out everything to focus on what Gio was trying to teach me.

Now that I had let everything back in, I could tell that there was some kind of conflict. Someone was fighting and Gio was determined to figure out why. We emerged from behind his throne into the common space. I was fixing my hair and my clothes trying to make myself presentable, which probably only made me look more suspicious. The intimate moment we had just run from had me feeling like the whole room could tell what had almost happened.

I saw Jordan wiping blood from the many cuts all over his face. They were already beginning to heal themselves. His fangs were out followed by an angry snarl that I have never heard from him. His eyes were bloodshot red and trained in on Veronica and her gossip crew across the room.

"Would someone like to tell me exactly what is going on?" Gio spoke to the crowd calmly. Everyone in the room froze in his presence but no one was speaking. "So, no one is going to tell me why they have interrupted my lessons with my new number two?" The room remained quiet, but Veronica rolled her eyes at the comment. Gio must have seen the gesture. "Is there something you want to say, Veronica?" he barked.

"No, my king, everything is fine, just a simple misunderstanding," she gave him a big fake smile, which I'm assuming he bought because he did not press any further. Jordan was my friend, and I was not going to just let this go.

"Are you telling us that you have nothing to do with what happened to Jordan's face?" I pushed past Gio.

"I don't have to answer to you, you are not my king!" she spat.

"But she is my number two, so you will answer her out of respect if that is what she demands, the same as you did for the one before her." Gio sat down on his throne before throwing his leg up over the side.

Veronica said nothing and she turned her back toward me, a clear sign of how much respect she had for me. He warned me that she was going to challenge me and that was fine, but taking it out on Jordan was not a part of the deal.

I turned to Gio. Maybe I was looking for some backup. Shouldn't we present ourselves as a united front? Wouldn't that help get everyone on our side? He slouched even deeper in his seat waiting for me to take control of this situation. Vampires respect power, that's what he told me earlier, and if I wanted this to work, I was going to have to play the game.

"Jordan, what happened?"

"Nothing, Kare," he said without even looking my way. Fucking vampires and their pride. It almost reminded me of all the hardheaded men back home. He wasn't going to say anything. He didn't want to look weak in front of everyone else. I needed to find another way in that wouldn't embarrass him.

Reprimanding Veronica now without cause wouldn't make anyone respect me. It would look like I was abusing the power they didn't think I deserved. I needed something to make her come to me, and after my lesson, I had the perfect idea.

"If no one will talk then I guess there is nothing to be done. However, I do have an announcement I would like to make since I have all of your attention." Gio finally sat up in his chair curious about what I planned to do. "After discussing it with the King, we have decided that compulsion against humans that live with us will be forbidden," the room erupted into separate conversations. "If any of you are holding people here against their will, you will release them immediately. If the humans would like to stay and be a part of our family, they are welcome, but it shall not be from pressure from a vampire," I projected my voice over the commotion.

"And if we do not agree with these new rules?" Veronica interrupted, turning back to me.

"Unfortunately, it is not for debate, Veronica. Though I will allow you to speak your peace," I smirk at her.

"Speak my peace?" She sounded insulted. "You just got here! Who the fuck do you think you are coming in and telling us what to do?" She was losing her temper. I'd seen Kole do this to Kyut plenty of times. Emotional opponents make mistakes. I just needed to remain calm.

"I am your superior, or have you forgotten?" I taunted.

"You're just Gio's pet whore!" Her voice reached a pitch I didn't even know was possible.

"You want to repeat yourself, Veronica?" I spun around to make sure I blocked out everything in the room. Her heart was racing, but she had no intention of backing down.

"You are Gio's princess pet whore, and the only reason you are here is because he felt bad for you! He should have let you die in that arena, but instead, he figures it would be better to keep you here, keep that Norse king happy. And why not get some pleasure out of the plaything while he is at it?" The veins in her throat looked like they were going to explode.

The entire cave was silent, or at least I thought it was. The only thing I could hear was her stupid heartbeat calling to the hunter in me. I looked back toward the vampire king wondering if he was going to comment, but he remained in his chair waiting.

"Anything else you need to say, you spoiled brat?" I closed the space between us in a blur. She was taller than me, but it meant nothing. I've seen Octavia take down people that were more than double her size. If it came down to it, I was sure I could take her.

Koel Alexander © 2024
Raven & Fire Series

"I think I've covered it," she seemed satisfied. I pulled away to look past her toward the others. The room was on the verge of chaos waiting for the next move. The truth is Veronica didn't deserve my anger, but this was about showing power and gaining respect. If she wanted to be the example, then so be it.

"Now that the show is over, I've told you all before that I am no longer a princess, but I am Norse." The pride of my family welled up inside me. I was an Alexsson before I was a vampire, and no one talked to us this way.

This was my moment, and it was now or never. Kole and Rollo would have loved this. The hunter inside was patient and waited for the right opportunity to pounce. The anticipation was exhilarating and the thought of not having to hold back would be satisfying. Either way, she needed to be addressed. I walked past Veronica to speak to the group.

"My brothers did most of the training back home, but all I did was watch them fight each other day in and day out. You can't help but learn as they demonstrate. Some of you want to know who I am. Good because I am going to show you. We Norse do not know fear, we thrive on it like a fuel to the largest fire. Our greatest moments are in the face of adversity. It breaks us down and molds us back into what we are. Death is but a phase. We all know it is coming for us, not meant to be feared but embraced!" I zipped back over to Veronica's face. "That's the reason why I jumped in front of the stake that would have killed your master because I was prepared to meet my Gods." I looked her right in her cold dead eyes. "Are you?"

Before she could answer I took all the strength I could muster, and my fist slammed into her face. I could hear the bones crack underneath the blow. I didn't know if it was mine or hers. Her body slid across the room and slammed against the wall. It did not take her long to spring up.

"You are going to regret that, princess." She wiped the blood from her mouth as the bones in her face were cracking and popping back into place as she healed. Even though it was disfigured and surely painful, she charged back across the room directly at me.

8 – Welcome to Ragnarsson - Rollo

Not really the way I wanted to welcome Marcella, but I hadn't planned on being attacked by a giant beast that was way smarter than any animal I'd ever encountered.

The soldiers checked the perimeter before we made the journey back. If that thing followed us home and hurt anyone, I would never forgive myself. My pride was already bruised considering I didn't manage to kill the damn thing. None of that mattered now I was back in Ragnarsson. My home, my kingdom. Pain and happiness choked me as I walked through the main gates.

The last time I was here everything was destroyed, but now after all this time has passed it feels like everything was alive again. A forever celebration, exactly the way my father would have wanted it. The memory of him slammed into the front of my mind. He would never get to see the kind of man I became. I would have to wait until we see each other in the great halls of Valhalla. We could feast and he could be proud of his son.

Once we passed through the gates, the people gathered as we made our way through the market. I glanced over to Marcella, and she was just taking in all the attention. I couldn't gauge if she was happy by such a warm welcome or if it was all too much in such a short time. Crowds of applause and cheers showered over us as we made our way to the longhouse. Only the Gods know how much I missed home.

"Are you okay?" I asked Marcella.

"I'm great, but don't worry about me. This is your homecoming, not mine," she smiled. "Enjoy it. You have worked hard and done a lot to deserve it. Some of these people have no idea what you went through." I smiled and turned my attention back to the crowd, but it didn't feel right to take credit for all of this when so many others played a part. I mean Kare literally died for this to happen.

"But I didn't do it by myself, you played a pretty big part as well, if I recall." I caught sight of one of my biggest accomplishments as I approached my family's longhouse. "And even if no one knows the part you played, I built something that should stand as a reminder." Sitting right behind the longhouse was the new marvel of Ragnarsson.

A dome sat right behind the longhouse. I was going to owe the builders my life because it was a masterpiece. It could keep out the sun with more than enough space for any vampires that decided to stay.

The structure was a little smaller than the longhouse itself but just as wide. The outside walls were built with the same wooden pillars I'd seen in Cosa. I asked Cassia to send them here myself. The builders used leather and the strongest ropes we could find to attach the pillars, creating a perfect oasis for my beautiful guest.

"Tell me what you think?" I turned to catch her full expression. She stopped in her tracks studying every inch of the dome. I couldn't read her expression she was standing so still.

She only had a couple more seconds of silence before I start to overthink this. After such an enlightening trip I really hope I didn't offend her with this. I hope I wasn't moving too fast.

"You hate it, don't you?" What if I had revealed my hand way too quickly. What the hell was I thinking assuming that she would want something like this? Why would I assume that she would even want to stay here this long? When it came to Marcella, I couldn't put my finger on it, but I always felt like I was a step behind.

My palms were sweating as I plummeted deeper into my own uncertainty over her reaction. I moved closer to her to start my three-part apology for overstepping, but before I could say anything Marcella grabbed my face with both hands and pressed her lips into mine.

My eyes widened, completely caught off guard by the kiss, but it did not take long to fall into her rhythm. This is what was missing to seal the deal on a glorious homecoming. I could ignore the world if I could just bottle up this moment for a little bit longer. I could feel the power starting to boil up from my center. The lightning started to drape down my arms, but I did not want to let this go.

The murmurs of the crowd must have knocked us back to reality. Marcella broke her lips away from mine and smiled, her fangs hanging barely visible behind her lips. My mind wondered what it would be like to have them pressed against me. Thor's beard, Rollo, get control of yourself.

"No one has ever been this kind to me, even when I was a human," she pressed her forehead against mine. "Thank you, Rollo. I will never forget this."

"It was nothing. For some reason I got a lot of pull around here," I teased.

"I can see that, and now that we got that kiss out of the way, I think it's time that I meet your mother and sister, and pray to the gods that they approve of me," she smiles. We continued through the crowd hand in hand.

We walked into the longhouse still being followed by a mob of people still cheering and applauding.

"The King is home!"

"Long live the king!"

"Long live Rollo!"

All of this positive energy felt so good. I scanned the room, and I was not disappointed. My mother changed nothing in the longhouse. It looked exactly the way it had when my father was king. Blue and silver silk hung from the ceiling and wrapped the pillars. Bales of ale in every corner as every Norse drank, danced, and celebrated like there was no tomorrow.

The throne sat in the middle of the room, the Thordsson symbol carved into the backside of the chair and the banner to match hanging directly above the seat. I watched my father tend over many issues in the kingdom from that chair while I sat in the corner drinking with Kole. These days I wish I paid more attention, but the past was the past. If it is Thor's will, I would be able to sit there for as long as he did... preferably longer.

"Son, finally you are home!" My beautiful mother rose from her seat which sat right next to my throne. My sister Aria was standing behind her. Last time we saw each other was at the wedding, but it feels like she gets bigger by the second.

"Mother, it's a pleasure to see you again. I've missed you." I made sure to bow as a show of respect, before awkwardly realizing I hadn't introduced Marcella properly. "Mother, this is..."

"The beautiful lady Marcella. I remember her from the wedding. You two were not exactly subtle about your affections toward each other," she smiled, and I dropped my head in embarrassment. My mother had seen me entertaining plenty of girls throughout the years, but this is the first time I've felt the need to protect it.

"Thank you for having me, Auslaug. I've heard about your country from Rollo, but words do not do it justice," she bowed to my mother, as well.

"Marcella, welcome to our home. I assume you must be very important to my son seeing as he has never seen anything through to completion in this kingdom, but for you he built this," she pointed in the direction of the dome.

"I mean, I wouldn't say I've never completed anything. That seems like an exaggeration." I laughed nervously.

"I would," Aria yelled out from behind my mother. "All you usually do is sit in the corner and drink with Kole, and flirt with girls." Mischief twinkled in her eyes, a family trait I'm learning.

"Okay, Ari that's enough." I interrupted, stealing a glance at Marcella, who was smiling back.

"The hour is late, and we have plenty of time to talk, but after your encounter on the way here I assume you would like to wash and get some rest." My mother waved to the servants to tend to our belongings. Those bright, deadly eyes of the beast flashed in my head. If this thing was going to haunt me my dreams too, I was going to be really annoyed.

"Yes, of course. I'll show Marcella where she is staying, and we will talk in the morning, mother." I bowed to her and my sister once more, then Marcella and I headed through the path connected to the longhouse into the dome.

I tried to relay from memory the way Cassia had the dome decorated in Cosa. I wanted to maintain the same feeling she had on the island. The high pillars were wrapped in gold vines and black silk. I told them to keep the furniture a light color since this area would be completely cut off from the sunlight. I didn't want Marcella to feel like this was just another cave. This could be a place that would feel more like a home.

She walked in and I followed behind her, trying to discern if she was pleased with the way it turned out. Her eyes examined every part of the dome as she ran her hands over the pillars and stepped towards the center, where I had the builders place a giant table for her to have her meals. Even though technically she doesn't eat. There were plenty of chairs in case she decided to have guests. Of course, she wouldn't have any friends here yet, and I wasn't even sure if she truly has any friends amongst the vampires she left behind.

"You built all of this to keep me here, huh?" She joked.

"I was hoping it would keep you around for some time. Why, is that creepy?"

"No, it's sweet. I've already met your family. The only thing left for us to do is get married," she smiled. I could not tell if she was serious or not, and this felt like one of those moments that was going to make or break whatever we were doing. So, I opted for silence. "Rollo, I'm kidding," she laughed, finally allowing me to let the air out of my lungs. "In all seriousness, this is amazing. Not only am I appreciative, but the vampires will also be happy to know that they have friends in your country." She rubbed her hands on the fur covering the chairs around her table.

"Do you need anything, food or drink?" I asked immediately regretting the question. I already knew she didn't eat.

"I'll take something to drink if it is not a bother to you," she said modestly. The topic of blood was always sort of a touchy subject. Or maybe I just got touchy around the subject.

"It's no bother. I'll be back in a minute. Make yourself comfortable." I went to walk out of the room before turning back. "Do you have a preference? Like man or woman, tall or short, fat or skinny?" I tried to hold in my smirk.

"Now there is the funny king I remember from the cave. No, your highness, I do not have a preference… unless you are offering." She shot her fangs out at me, causing me to flinch, before she plopped herself down in a chair laughing at my reaction.

"I'll be right back," I huffed and marched back down to the longhouse, trying to completely ignore how unbelievably arousing that was. Rollo, you are a sick man.

I managed to convince one of the servants to provide me with some blood. I was going to have to investigate a more permanent solution if Marcella and Kare were going to stay here. I had a servant bring Marcella the blood while I retrieved some food from the kitchens for myself. I was picking through my food like a bird, further attempting to not embarrass myself. My meals usually didn't last for more than a couple of seconds but there was a lady around. I had to make sure I at least appeared civilized.

"I never asked if you wanted to share a meal tonight. I just kind of invited myself," I noted.

"I think what happened at the gates was clear that I wanted you to spend the evening with me, and you don't have to ask. Are you not in charge?" She replied with a smirk.

"I try not to walk around using the king card unless I have to." I pour myself a cup of ale.

"A very smart decision. We have had enough cruel and arrogant rulers. The world does not need anymore." She lifted the cup and drank, the tension almost immediately seeping from her body that I didn't even notice was there.

"You have no idea how much I agree." We sat in silence for a little while, just enjoying each other's company. Everything she did was done with so much grace. She was perfect in so many ways, and the monster underneath her surface stirred the storm in me whenever I was near her.

"I can see you balancing the scales of the world in your head, my king." Her words stole my attention.

"Your king?" I questioned surprised.

"Am I not in your kingdom? Am I not under your roof?" Everything she said was followed by a smirk.

"And when you aren't under my roof?" I asked, terrified of the answer.

"I believe I can make some room for you. Just don't tell Gio. He doesn't like to share me very much." Her king, I repeated to myself mentally. Maybe I was jumping too far ahead, but it was too late. I was already prepared to jump over the edge for her.

This must have been how Kole felt when he met Octavia. This must be why no matter what happened he could not leave her side. I knew sitting across from her right now that I would not let anything or anyone harm her.

"It's not just you, by the way," she interrupted my thoughts again.

"What do you mean?"

"I mean I feel it too," I sat back in my chair trying to stop the blood from rushing to my face. "Whatever it is between us, I feel it, and because of that I feel that now is the time that I should tell you more of my story." She shifted uncomfortably in her chair. I already knew from experience how this subject made her feel.

"I told you before that there is nothing you can tell me to make me feel any differently about you," I reiterated, hoping my reassurance eased her nerves.

"And I believe you, but I need you to know all of me. The good and the bad, the calm and the ruthless." Her words sent a chill down my spine. I didn't know the specifics yet, but I knew it had to do with her father, and I had no sympathy for the man. If he was standing in front of me right now, I would kill him myself. I waved for the servants to bring more ale.

"I'm all ears." I sat back in my seat as she continued her story.

"After the run-in with my father at my sister's grave, I went back and forth over the idea of how to kill him. Should I just snap his neck and make it quick? Should I rip into his neck and watch him bleed out?" Her body tensed as her anger started to build. "I even considered digging a hole and burying him alive right next to the child he should have been protecting, but that monster didn't deserve to be anywhere near my sister." I leaned up intently because it seemed like I was finally going to find out what happened to him.

"What did you do with him?" I asked.

"I knocked him out cold and dragged him to the closest cave I could find. The sun was going to come up soon and killing him right away would have been a kindness. I wanted him to look me in the eyes and face what he had done. Are you listening, Rollo?"

"Of course, I am. I guess I'm just confused as to why you're clearly concerned I'll see you differently for whatever horrors you think you've committed. I have no sympathy for the coward. I'm sure whatever justice you served was fitting."

"Don't count me out, yet," she grimaced. "I tied him upside down and waited for him to wake up."

"Upside down?!" I almost choked on my drink. "Why upside down?" Her eyes locked with mine and the monster that lived inside flared.

"The blood drains from the body much easier when you are upside down." She dragged her tongue over her fangs. I sat back in my seat, unsure what to say or how to feel. "But before I drained him, I had some things that I needed to say." I imagined she had an army's worth of questions. Surely he would be hanging for a while.

"What did you say when he came to?" I asked intently.

"Frankly I'm not sure what I expected him to say, nor what I planned to ask. He was a degenerate drunk, and I was being impulsive. Why should I even believe anything that came out of his mouth, no matter what I asked? Nevertheless, I didn't really need to rely on him telling the truth. I had my ways to pry the truth from his lips." She took a long-drawn-out gulp from her cup.

"What happened next?"

"Depends on your definition of next, because that was only the first night. My revenge needed to mimic every minute of suffering that he put my sister and I through. So, with that being said, the first thing I did was leave him hanging for hours. I would only return him upright so that he could have a cup of water, before I returned him to his torture." Silence followed as I didn't exactly know what to say and she clearly was nowhere near done. "I wanted him to feel what it was like to starve the same way he made us starve all those nights. He squandered our money on drink and women."

"Sure, could be seen as somewhat barbaric but I can't say he didn't deserve that so far."

She locked eyes with me, ensuring I was paying close attention for what was coming next. "At the time, I called it my three steps of revenge. The first was preparation."

"Preparation?"

"Yes, I was preparing him for the worst moment of his life. He should be thanking me because no one prepared me for the worst in mine. I'm sure you can understand that sentiment, considering the betrayal you faced."

"I guess you have a point. What is the second part?"

"The second part is experience. Which is just a short word for torture. I can share the details if you would like?" she smiled.

"I think I get the gist of it. Torture comes in many forms, but is largely all the same. Why don't you tell me what the last step is?" Her eyes burned with intensity as she said the word slowly.

"Hope."

"Hope?" I questioned.

"After many grueling days in the cave, I may have accidentally left his binds loose, and I hadn't returned that evening."

"Wait what? After all of that you let him go?" I asked confused.

"Or so he'd hoped," a grim grin followed. "You see, for a moment he believed that he had a chance to survive. After all the torture and counting his days knowing that he was about to die at my hand, he had somehow survived. When he managed to get out of the cave, a sliver of hope crossed his mind."

"Ohhhh," I tried to refrain from looking stupid. Of course the hunter had a plan.

"I let him believe he escaped me, and for many moons. Do you know what he did in all that time, Rollo?" I didn't respond, assuming the question was rhetorical. "He went right back to gambling and whoring, right back into the life that got him there in the first place."

"Thor's beard," I put my head in my hands.

"So, I let him enjoy that hope, and I just waited and watched. I watched as he squandered away the reprieve he received. One night, as he was leaving the tavern, I watched him look to the sky and thank the gods for sparing his life and cursing his abomination of a daughter. What was left of her anyway. And before the blessing could leave his lips, my fangs attached to his throat and I crushed his spine in my hands. His body gave up as he could not hold up his weight, so I held him, crushing as many bones as I could. As he bled into my mouth, I counted every single breath as he left this world."

Yup, I was completely speechless. Her body language was reliving the kill. She twitched, and her fangs rumbled as she recalled taking his life. I could feel it stirring inside her.

"And I would do it all again. A thousand times, maybe drag it out even longer. I am a monster, stalker, and a hunter. Exactly what I was meant to be. Now you tell me if I am still worth your affection, my king." I did the only thing I could think of doing at that moment. Leaning over, I grabbed her and pulled her close to me, then kissed her soft lips. As crazy as she was, everything, including the story, only made me want her even more.

"You are more than worth it."

Koel Alexander © 2024
Raven & Fire Series

9 – Worth Every Bite - Rollo

Now that we got all the blood and gore of the past out of the way, I was able to enjoy the next few nights, showing Marcella around Ragnarsson. We toured the longhouse where we hold all our gatherings, the training pit where Kole and I spent hours fighting each other, and the lively market which thrived every single night. We ended the tour on a hill right above the docks, watching the boats come in and taking in the perfect breeze of home.

"Your home is beautiful, Rollo. Thank you again for everything you have done," she smiled, and weaved her hands through mine.

"Thank you for coming with me and trusting me." I didn't know what to say next as the silence hung between us... until Marcella started to lean in slowly, so I followed suit and waited for her soft lips to press against mine. I couldn't get enough of her, and I wanted to spend every moment I had left staring into her eyes and kissing her lips.

"At some point, you are going to have to act like a king. You do know that, right?" She broke away from me with a smile.

"I am acting like a king right now. Who else could sit on a hill ignoring all of their responsibilities to spend time with a beautiful woman?" I laughed.

"The flattery is appreciated, but I'm serious. While I'm away from Gio, and Kole and the vampire hater are gone, we need to tell someone about the creature that attacked us." Her tone was serious, so I knew I should probably tone down the jokes for the moment.

"Are you sure we can't just pretend it didn't happen? Are we not having a great time?" I countered.

"We are, but I think we need to investigate what it is and what it was after," she repeated.

"You're probably right, but before we do that, I did promise Kole I would check out what was going on up north and keep an eye on what Ivar is up to." I got up off the ground. The mention of Ivar's name always tugged at my temper. The Gods spared him once, but I know I won't be so merciful a second time if I find out he is up to no good.

"Ivar is the son of the man that started all of this, correct?" Keeping up with everyone involved was probably difficult for her, but she was doing well.

"Yea. Kole spared him and sent him and his own brother to run the kingdom up north, but for some reason they have stopped all communication."

"And you think that the thing that attacked us in the woods is connected?" she asked.

Koel Alexander © 2024
Raven & Fire Series

"If I have learned anything from my time dealing with the Gods, evil spirits, and curses is that everything is always connected. Now that you have stirred the pot, the king has some work to do. How about we go to the throne room, and you can watch me do my thing?" I offered her a hand up.

"It would be my pleasure, King Rollo." I loved the way she said my name.

We walked back to the longhouse where the party was still raging on. It was exactly the kingdom that I would want to rule over. I took a minute to take in everything that I had been missing while I was stuck winning Gracia back for my friends. Now, I was going to sit on the throne, whether I wanted to or not. All these people are going to be looking to me for guidance, and Thor willing I was going to make the right choices.

I made my way through the room when I realized that I had nowhere for Marcella to sit. I would be the king of moving too fast if I asked her to sit right beside me, but I did not want her to think that she wasn't important. As I got closer to the throne, I started to panic.

"I...uhh maybe you stand beside me," I could not stop stuttering.

"I will just sit at the table in the front, Rollo. I'll be fine, just take care of your business. Unless, of course, you want to get married right now?" she replied with mirth in her voice.

"You would be the Queen of Ragnarsson for an eternity," I say out loud.

"Yes, I guess technically I would," she smiled and made her way to her seat.

My mother and my sister practically ushered me to my seat. The bottom of the seat was hard as stone. How my father sat on this thing for hours at a time was a mystery to me. The seat wasn't very comfortable. That would probably be the first thing I change.

"All rise!" My mother spoke loudly, "my son, your king has returned from his triumph in the Roman lands."

The crowd cheered loudly slamming their cups and stomping their feet. I nodded my head in a silent thank you for the tribute. I leaned forward to speak, but apparently my introduction was not done.

"The stories of his conquest will be sung in Valhalla so that his father Eirik can hear them. He has been blessed by the Gods themselves, and under his rule he will lead us into prosperity and glory. LONG LIVE THE KING!" She raised her cup, and the rest of the longhouse joined her in unison.

My sister walked to the front of the throne and opened a box that held my father's crown. It was made from a shiny black metal, the same color as our flag with the trim was covered in blue stones. My mother grabbed the crown and placed it on my head for all my city to see. If it didn't feel real before, it certainly does now.

I waited for the cheers to subside. Although the welcome party was meant to be a celebration, I had some real concerns I needed to investigate. Especially since Kole and Octavia have been gone for some time, and I had yet to look into this matter with Ivar. Part of me was starting to worry for Kole, as I wasn't expecting him to be gone this long, but he did deserve the break for his role in saving us all. Even if the entire thing was my idea.

"Good people of Ragnarsson, I want to thank you from the bottom of my heart for your support as I've returned home. I want to first thank all the men and women who put their lives on the line to come to our aid in Gracia," I raised my cup. "Those that did not return are dining with my father in Valhalla, knowing that their sacrifice was not in vain. I have gained so much from this journey. New family and friends," I slid my eyes over to Marcella as she smiled from her table. "A new treaty has been formed to maintain our long-lasting peace between the Norse, Romans, and the vampires." Some people in the crowd looked confused when I used the word, but they would learn eventually. A man raised his hand signaling he wanted to speak.

"What about the beast that attacked you on the road, my lord?" A scowl replaced the smile on my face. It wasn't his fault to bring it up but what a way to sour the mood. After my mother promised prosperity, I didn't want to have anyone worried about being safe.

"My mother and the rest of the leaders will be discussing what occurred in the forest when we have more details. An investigation is under way and we'll have more to share soon," my tone portraying both confidence and finality.

"And what about Kyut and Ivar up north, my lord?" The man interrupted again, further testing my patience. The mention of that rat's very name boiled my blood.

"King Kole has agreed to let me inquire on what is going on in the north. Taxes are owed, and even though Kole decided to spare his brother and Ivar, they have turned their backs on him once again. This will not go unpunished, and after I spend some time here with my people, I will be heading up north to get answers myself."

I waited another couple of seconds making sure there were no other questions. This was insanely tedious and taxing. All I wanted was to drink and relax after such a long journey.

"Enough with all this seriousness. Let us drink and celebrate the return of your king and the victory that will lead us into the future. SKOL!"

We all clanged our cups and downed our ale to the sound of the drums before breaking out into a glorious song.

"You sure know how to give a speech. I didn't know you had it in you," Marcella joked.

"Me either. I just figured if I nailed it then I could get off that chair faster. My ass is killing me!" I rubbed my backside and we laughed together. A tiny figure snuck up beside us.

"So, this is the vampire that everyone is talking about," my sister's voice rudely popped into my ears behind me.

"Ari, don't be rude. Marcella, this is my sister, Ari." My embarrassment likely showing with the redness of my face.

"Nice to meet you, Ari. Yes, I am a vampire, but I wouldn't say that I'm THE vampire." Marcella smirked just enough so you could see the curve of her fangs.

"Is it true that you don't age?" she asked.

"Ari!" I yelled annoyingly.

"It's okay, Rollo. She's just curious. It is true I do not age, technically," Marcella replied patiently.

"Then how old are you?" she asked. I put my head in both my hands because there was no way I would ever be more embarrassed than I am at this second.

"I am old enough," Marcella teased.

"Mhmm I see. Well enjoy your stay here. You must be important since the first thing my brother did was build you a house," she placed a cup down in front of her before turning to me and walking away.

"I'm not sure if your family likes me or not," she surmised.

"I'm not sure if they even like me, to be honest. I'm going to eat and drink and pretend that the whole conversation didn't happen."

"That's a shame. I like her. Maybe I can get used to this place." She followed.

"Anything is better than an old, dark, musty cave," I joked.

"Careful, your majesty," she made sure to stretch the word. "That cave was my home for a long time, but yes, I would have to agree with you."

The crowd sang and drank, basking in the return of their king. With a little more work, maybe I could get Marcella to stay longer than she intended. Guests came over to our table to pay their respects and thank me for the victory.

All of it was so new to me, the blind loyalty and respect were intoxicating. I could understand how men could get lost in that kind of power. You held the very life of the kingdom in your hands, and with one word you could change everything.

From the corner of my eye, I watched as my mother approached the table and interjected. "I'm sorry to interrupt the party, son, but we have the war room ready. We need to talk about what we are going to do next."

"First thing tomorrow, mother. Tonight, I want to enjoy the festivities," I said.

"Rollo, I understand that you've had a long journey and want to celebrate with our people, but you have responsibilities now beyond being the life of the party," she said sternly.

"I'm aware of that, but look around, mother. Everyone is drunk and enjoying themselves. Nothing of note will come from the meeting tonight. Tomorrow, I promise I'll be the first one there." She hesitated, but inevitably nodded her head and left me alone for the night.

"Good night, mother!" I yelled as Marcella got up from her seat and walked around to my side of the table.

"I'm glad you dedicated the night to the party, but what would it take to get you to leave with me?" Her mouth grazed the top of my ear.

"It wouldn't take much at all, but I remember what you said when we started this journey." I turned my head to hers.

"And what was that?" she teased.

"You said this was a journey together to my home and nothing more," I smiled. She drops her lips just inches away from mine daring me to lean forward and press against hers. I gathered the courage to move closer and, in a blink, she was behind me again whispering.

Koel Alexander © 2024
Raven & Fire Series

"The journey is done, your Majesty. Maybe now I'm ready for more," her sultry words whispered in my ear lighting the spark in my body.

"Let's get the hell out of this party!" I smiled.

I didn't think we could get back to the dome any faster. Our lips sealed together as we removed any piece of clothing we could grab. Her hands trailed up and down my chest as she opened her mouth more, allowing me to devour her. I was completely lost in desire; I could barely get my thoughts straight. I grabbed her waist and pulled her even tighter against me. She used her strength to break away and look down before she returned her eyes to mine and smiled.

"I can see that every bit of you is a King," she whispered to herself. Making me want her even more than I thought was possible.

She dashed back over to me forcing me down into a chair as she removed her dress slowly. It slid down off her shoulders showing her immaculate breasts traced right along the edge of the dress as it disappeared entirely. Her hips swayed back and forth, and my eyes followed them. Marcella was astonishing, more than perfect. She was a vision of the Gods. She straddled me in the chair I was frozen in.

"I hope everything is to your liking, my king." The lust was pouring out of her pushing against my own.

"I have never seen anything more beautiful in this world," the words were cliché but I don't think I've ever been more sincere. I rubbed my thumb along the scar and pulled her down to kiss her even deeper than before.

Moans escaped us both as we matched our rhythm, Marcella moving her hips harder slamming against my body. I couldn't maintain my restraint much longer, I needed so much more.

I lifted her up and she slowly brought herself back down onto me, allowing to experience what utopia feels like. We stared into each other, those grey eyes breaking me down as she moved up and down on top me. I matched her movement with my own, every thrust forcing her to vocalize her pleasure. My hand squeezed her thighs as the other explored the rest of her body. Gliding over her breasts, her nipples, and her tiny waist. Marcella commanded my focus, knowing exactly what she was doing.

She tilted her hips, grinding harder against me, forcing a moan from me which excited her so much her fangs shot out without warning. That monstrous smile stared me down as her movements never stopped. It finally clicked in my head what was going to happen next, and for a split second I was afraid, but watching her work made all my hesitance go away. If I was going to do it, now would be the time before I talked myself out of it.

"Are you certain?" she asked tentatively. I exposed my neck to her and nodded to her giving my permission. Just like a snake, she struck quick and true. I felt a tight pinch of pain replaced by a warm feeling of relief as she drank.

She grabbed my neck sucking deeply, grinding harder and harder, moaning in my ear while the blood flowed from her lips as we both found our way to a blissful climax. I screamed her name to the Gods and felt no shame about it at all.

She pulled back off my neck, her face in pure ecstasy, and we folded into each other right there on the chair. What a fucking way to be welcomed home.

10 – ANOTHER ONE - KOLE

The All-father and the God of War spent the next couple of minutes stretching and getting themselves situated since they fell out of the tear in the sky. Despite Octavia almost killing us both, the plan worked. Maybe these two could finally give us the chance we needed to get out of here and warn the others. We sat quietly waiting for the Gods to acknowledge us. We didn't know what kind of mood they would be in.

Odin snapped his fingers and a chair covered in runes appeared right next to him. A skeleton throne appeared allowing Mars to sit, as well. They seemed extremely agitated, so we opted to remain silent until Odin finally looked down at us.

"I mean how long were you two going to wait, honestly?" His voice roared in our heads. "We have been on the outside looking in for far too long and you two barely noticed," his knuckles tensed, indicating he was clearly angry with us. All I could do was laugh to keep my temper under control.

"We have done everything that you tasked us with doing. Apologies if we wanted to take a much-deserved break, that turned into a literal trap forced on us by a vengeful spirit." I tried to keep the anger out of my voice.

"It didn't seem like you were taking a break when you got here," Mars shouted.

"You were watching us?" Octavia interrupted.

"It was not hard to miss. The two of you did not hide what you were doing," Odin said lowly. I looked back at Octavia with a smirk, and she was trying to hide, the blood rushing to her cheeks.

"That's not the point. As you know, we have a real problem, and we need to get the fuck out of here," I reminded Odin.

"Clearly!" His rage was palpable in the air.

"So, what are we going to do? Can you get us out?"

"It's not that simple, young king," he replied much more calmly.

"What do you mean it's not that simple? What is the benefit of being all-powerful if not to fix things that are complicated?" My voice keeps elevating as my frustration builds over his non-answers. In my gut, I know I should be more respectful. This is the All-father I am speaking to… but I've had about enough of the Gods and all their games.

"That question is exactly why I sought out the means to be powerful, but your altercation with the spirit has shifted even more Gods against our cause." His voice boomed in response.

"I warned you about that parasite," Mars directed his words toward Octavia.

"I have a vested interest in his preservation. The same way you preserved that worm Ivar, who is now going to be used to hurt my people. I need to get out of here." I took a step closer to them.

"Octavia ripped a hole through the barrier Delphi placed around Midselium allowing us to slip through. I sent Thor to warn your friend Rollo for the time being, but before we free you, Mars needs to tell you how to stop the spirit. For after we free you, we will have used all our power, and we won't be able to contact you again until we have had time to replenish our strength. Although by then you should be able to complete your journey." He sat back in his chair as a raven landed on his shoulder.

"Of course, another damn quest to clean up your mess, which is to be followed by a riddle, I assume," Octavia said sarcastically.

"Is this mess ours, my child? You should have listened to your instincts and rid the vampire from this world. If you would have done that we wouldn't be in this predicament," Mars rolled his eyes as he replied.

"One of those vampires is my sister, and I swear I will burn down Olympus to the ground before I let you hurt her." I grabbed my axe and stepped towards Mars.

"You must have been here too long, mortal, and built an abundance of arrogance along with it. How dare you step to a God? I could crush you with a pinky, with a mere thought."

Mars' voice knocked me back off my feet as the flames poured from his eyes.

"You need us!" I yelled from the ground. "If I'm wrong, strike me down now and get it over with. If not, speak and tell us how to get rid of this spirit so we can get back to our kingdom and save it yet again." Odin held up his hand to calm the God of War, who I'm sure wanted to burn me alive.

"The spirit cannot be killed, but it can be contained. An ancient artifact was created that could keep her from spreading her influence. Jupiter would never create anything without having its counterpart, a balance of nature to bring it under control if its ambition got too big," Mars explained.

"Why doesn't Jupiter bring Delphi back to the fold? The destruction of our world is more than enough ambition?" I interjected. Mars and Odin exchanged a glance but said nothing in response.

Octavia reached over and grabbed my shoulder with a frown on her face. "He doesn't care if we live or die. He will wipe the earth and start over if need be. We are but mere pawns as usual," she said softly, completely disappointed to be continuously reminded that we were not important. "So where is it?" Octavia stepped forward.

"That is the problem. The Gods have relied on the oracle for so long that no one has kept track of the artifact. We have been too busy quarreling with each other over the years," Mars said.

"Of course," we responded in unison.

"What I do know is that it was last hidden in Norse territory to make sure that no Roman went looking for a way to trap the spirit. That knowledge was entrusted to one God, the keeper and patron of all knowledge and wisdom." Before he finished, my eyes shot over to Odin, that devilish grin once again waiting to lead me down a complicated path.

"You know where it is? This whole fucking time!" I yelled.

"I didn't tell you because I needed to know if I could trust you," Odin said calmly.

"And killing my father wasn't enough for you to trust me?!" I was completely enraged.

"It was a start," he smirked. Fucking smirked.

"Fuck you!" I felt the darkness rise quickly on its own. Odin raised his hand and stuffed it back down before snapping his fingers, bringing me to my knees.

"I know you have accomplished much, my son, but be mindful of who you are speaking to. Time will not allow me to explain all the reasons you should never speak to me that way." I shifted uncomfortably on my knees waiting for him to finish explaining why he continues to lead me two steps forward and five steps back every time he opens his mouth. "I do not know the exact location of the artifact," he said. Octavia sighed in disappointment, and I just tried to burn a hole in his head with my glare. "While it was entrusted to me, there were still fail safes taken to make sure that I myself didn't try to wield it. It was a pretty good idea, for Romans anyway," he shrugged, and a low growl came from Mars as he took the insult on the chin.

"Are you going to tell us what we need to do or are we going to sit here basking in each other's company for the rest of time?" I was still restrained by Odin's power.

"I suppose I can move on with my story. I wouldn't be in such a rush to be out of our presence. As we told you before, once we free you, we will not be able to assist you anymore on this leg of your journey. Getting you out will take all our strength." He rubbed the bird on his shoulder.

"Yes, we get it, heard you loud and clear. Can you tell us now?" Octavia interrupted impatiently.

"The artifact is hidden in the north, high in the mountains above your brother's kingdom. I assume you know the place." It is exactly where I banished Kyut and sent that snake Ivar along with him at the behest of the God that was supposed to be guiding me.

This whole time? Was that a part of the plan? Was this the only reason that he wanted Ivar alive? What did he have to do with the artifact? What was Delphi using him for? Or was she lying about using him? This shit was so confusing.

"Only the head of the cursed can find the artifact, and only a human can wield it," Odin waved his hand and finally let me up off my knees. "You will need to lead the spirit back to the center of the world, and when she inhabits a body, use the artifact on her to trap her in this place and in that body, containing her powers and influence," he sat back in his chair as he finished his explanation.

"Head of the cursed?" I turned back to Octavia hoping she understood something that I didn't. "What does that even mean?"

"I have no idea, but whatever it is our answers are up north... which means that the silence from up there is no coincidence." Her eyes were burning with concern.

"Can you tell us anything about this curse, and does it have anything to do with Delphi's counter to our deal?" I asked.

"You know we can't answer that," Mars barked coldly.

"Of course," I shook my head. I wish I could say my disappointment wasn't expected. "What does this artifact look like?" Octavia asked, trying to glean any amount of useful information she can out of the Gods of confusion.

"I am not sure actually, but it is powerful. You will know what it is when you come across it. Especially you, my child. It was forged in Roman lands," Mars said.

"Is there anything else you can tell us?" My head was spinning with all this new information or lack thereof, and I was ready to leave this place. "Anything else at all?"

"No, that will be all. You two have been chosen for a purpose beyond just being rulers of your people." Mars started to speak.

"Yea, we know, we know. Chosen by you, we get it," Octavia droned on sarcastically.

I stepped up to make sure both Gods could hear me because I had finally reached my limit. While trying to do what I thought I was supposed to do, I fell right back into the pattern of being used by them, but this was the last time.

"After we finish this and bring Delphi down, we are going to have a sit down with you, and whoever else needs to be in attendance because enough is enough. You clearly need us, or we would have been dead many times over already. It's far past time you stop treating us as chess pieces in your game and start treating us as your chosen victors." I stood tall and waited for them to either answer or kill me. An answer would be preferable.

"If you succeed, then we will speak. You are imbued with my spirit, so I expect nothing less than this display of strength. Let the raven guide you, my son, because I will not be able to. If this is the last time we speak, just know that regardless of how you feel about my methods you have impressed me." Odin inclined his head after he spoke.

"You as well, princess. You are the epitome of the Roman spirit, and I have no doubt you will succeed," Mars echoed, though neither he nor Odin waited for us to acknowledge their words. They shot into the sky in a ray of blinding light.

The lights danced across the skyline clearing the eternal darkness that Delphi bestowed upon us when we arrived here. The lights headed back to the villa and slammed directly into the center. Octavia looked up at me and smiled. We were finally going to go home thanks to the same Gods that caused all of this in the first place. My life seeped in irony.

"Let's go home!" We started to walk back toward the villa.

"Going so soon!" I knew I recognized the voice no matter what body it was in. A decomposed soldier came limping behind us, his eyes coated in the same green mist I'd grown accustomed to seeing.

"This bitch really won't go away," Octavia turned to face the soldier.

"They have made it so you can get out. That will not save you from what's waiting for you on the other side," the soldier smiled. "I'm just as powerful out there as I am in here." I reached down into the darkness and dragged my powers to the surface.

"We will see you real soon, Delphi. Come and find us if you can," I opened a portal in front of us, and we stepped through dropping us off directly in front of the swirling portal at the center of the villa. The water was back to normal. I grabbed Octavia's hand and we plunged into the water, willing it to take us back home. We had to get all the others back together and save the kingdom one last time.

Koel Alexander © 2024
Raven & Fire Series

11 – I Hate It Here - Octavia

The feeling of falling through the void would never be enjoyable or familiar. If I never jump into that portal again, I would be a happy woman. It let us out flat on our backs in the middle of the forest, and immediately the cold air swept over me.

The forest was dark, but as my eyes adjusted and searched the area, the feeling of familiarity began to creep in, as did my disdain for where I was. Out of all the places I wanted the portal to take us, why did it have to be here? Kole landed right next to me, releasing a deep breath with what sounded like relief. Midselium was supposed to be a getaway for us, but it ended up becoming a prison, and it felt good to finally be free.

"Any reason why we ended up here?" I asked him.

"I don't know. I was thinking about who would need me the most as we went through the portal, and it sent us here. I thought it would take me straight to Rollo," he remarked as he got up and brushed the dirt off his clothes.

"Why in the world would this psycho need our help?" I made no effort to shield my words. Kole gave me a look and I knew he wasn't necessarily happy about my discourse toward Gio.

"Maybe he isn't the one that needs our help," Kole stated and started walking toward the cave.

As usual, the cave was alive. Gio must be throwing another one of his bloody parties. Bloody parties, I shook my head at my word choice. It was rare not to see one of his vampires guarding the entrance, but now that they lived out in the open it was probably overkill.

I followed behind Kole down the path heading toward the commotion. The closer we got the faint beating of the drum started to build in the back of my mind. The influence from Mars was missing in Midselium as we were unknowingly being cut off from the real world, but now that I was back, I would have to fight to suppress it as I did before.

A loud crash stopped us in our tracks. Another crash followed which quickened our pace down into the cave. Cheers followed as another crash ensued. Now I was completely confused as to what was going on down here.

My memory sent me back to the day the travelers found their way down to the cave, and instead of releasing them, he fed all the people to his children. I thought the image had shaken its way loose from my mind over time, but it was firmly implanted there and made no attempt at escaping. Our eyes locked and without words, we were sprinting directly toward the commotion with no thought of the danger that we would be running into.

We turned the corner and emerged into the center of the cave. The first thing I saw was that ugly chair. Sitting comfortably without a care in the world was Gio. He showed no interest in what was happening as it seemed that two vampires were trying to rip each other apart while the others cheered in encouragement. Snarls and growls followed by punches raged on as the vampire traded blows.

"What the fuck is going on?" I leaned over to Kole as we came to a complete stop at the entrance.

"I have no idea, but for whatever reason the portal has brought us here." He walked closer to the crowd trying to figure out what was going on. I pushed my way to the front, fighting the urge to pull out my daggers and solve the dispute myself. The two vampires broke apart to take a breath and that's when I noticed her. The curly hair and the perfect brown skin even when covered in blood put mine to shame.

"Kare?" I gasped surprisingly. She turned at the sound of my voice completely ignoring her opponent.

"Tav?" she brushed her curls out of her face right before the other woman's fist almost knocked her off her feet.

"Odin's beard, Kare, what are you doing?" Kole pushed his way forward, but Gio sped over blocking his way.

"I'm glad you're back, young king, but you must not interfere," he spoke plainly.

"Gio, I know we have made strides in our friendship, but if you don't move out of my way, we are going to have a big problem," Kole hissed.

"I mean no disrespect to either of you. I wouldn't want your queen to try to smash my face in again," he drawled as he sent a smirk my way. Arrogant prick. "But Kare was challenged publicly, and if she wants to have any respect among us, she needs to stand on her own. Being Norse I'm sure you understand." Kole must have understood because his shoulders relaxed, but the look on his face told me he was not any happier with the explanation.

Kare regained her balance and wiped the blood from the corner of her mouth. She looked over to us, waiting for our nod of support, which we gave instantly. Better for her to know we are on her side so she can concentrate on her opponent. I leaned over to Gio to make sure that he could hear me over the commotion.

"Just to be clear, if anything happens to Kare, you and I will be replaying what happened the last time I left you with her." My gaze didn't escape his, so he knew how deadly serious I was.

"So safe to say that the honeymoon could have gone better," he implied.

Kare seemed to settle down now that we were here, while the other vampire was low to the ground snarling with anger. She charged with incredible speed, similar to what I had seen in the arena when they helped us fight Marcus.

It seemed wrong. Why should Kare have to go through this just for the sake of appearance? The other vampire extended her nails and swiped ferociously, trying to dig into Kare's face. She dodged easily finally catching one of her arms to stop her advance. She planted her foot directly into her chest knocking her off balance. I'd seen Kole use the same move before. Maybe Kare was doing more than just watching her brothers fight on that balcony. She must have picked up some of their moves.

"Veronica, we don't need to do this. I am not your enemy," Kare yelled to her as the vampire made her way back to her feet.

"You are my enemy. Why should we have to listen to you? A newcomer that knows nothing of our ways. I won't have it!" Veronica charged again.

Kare rested her shoulder and braced her stance as the other vampire closed the distance between them. She slammed into Kare with unbelievable force, but Kare managed to hold her ground. Veronica was infuriated, the feral growls coming from her throat purely animalistic. There was nothing human about this display. I looked over to Kole expecting him to be as uncomfortable as I was, but he had a smile on his face.

"What could you possibly be smiling about?" I questioned dryly.

"Because I'm a proud older brother," he said quietly. What was he proud of? This whole thing was ridiculous. He must have seen something I didn't, which is usually the case, but this time I wish he would elaborate.

Kare was still holding Veronica off as she snapped those giant teeth at her over and over, attempting to bite anything that she could. I could barely keep track of their movements, but Kare landed a punch to her stomach causing Veronica to gasp for air. In one smooth motion, she grabbed her by the neck and slammed her over her shoulder using her own weight. Veronica crashed onto the floor of the cave and the ground cracked beneath her. Kare was suddenly on top of her, pinning her throat to the ground with both hands.

"Holy shit!" I said it out loud before I looked over to my husband whose smile was even bigger.

"Come on, love. She's an Alexsson. I never had a doubt in my mind. I've pulled that move on Kyut a thousand times," he said happily.

"She is most definitely impressive," Gio said under his breath.

"I still don't see why this was necessary in the first place," I turned to address him. "You could have solved this in two seconds without this fight. Just throw around that authority you love so much."

"You're right, I could have, but who would that help? A show of force guarantees that she will not be challenged again so easily," he didn't turn to speak with me directly, poking at the anger that I was trying so hard to keep down.

"Yes, but you also put a target on her back. One that she never asked for. She's not a soldier in your army," I spat at him.

"Nor have I treated her like one. She has all the freedom she wants, but this is our way. Better to embrace it if she is going to live here." I knew arguing with him would be useless, so I saved my breath.

The crowd was waiting patiently to see what was going to happen next. Kare still had Veronica pinned down. Veronica was doing her best to thrash her body to shake the hold Kare had on her throat.

"Yield Veronica. It's over and I don't want to hurt you," Kare urged.

"Fuck you!" she squeezed the words out. "I don't yield to pets," she spit blood into Kare's face, and I saw a complete switch in her demeanor. I could feel Kare's anger. She lifted one hand off her throat and slammed her fist into Veronica's face, causing her head to bounce off the floor of the cave.

"Yield!" she yelled and when Veronica refused, she punched again and again. "Yield!" Her fist landed again. The crowd began to recognize how serious this was, and the cheers started to die down.

Gio remained still, but he never took his eyes off what was happening. Then Kare leaned in closer, leaving barely any space between her and Veronica as she spoke calmly and powerfully.

"Yield!" Something washed over Veronica because without any pushback she looked up to Kare and spoke.

"I yield," she spoke the words softly and Kare released her.

"That's impossible," Gio remarked surprisingly.

"What is?" I asked. It was the first time he looked at me when he spoke.

"I'm not really sure yet, but I think Kare is even more special than I thought." He walked over to help Veronica up before passing her over to the other servants. Her face was already beginning to heal from the beating. "Please come in and join us. We want to hear all about your magnificent honeymoon," Gio switched subjects smoothly and walked back to his throne as if nothing happened. Kare ran over to us and hugged both of us as tight as she could.

"I'm so happy you guys are back. There is so much we need to talk about. Sorry about all that, by the way. I really didn't mean for you to see that. I promise I'm being treated very well here," she sputtered as she could not stop rambling.

"Kare! Kare, relax." Kole rubbed her shoulders. "We have plenty of time to hear about how much fun you are having here, but we have a lot we need to talk about. More than you could possibly know," he said.

"I promise you while we all enjoy a nice provocative story, I'm sure you can skip all of the intimate parts of your honeymoon," Gio scoffed from his ugly chair.

"Don't be an ass, Gio. This is serious. We thought you would be happy to hear that this story happens to center around your favorite spirit." The smile on his face faded.

"That fucking bitch!"

We sat down to share a long overdue meal. I wouldn't say that I was enthused about being back in this cave, eating this mystery food. Hearing that Kare was learning how to hunt and bringing food back for the humans warmed my heart.

She was a vampire, but there were so many parts of that kind heart spilling out. It helped deal with the urges, apparently. She was still compassionate and caring, even to her own food. She was so anxious to tell us everything that she had learned since we left. Her experience so far as a vampire sounded like an entirely new adventure, almost as if she was finally living and truly coming into her own.

She assured us that Gio had kept his promise and was personally walking her through everything she needed to know. It killed us to spoil the reunion with all the bad news about Delphi. She sounded like she found a position and a purpose here. She was Gio's number two now that Marcella was traveling with Rollo, and she was perfect for that role considering she was always a voice of reason for all of us.

While she spoke, I could see that Gio had never taken his eyes off her, studying her for some reason... almost with what looked like a sense of adoration. Kole nudged my shoulder. He must have noticed that I was staring at Gio. Maybe I was just projecting my own situation with Kole on them and overthinking it. Though, I know better than anyone what some forced proximity, mutual attraction, and a shared purpose can build between a man and woman. Something in my gut was telling me to bookmark that look of his to consider at another time.

"You sound like you're fitting in well, sister, all things considered," he nodded his head toward the other vampires.

"I am, but I'm so happy you guys are back. I missed you both," she said happily. "We thought maybe you guys weren't coming back, it's been such a long time. Longer than I thought you'd be willing to take."

"Trust me, our prolonged absence was anything but willing. If someone had their way, we wouldn't have made it back at all," I looked over to Kole.

"Gross!" Kare whispered. I tried to hide my smirk because I knew where her mind went, but it was time to get serious. The true reason we were held behind had little to do with our nuptials, and everything to do with a certain vengeful spirit. Only the Gods know how much time we have to sort through this new mess. It didn't seem like we were gone for all that long, but there was no way to tell how long we were in Midselieum. Time there just didn't work the same as it does out here.

"While we are happy to see you both, and reflecting on the time that has gone between us has been riveting, I'm sure there is a reason you have rushed back here," Gio said seriously.

We filled them both in on everything that happened after Delphi trapped us in Midselieum. We told them about her plans with the curse. We explained how we managed to escape, and the message we received from Odin and Mars, somewhat dancing around the cursed head part. By reading their body language they were just as surprised as we were.

"I knew this was going to happen. I knew we shouldn't have made that fucking deal!" Gio snarled.

"It was your life that was saved because of the deal," I countered. "And not to mention after we saved you once, Kare saved you again right after that." He sat back in his chair silently with that comment.

"What about Rollo?" Kare asked.

"Odin told us that he sent Thor to warn him. I just hope he makes it in time before he walks into danger up north." Kole spoke as tensely as he looked.

"We need to bring everyone to the table and figure out what the next move is. Have you been in contact with Cassia?" I asked Gio, but he brushed off my question and rolled his eyes. "Gio, have you reached out to Cassia?" I asked again.

"I rarely have the time for myself, let alone keeping up with others, my queen. She should have everything under control," he replied nonchalantly.

"You have got to be fucking kidding me," I slammed the cup down as the drums began to pound in response to my anger.

How could he just let everything that we worked for be left unattended? The voices crept up to the front of my mind, and then I felt a hand hover over mine. I looked down at Kole's hand and felt the calming energy immediately. His look urged me to relax, so I took a deep breath and quelled the voices back down. Think happy thoughts, I told myself on repeat.

"I can go and retrieve Cassia and come right back. I've never opened a portal that far before, but I can make my way there shortly. After that we can head to Ragnarsson to meet with Rollo so we can all head up north together," he spoke to the group.

"Fine," I muttered.

"I'll leave as soon as possible. Are you going to be okay here until I get back?" he turned to me and asked. I can't believe I was going to spend another night in this godforsaken cave, but Kole could move faster if I stayed behind.

"Yes, I'll be okay. Just hurry back please," I pleaded.

"I'll be back before you know it," he kissed me and headed back outside the cave.

12 – A Gift Worth Giving - Cassia

When I accepted this role to watch over Alexandria as a favor to the new queen, I thought it would be temporary. For too long I have been stuck traveling back and forth from Cosa to Alexandria, making sure that we didn't have any more issues after eliminating Marcus.

There had been small uprisings here and there, but nothing serious. I'd placed some officers that I trusted to keep track of the day-to-day issues. Anything major that came along was to be passed to me immediately. I was under the impression that this new age of life was a collective, but honestly ever since the wedding I haven't heard much from the others.

The newlyweds were still on their honeymoon, enjoying life while I tried to rebuild the city after all the death and destruction that was caused by the Bellators. All while trying to maintain the beautiful way of life we had in Cosa. When my father died, I did not want to be a queen. However, since I've been thrust into this position, I've decided to be the best queen the country has ever seen. Admittedly, watching over a city that was not mine on top of all that was exhausting. The vampires weren't far from here, but Gio has made it very clear by his silence that he did not have the desire to be helpful to Alexandria. The distrust of us Romans was not going to wash away just because we won a battle together.

I was sitting in this empty throne room, drinking wine, talking to myself, and wondering when I would get to sail back home. Other than the boredom, things were thankfully going according to plan.

The construction in the market was almost complete. The arena would take some time, but it was coming along, as well. I sailed back to Alexandria on the guise of some great news. It would be laid at my feet shortly, and when the queen sees the gift I have for her, she would definitely consider allowing me to rule both Alexandria and Cosa. If it wasn't temporary, maybe my attitude towards ruling both would change.

"How long until they get back?" I yelled to my commander.

"They have just docked, my queen. They are on their way up to the villa now," he answered. I had my agenda in this game, but what I was doing was good for our country. Gracia would thrive under my full control. I just needed the others to see it, and this was going to be the perfect start. Two more commanders ran into the throne room completely out of breath.

"What is wrong with you two?" I sprung up out of my seat. "Is there a problem with the package?" The soldiers hunched over to catch their breath before speaking again.

"No, my queen. The package is still secure, but we have another visitor," he spoke through his deep breaths.

"Okay, well spit it out already. Who is the visitor that has you running for your lives, and why was I not notified that we had other visitors arriving today?" I pressed.

Around the corner came Kole dressed in his dark cloak and black armor with the raven of his house stamped on the front. He stopped at the entrance before he approached the throne smiling. Clearly, my men scrambling was amusing to him.

"King Kole, welcome. I was not expecting you. I would have made for a proper entrance." I shot a death stare at my soldiers.

"Good to see you, Cassia. No need to blame them. I know I am unexpected. I did not have time to send proper word," he walked over to the bar and poured himself a drink.

"I assume your honeymoon was great. You have been gone for some time."

"Eventful would be a better word, and it feels good to be back. Unfortunately, I don't return with the best news. We need to gather all the kings and queens to meet on a very urgent matter," he took a sip out of his cup before making a weird face at the taste.

"Urgent matter, you say. Straight to business, then." I waited somewhat impatiently for him to explain.

"Normally I would caution against too much business but, seeing as we have another world-ending problem, we need to meet and figure out how to proceed. I can fill you in on the details on the way." He placed the cup down abruptly and turned my way.

"On the way? To where exactly?"

"Yes, on the way back to the Delphi caves. I don't have a whole lot of time..." He turned toward the door and I could hear the chains dragging down the hallway. It was perfect timing for me to place myself in the good graces of the new king and queen.

"All right, Kole. Understood. But first I have a gift for you and Octavia, one that I would love to bring to her myself, seeing as we are all meeting." I smiled in triumph.

"Of course. What is this gift anyway? I hope it's not too big to carry back," he joked.

"Oh, I think we will be just fine. No matter what it takes you are going to want to bring this gift back to your wife." I waved my hands to signal for the other soldiers to bring in my gift.

They dragged in the man, his blonde hair covered in dirt. He was shackled around his hands and feet. He fought the grip of the soldiers as they threw him down at the feet of Kole. Behind the man was a slender woman walking slowly, no need for the guards to wrestle with her as she came along willingly.

"My king, I believe that you were looking for these two." My exuberance I'm sure could be felt as much as seen on my face. Kole walked over to the man and lifted his axe under his chin so that his eyes met his.

"Titus Bellator," he said calmly. "The Gods have brought us back together." He couldn't hide how surprised he was, as he looked past Titus to the woman behind him. Nothing but pain and betrayal filled his eyes for a woman he barely knew. "I will not be passing any judgment on you. That right alone belongs to the woman you stabbed in the back. The woman that would have laid down her entire life for you to have a better one." There was no space between them as he released the contempt in his words to her. "The woman that fought the Gods tooth and nail to make sure she had enough to come back and save you." His eyes went pitch black with the contempt he felt towards her, and I could feel the darkness emanating off him.

"My king," I cautioned. Kole looked back toward me and attempted to calm himself down. He shifted over to Titus and punched him in the jaw without warning. The man fell flat onto his face completely unconscious. I guess that's one way to work out your anger.

"Grab your things. We leave as soon as possible. Make sure he does not speak, or I may not be able to stop myself from killing him," he said as he walked out of the throne room.

Koel Alexander © 2024
Raven & Fire Series

13 – Death's Kiss - Kare

Octavia was trying, but I could tell that she was still apprehensive when it came to Gio. I appreciate her attempt to put her feelings aside just for me. It was probably harder than we all realized. Mars instilled his resentment into her, and I was no stranger to warring with yourself.

She decided to find a room and get some rest while she waited for my brother to get back. She must have been exhausted from all the obstacles they had to endure. They are the strongest people that I know, because what Delphi put them through in Midselium sounded cruel and miserable. On top of that, we have yet another mystery threat looming over our heads.

Things could only get more complicated from here. The cave was reaching its breaking point, especially after my fight with Veronica. You could taste the tension in the air. I never intended to hurt her, and on some level I couldn't... but my instinct took over and it was kill or be killed. Maybe now I garnered some respect as a number two from the other vampires, or I might have gained a handful of new enemies. Crapshoot either way, but I guess that's just how these things go.

I was worried about how Gio was going to take all this news. We knew that the deal Kole made in the arena would come back to haunt us, but not knowing made everything extremely frustrating. If I'm being honest, after he received some closure from Selene at the wedding, he was in a much better mood, but this had to open old wounds. I decided to go and check on him. He always felt like he was alone in this. Maybe I could help pull him out of that abyss.

I pushed past the thin curtain separating his room from the throne room. He had candles lit as he rested in a chair, goblet in his hand with his feet elevated on the table. I could tell by his posture that he had indulged in a fair share of blood. I know he heard me walk in, but he did not acknowledge me as I moved closer to the table.

"Have you come to check on my emotional state, little flower?" He didn't even bother to turn to me as he spoke, so I took a seat on the other side of the table. He was slouched in the chair, his shirt half open pulling my eyes to trace his muscles down his stomach.

"I just wanted to see how you were doing after hearing what my brother and Octavia shared." I tried to force myself to not let my eyes continue to wander. He was too sharp to not catch me staring.

"While I am glad that the king and queen have returned, I would have enjoyed some good news for a change, but I have been expecting the bitch to poke her head back out sooner rather than later." He downed the cup in a single gulp, though I'm sure he wishes he could do the same with his sorrows right now. I didn't want to admit to snooping, but I figured now would be a good time to ask about the papers I found on the floor the other night.

"I saw the papers on your floor the other day were covered in Latin. Were you looking for a way to get rid of Delphi for good?" I inquired. He let out a deep sigh and sat up in his chair.

"I was looking for any clue that she has been confined at any point in history. There was a mention of an artifact in some of the text. Octavia and Kole have filled in the holes at least, solving that mystery," he admitted somberly.

"Then why do you still seem so upset?"

"I'm not upset, Kare. I've lived for almost two hundred years harboring this hate for the spirit, even after I thought I killed her. I spent all those years miserable and aching for Selene only to find out that the revenge that I thought I enacted did not stick. I'm just.... I'm just tired," he said softly. "Time as a vampire is forever moving, but forever stagnant. Life moves through you, not with you. Do you know how many nights I've pondered this existence?" I was speechless as he continued the rant. "It's endless and exhausting, and it took me decades to realize it," he dropped his head in defeat.

I walked over to his chair and put my hand on his shoulder to comfort him. I could not even grasp what it must feel like to carry this for over two lifetimes.

"The past is the past, and though it hurts we have the power to move us toward the future. I didn't become immortal to only get to live a couple of months of it," I joked.

Gio looked up, and in a blink of an eye had us both on our feet with his face and body dangerously close to mine. I gasped, almost stumbling back from the unexpected closeness. My body started to tense, followed by the chills flooding over every limb. I hated when he did this, but I wouldn't dare push him away. My body called for whatever was going to come next.

"The future is you, little flower. You will be the best of us all, and you don't even know it," he spoke softly. "As much as I hate the design of the Gods, I believe that they placed you here to lead us into something new. The same way they placed your brother to bring in a new age to this miserable country," he spoke with intent.

"Why do you think I'm so special?" I pressed for an answer.

"You are only scratching the surface of what you are capable of, trust me," he moved even closer, which I didn't know was possible. My heart was slamming against my chest as my head tilted up toward him, inviting him to make his next move, begging him to let go of some of that damn restraint. He dragged his tongue across his fangs and my eyes followed.

"With your permission, of course," he didn't get to finish as I grabbed the bottom of his shirt and forced his mouth down onto mine. The taste of blood on his lips and his tongue ignited the hunger in my stomach, so I pulled him closer. Something I was not sure that I wanted but now there was no question.

Koel Alexander © 2024
Raven & Fire Series

My hands reached up as I wrapped them around his neck, refusing to let him break the embrace. His hands grasped firmly against my waist as he lifted me onto the table and placed himself in between my thighs, making room for his body against mine. I was lost in a tidal wave of sensation every time his skin touched mine. I gasped and reveled for more. Being a vampire made even the most normal interaction intoxicating. Every feeling was dialed up to an immeasurable amount, and the way Gio moved his hands was going to break me.

I could feel him getting aroused further, exciting me and heating me at the center of my body. He pulled his head back and kissed his way down my neck, pressing his fangs along my skin. Everything inside me anticipated the bite, which is something I would have never thought I would want.

I only know that right now my body pleaded for him to plunge his fangs into me. He must have felt me leaning my neck, urging him to do what needed to be done, because he widened his mouth prepared to bite until I heard someone walking through the curtain. Standing in the center of the room, her mouth wide in complete surprise, was Octavia. I pushed Gio back completely embarrassed, even though I was doing nothing wrong.

"Perfect timing as usual, my queen," Gio muttered sarcastically, covering up the bulge in his pants.

"Octavia I...I," I started to try to come up with words to explain what she walked in on.

"It's fine, Kare," her face said the opposite.

"Are you sure it is fine, Tav? No offense, but I can hear your heartbeat from here, and you do not seem happy."

"Just a bit of shock, that's all. I came to tell Gio that Kole was back, and he needed to see us all. I hear that he brought something important back from Alexandria." She stood unreasonably still, but her heart was still thumping, reinforcing her unhappiness.

"Well, we should all join him. I will need a couple of minutes to gather myself," he turned back to me and winked as a smirk lit up his face. Octavia was not amused.

"Can you cut it out, Gio?" I mumbled quietly.

"Yea, gather yourself. While you're at it, how about I leave it to you to tell Kole what you were about to do with his little sister?" She shot back before she walked out of the room. We sat silent for a time trying to make sense of what transcribed between us, the cloudiness in my mind clearing with every passing second.

"I think that was better than I expected," Gio joked.

"I guess so since she didn't pummel your face this time," I agreed casually as I fixed my dress so that my brother wouldn't think less of me.

"Maybe we can finish this discussion some other time," he rubbed his hands along mine.

"Yeah, maybe. Let's go see what my brother has brought back, trap the spirit, and save the world. Only then can we revisit this talk." I gave him a smirk.

"Playing hard to get. Excellent. I've always enjoyed the hunt," he smiled.

Koel Alexander © 2024
Raven & Fire Series

The other vampires stood in the background in the throne room having dozens of side conversations. So much has happened here in the last couple of days, so most things failed to hold their attention. I emerged from behind the throne, walking side by side with Gio. I was getting fewer sneers and stares after my disagreement with Veronica. She stood in the back with her usual crew of followers, but her eyes averted mine.

Jordan was sitting at the tables with a group. When he saw me, he smiled and waved in my direction. I'm glad he was okay, but he never did tell me what happened. Just because we can heal doesn't mean that Veronica should have put her hands on him. Hopefully all of that was finished now, but I could only be so lucky.

My brother walked down into the throne room slowly. Thank the Gods Octavia wasn't going to tell him what she walked in on. I felt maybe fate was on my side because he had a scowl on his face already. Octavia ran to greet him as he made his way down, and I sent a smile his way. Gio sat on the throne as he usually did, waiting for what we all needed to be present for.

"Welcome back, brother," I spoke before everyone else, testing the temperature in his mood.

"Good to see you, sister," he smiled and wrapped his arms around Octavia. I loved seeing them together. They really did complete each other. Never too high, never too low, just right.

"I assume your trip was successful, my young king," Gio asked. Kole didn't say anything, but he whispered something into Octavia's ear and her entire body went rigid. I know I shouldn't listen, but her heart pounded ferociously in response to his words. I have no idea what could have made her so upset until Kole signaled for the rest of the company to walk in.

I recognized the queen of Cosa, Cassia. I could never forget her piercing blue eyes and bright blonde hair. She was watching over Alexandria while my brother and Tav were gone. She seemed to be in good spirits.

Behind her a man was being dragged in chains. I recognized him from the balcony. The man who made my first trip to Gracia one of the worst things I've ever been through. It was Marcus' son. I couldn't remember his name, but the woman who followed behind him I knew all too well. The one who betrayed her own kin, Floria, walked in unchained, her head down watching the ground and avoiding her sister's gaze... the same way she did when she gave us over to that monster.

14 – Fun While It Lasted - Rollo

I wanted to sleep the day away and never leave her side. After last night, I have never felt so alive in my whole life. I rubbed my hands across my neck reliving the memory. The puncture marks were gone, but I would never forget how they felt. Those teeth of hers were both terrifying and exhilarating.

The fear and the thrill mixed into one giant bowl of pleasure. How was I supposed to put that into words? I decided to walk down to the water and enjoy some of this beautiful weather before I traveled up north, where I was sure to freeze my balls off. Fucking Ivar. After everything that has happened, he managed to walk away with his head, and this is shit he decided to pull.

"My king," a soldier came running over interrupting my pestering inner hatred for Ivar.

"What do you need, soldier?" I asked and he handed me a parchment.

"A letter was sent from the vampire king."

"Interesting. I wonder if he wants me to return his only friend yet," I joked. I ripped open the letter but before I could start reading, the skies got dark as storm clouds started to roll in. This was weird because I wasn't doing it, and it was sunny seconds ago. "What the hell is going on?" I jumped up from the grass, stashing the parchment inside my pants. The hair on my neck and arms rose in response to the lightning I could feel building above me in the clouds. I turned to run, but a streak of lightning struck me directly in the chest, knocking the world into darkness.

I woke up in the center of a giant ship. The water washed up over the edges, but somehow the hull remained dry. Violent streaks of lightning slammed into the water illuminating the aggressive waves. The sound of the thunder was not only vibrating my ears but the entire boat. How it managed to not capsize was an act of the Gods themselves. I picked myself up off the hull trying to figure out where I was.

All I remembered was walking by the water at home and then being slammed by lightning. I checked for injuries, but I felt no pain. I reached for my hammer, which I never leave behind, only to find out that it was gone. I must have lost it when I got hit by that lightning.

I walked to the front of the boat to see if I could make some sense of this because I was starting to get freaked out. Something massive crashed at the other end of the boat, almost flipping it entirely. I turned my head to see what had landed on this boat. How I could have possibly missed something that big fall from the sky?

A gigantic man, easily almost eight feet tall, stretched his arms in a giant yawn. I recognized him immediately from the time we spent at the omega in Midselium. His long red beard matched his messy long hair.

"Holy Helheim!" I said to myself as the God of Thunder reached his right hand into the sky. On command, his mystical hammer Mjolnir came twirling through the smoke and settling in his hands. The God trained his eyes on me and bellowed out a giant laugh. It was comforting and frightening at the same time.

"Rollo, my boy!" he exclaimed. I had no idea how I was supposed to respond. Should I bow out of respect or just remain quiet? Kole and Octavia were the ones that did all the talking to the Gods, I usually just stand in the back and try not to get killed. "Loosen up, my boy. Why so tense?" His words surprised me even more.

"I'm not tense," I replied slightly self-conscious. "It's not every day the God of Thunder slams you in the chest with lightning just so he can talk to you on a boat that is unable to sink." I tried to rationalize it, but no words could make this make sense to common man.

"Who said this boat couldn't sink?" His smirk was filled with mischief and mirth. I could see how similar we were...

"Well, I just figured it wouldn't since you jumped down from the sky and it's still in one piece." As I spoke, the God of Thunder began to stomp on the hull with both feet rocking the boat as hard as he could. "Uhhh, what are you doing?" I practically screeched as I tried to hold on for dear life. Thor's laugh pulsated through my head in every direction. "If you brought me here to kill me, this is not the way I planned to die." The movement of the boat stopped immediately, and the God's eyes pierced mine, the violent storm still dancing across his pupils.

"Kill you?" He asked. "Why would I kill you? I just thought we were having a little fun. These meetings are always so formal. I just figured a man of your taste would enjoy a bit of excitement. You are molded after me, my son." He spoke as if I was spoiling all the fun he was having.

"Not to be a pain in the ass, sir, but I'm kind of on a time crunch," I explained cautiously. Thor seemed unimpressed, like I stole the wind from his sails.

"I guess you are like the others, all business." He didn't wait for me to respond before he waved his hand and dropped us in the middle of an empty tavern.

While this is more of my scene, I really needed to get back. A king disappearing in the middle of the day was not going to look very good on my part.

"I know you're in a hurry, kid, but have a drink. There are things we must discuss," he pulled out one of the biggest cups I have ever seen and poured the ale to the brim.

"Thank you!" It took me two hands to slide the cup in front of me, and I had to stand on my feet to take a sip.

"Since you're all about business, Rollo, let's get straight to the reason I invited you to my favorite tavern," he sat down and grabbed his cup with ease.

"Is it because there are no lines?" I joked. The God of Thunder bellowed with laughter while rubbing the foam out of his messy beard.

"I knew I liked you. In all seriousness, it's about your friends in Midselium."

"Kole and Octavia? Are they okay?" I asked.

"Now they are. That nasty spirit trapped them there unexpectedly," he took another sip from the giant cup.

"Delphi trapped them there? How is that even possible?"

"I honestly don't know. It's so hard to keep track of who can do what these days. What I do know is that my father has been missing for weeks, and man has it been glorious without him always barking orders. Thor, go do this. Thor, go do that. Thor, wipe out my enemies. Thor, stop drinking so much." He rambled on and on in between gulps.

"Where are they now?" I asked, trying to get him back on the topic at hand.

"Don't jump ahead, Rollo. I've been enjoying this brief bit of freedom. Jumping to every beck and call of the All-father is exhausting. Unfortunately, a few days ago, I felt my father's presence return. The spirit had locked him out of Midselium, and he spent all his time trying to contact your friends."

"So, since you could feel him again that means that he's back and he can get them out, right?" Thor slammed down his cup and gave me a sneer which meant that was my last chance to stop interrupting the story.

"Now me, I'm not so good at the prophecy stuff. I prefer to talk with my hammer, but Odin has his own way of doing things. He returned and came to me and requested I bring you a message while he works on freeing your friends." I nodded in agreement not offering any input. I made the decision that living was more important than vomiting the thousands of questions that I had. "So, listen carefully, even though I'm likely to forget some of the things he told me. Odin says that the curse is loose."

"The curse is loose," I said to myself. Thor continued to speak.

"There is an artifact hidden in the northern lands of the Norse, one that can help neutralize your spirit problem," he said, then paused.

"Anything else?" I asked.

"I'm trying to remember," he barked, clearly agitated. "You know how difficult it is the remember all the prophecies I have heard?"

"I can't even imagine, sir."

He scoffed, maybe finding me amusing or irritating. I'm not sure which nor do I care so long as I leave this interaction with my head firmly on my body. "Odin said something about the head of the cursed will show you the way or be the way maybe... I'm not sure but something about a cursed head should help." I stared at him completely baffled. How could you not remember the words to a prophecy that could lead to me living or dying? Maybe this is why my mother insists I not drink so much. Thor's beard.

"Okay, so I know where to start at least." I started to work out a plan in my mind as I got up from my seat and moved away from the table.

"So, you know what you need to do, young warrior?" Thor asked.

"Yes. I need to head north, take care of that traitor Ivar, and find Kole's brother so we can find this cursed head and this artifact to stop Delphi." I reiterated methodically.

"That's the spirit! Truly a descendant of mine. Grab your hammer, head up north and be the hero!" He roared before taking another giant gulp from the cup. It's like the cup never ended.

"You wouldn't know anything about any giant beasts terrorizing the woods around Ragnarsson, would you?" I asked hoping he could solve another mystery for me.

"Nope, and even if I did, I wouldn't be able to tell you. You know the Gods and their rules and all. If all else fails, I say kill it," he shrugged. "Now, get back home and do what you need to do," he said as he clanged his cup against mine. My muscles strained to keep the cup up straight. I thought he would just send me back after we finished talking, but he kept nodding toward my cup. It took me a minute to get the hint and I wished I didn't. He was going to make me chug this giant cup.

"Have some respect, Rollo. Never leave a drink behind," he laughed.

"Seriously?" I asked. He smiled and tilted the cup to the sky, chugging the rest of the ale. I followed suit knowing that I would regret this later.

I woke up in the middle of the field alone, in disbelief that not only have I seen the God of Thunder twice, but I drank with him too. I don't know if the ale was real, but I don't feel like I chugged a gallon's worth, so that's a good thing. I brushed off the dirt and headed back to the dome. If I was going to see what this curse was about, I definitely needed some backup.

Kole and Octavia were being held hostage this entire time. That explains a lot. I didn't expect them to go on their honeymoon and fall off the face of the earth for so long. It must have been horrible being imprisoned there. Somehow that wicked spirit managed to rope Ivar into this, which gave me a real reason to make sure that he ended up dead this time.

I needed to get up there quickly before Kole reached out. I wanted to have something to show for all the time that he was gone. I was supposed to take care of this for him, to alleviate some of the pressure he was under. Not that I needed to prove anything, but I wanted to do it as his best friend. The same way he would do for me. I filled Marcella in on my talk with Thor and found it odd that she was not at all shaken by the information.

"I know everything is happening very quickly, but you don't want to at least talk about what happened last night?" she inquired.

"If I talk about it then there is no way we are leaving here," I replied smugly.

"So, it is safe to assume you enjoyed yourself?" She closed the gap between us.

"Of course, I enjoyed myself!" I pulled her even closer.

"And you enjoyed all of it?" she searched my face for a very specific answer, and I knew what she was referring to as I rubbed my neck over the area where her bite marks used to be.

"All of it, though maybe a little less teeth next time," I laughed.

"I'll work on my technique. It's been a while since I've used them for pleasure," she rubbed her tongue along the tips of her fangs forcing me to question my composure.

"But since you are all about business today, let's focus on what we need to do." She turned quickly, breaking me from the trance she had me under.

"I just need one more thing, then we can worry about business," I pulled her back, wrapped her up in my arms and kissed her like it was the last thing I would do.

"Maybe you are right. Let's get moving or I will never let you leave this dome," she smiled.

I summoned the company to put together a small group to travel with us up north. The sun was beginning to set and now was the time to move. My mother and sister waited at the gates. They were unhappy that I was leaving so soon, but they understood what I had to do. If it all worked out, I'll be back home in no time.

"It saddens me that you have to leave already, my son. You just returned to us," my mother hugged me.

"I know, mother, but I promised Kole I would look into what is going on up north, and now with all this new information it's imperative that I leave immediately." I returned her embrace, squeezing tighter than she could probably handle. "Sister, take care of our mother. I will return shortly."

"I will. At this point, might as well be my kingdom," she joked.

"Maybe one day, sister, but for now just watch over it for me." I kissed her on the forehead.

"It was a pleasure meeting you all. Auslaug, Aria, thank you for all the hospitality, and if it pleases you both I would love to spend more time in Ragnarsson. Everything here is sensational." Marcella gave a slight bow.

"You are always welcome here, my dear. You have lit a fire under my son. He is destined to burn bright, and maybe you are what he needs to get him there," my mother spoke softly.

"Yeah, that and a brain," my sister interrupted. They all shared a laugh and we prepared to make our farewell as we journeyed up to the wasteland to solve this once and for all. I reached into my armor to make sure that the parchment was still there, I decided I would read it later on. Getting up north as soon as possible was the most important thing. Gio would have to wait. I hadn't heard anything from him since Marcella and I left, and Kare was safe with the vampires so no need to worry.

"How long do you think it will take us to get there?" Marcella asked.

"A couple of days, max. The group we are traveling with is small, so we should be able to cover ground fairly quickly."

"And what about the sun?" she pressed, rightfully concerned.

Koel Alexander © 2024
Raven & Fire Series

"I have sent others ahead to find us shelter. We will stay on the trail, and when they find a suitable place for us to camp, they will signal."

"I see you are very attentive, a necessary trait for a king," she teased.

"I think I'm doing a good job my first couple of months on the job," I said confidently.

"I think you are, as well," she agreed.

15 – Romans Revenge - Octavia

All the pain and rage flooded back, while what I walked in on between Kare and Gio faded to the back of my mind. The drums and voices were on a rampage. It was taking everything in my power to keep my fury contained. It sounded like an entire legion was marching into battle in my head. I allowed myself some peace while I was in Midselium, ignoring the fact that Floria was still on the run. I made a choice to live in the bliss of my own ignorance. Every day was a struggle, but while Kole and I were together he made it easy to not think of her.

A small part of me would have been content to pretend that she never did what she did. She is my baby sister after all, and all I have left of my family in this world. We shared a love that I thought would never fizzle, something that nothing could come in between. Now, all I feel are flames and it is making me numb. I tried to convince myself I left all that betrayal back in Alexandria. I wanted it all to be a dream, that she didn't shove a knife directly into my heart and twist it around for good measure. But here she was standing before me, avoiding my gaze the same way she did when she tipped off Marcus and her pathetic husband.

Alexandria's flower covered in mud next to the enemy that she chose over her flesh and blood. All of it rooted in some dark jealousy of wanting to be queen. How long had she quietly resented me for being next in line, for something that I never wanted? How long did the snake slither right next to me while I had no idea I was in danger?

"Clear the room!" Gio commanded.

Kole stood behind me instinctively, staying close just in case I managed to lose control of my temper. As the rest of the crowd cleared the main space, I was running through all the different things I wanted to say to her. What was there left to say that I didn't say before? My mouth was dry, and my palms were sweaty with anticipation, but I had a knot in the pit of my stomach the size of Olympus. Strong arms wrapped around me from behind, snapping me out of my thoughts.

"Good to see you, Queen Octavia," Cassia's bright blue eyes stared back at me. Kole let me go once he felt some of the tension leave my body.

"Good to see you as well, Cassia. How are things in Cosa?" I asked, trying to ignore the prisoners.

"Cosa is great, when I actually get to spend some time there. I did not expect you and Kole to be away for so long," she admitted.

"We ran into some unforeseen circumstances while we were trying to enjoy ourselves," I said modestly.

"Your husband informed me on the way here," she looked back towards Kole. "By the way, I prefer to never travel in your fancy portals again. I'm pretty sure I almost lost my lunch," she chuckled.

"It takes some getting used to," he interrupted us.

"But more importantly, I wanted to show that even after you left, I never gave up searching for the traitors that put you all in danger. With a show of good faith and our continued alliance, I brought them straight to you," she waved her hand in a display of the prisoners.

"I appreciate that, Cassia. You are exactly what Gracia needs right now in a ruler. I am grateful my people of Alexandria could rely on you while I was gone." I pushed past her and walked over to Titus. He had a massive bruise on the side of his face, covered in dirt, smelling and looking worse for wear. I needed to get some answers from him about where he had been this entire time, but I'm not sure I could refrain from killing him as soon as I heard his voice.

This man killed my brother and deserved nothing short of an excruciating death, but I wasn't a coward like him or my sister. It had to be done the right way. I slowly walked over to them. Floria's eyes remained on the ground still, but Titus forced his eyes to meet mine.

"I remember it like it was yesterday, you know. The day you showed up in my home and told me that I would bow before you and you would crush me," he remained silent. "For a second in Alexandria, I bet you thought you were closer to your goal.

Even though you managed to turn my sister against me, you are the one on your knees before me." My gaze shifted to my sister.

"You and I have much to discuss, but I'm barely holding it together as it is. You can pretend to be ashamed all you want, Floria, but I'll never let you forget that you dishonored our parent's memory. You dishonored Tiberius' memory, and you put your jealousy and personal ambitions above everything and everyone. The Gods have shown you the karma of your decisions. Take her away!" Cassia grabbed her arm and marched her out of the common area.

Kole rested his hand on my shoulder, the constant comfort that I needed to not lose my cool. I turned my attention back to my brother's killer. Now that my real emotional trigger was out of the room, I could get the answers that I need.

"I'm surprised you're so quiet, Titus. If I recall correctly, last I saw you, you couldn't keep your mouth shut," Kole teased but Titus remained silent. "Where is that big, brave Roman that was in my face telling me how I would never be his equal? How you would never give up the kingdom to someone like me? A dog, isn't that what you called me?" He kneeled down so that he was at eye level with Titus, who still refused to say a word. Maybe he needed a little bit of a push.

"He doesn't have much to say now, my love. He has lost it all. It was all taken from him, the same way he took it from me." I leaned closer to make sure that he could hear me. "I only wish that I could have been down on the sands when your brother took his last breath." Titus jumped up in his chains, reaching to try to grab any part of me. The chains on his feet sent him falling to the ground, but maybe he was finally ready to speak.

"We should have killed you as soon as you got off that dog's boat. You and that handmaiden bitch behind you!" Kole stepped forward, but I stopped him before he got to Titus. Now that he was talking, maybe he could tell us where he was hiding. "You're still a filthy Norse animal, always have been and always will be. A crown won't change that, King!" He spit at our feet.

"I'd say my worth has changed. Only one of us is chained up in a cave, covered in dirt. Not to mention only one of us ran into hiding. Wherever you were, did they tell you that I hunted down all those loyal to your father and killed them myself? I'm sure word would have reached you, unless you and the princess dug a nice hole to live in," Kole teased.

"My father was a fool clouded by tradition and a puppet in the grand schemes of his Gods. The people of Rae do not mourn for him, they love their prince. He is a stain to our name and I'm glad he's gone!" he spoke like a wounded puppy.

"At least he was a challenge," Kole shrugged ignoring his words, but I was paying very close attention. "Your father almost killed me in the arena, but I'm sure I could snap you in half without breaking a sweat."

"So that's where you stayed. I will make sure I take a visit to Rae to let them know the part you played in this war. I'm sure they will change their minds about their prince when they find out you ran like a coward," I smiled.

Whatever lies he spun in his retreat to Rae needed to be handled. Who knows how deep the blind loyalty runs. Those people still may not accept that information from me. There has always been tension between our countries. The news would have to come from someone neutral in order to win them over. One thing is for sure, their prince will not be returning to them.

Floria would have been perfect for this, but I couldn't trust her anymore. I was not entirely sure what I would even do with her now. Kole exiled his brother allowing him to live, but with everything that has happened since I wouldn't be surprised if he was regretting that decision.

"Are you going to kill me already, because honestly, this cave is miserable. No wonder my father kept these bottom feeders down here," he gestured toward Gio, who rose from his seat slowly.

"I assure you that I am not the one to antagonize, Roman. I am the one that ripped the head off your father," his fangs were exposed, followed by a deep growl in his throat. Titus jumped back in surprise. I was going to have to spend this entire time keeping everyone from killing him.

"Your mouth will be the death of you, Titus, but I won't let anyone here kill you except for me." His face relaxed into an evil smile.

"Well, we all know how that ended up the last time. Are you in a hurry to be reunited with your dead relatives?" Kole stepped forward, but I restrained him again. I know that he would have love the idea of taking care of him the same way he did Lucius, but I needed to do this on my own.

"The girl you fought that night in the ambush is long gone, and I assure you this won't play out the same way." I walked over to the others. "Set up the square, this ends tonight," I ordered and started to walk off, when Kole grabbed my arm.

"I assume there is no way to talk you out of this?" he asked.

"You already know what I'm going to say." He didn't like my response, but he'll just have to get over it.

There was a clearing just north of the cave. Gio had the other vampires clear a space and build a makeshift barrier for the square. I needed to end this tonight. It was the only way that I could move past it.

My family was gone, my sister a traitor, and the man in the mask still living and breathing. When Kole killed Lucius that should have made me feel better, but the fire still burned to get the revenge I was owed. Revenge that my conscious demanded, and Mars made sure that it was burning bright inside me. All of it I planned to unleash on Titus this very night.

I asked Gio to provide him a place to rest for the fight and make sure he received food and water. I would get no satisfaction in killing him if he was frail and weak. When the sun falls, he will be going with it.

My daggers were holstered to my side and a spear strapped to my back as I waited patiently for the traitor to be walked to his death. Every second was an eternity, the drums and the voices pounded begging for blood. Kole, Gio, and Kare stood behind me as Cassia walked back into the cave to escort Titus into the square.

"What's taking them so long?" I said impatiently.

"They are coming now, Tav. I can hear them," Kare said. I couldn't hear anything over the fury brewing inside me. I needed to calm myself. Fighting this way would surely have history repeating itself. Through the trees emerged Titus, still chained at his hands and feet but dressed in whatever Roman armor he managed to salvage in the cave.

Floria followed behind him, escorted by two of Cassia's men. They kept her close even though I would not expect her to try to escape a second time.

The sight of him triggered the flame instantly. I didn't have to look down to tell that my hands had begun to glow. As if he could sense my anxiousness, Kole rested his hand on my shoulder.

"Be calm," he whispered to me.

"I am calm," I replied as the tickle of the flame ignited at my fingertips.

"You don't look calm," he reached down and set his hand into mine. "You are the fire of Gracia and a queen. He is beneath you. If I can't talk you out of this, then I will encourage you to complete this task quickly and take a step closer to making yourself whole again. What he has taken from you cannot be replaced. I know that. The Gods will make sure he is put where he belongs, and I know you are the perfect person to see this through." He smiled, reassuring me with every word and gesture. There will always be something about my husband, he just always knows what to say.

"Can we get this over with?" Gio implored from behind us. "Psycho spirit is still on the loose, unknown curse running rampant up north, and mystery artifact to retrieve before we even have a chance at moving forward, yet again. You should have just let me rip him to pieces like his father," he suggested.

"No, I need to do this myself." Titus stood right across from me as Cassia removed his restraints and handed him a sword. He twirled the weapon in his hands, measuring its weight and balance. Even now in the wake of his death, he moved with arrogance.

"It's a shame that after I kill you, I probably won't make it away from here alive. I could take most of you down, but whatever that monster is, he is most likely pretty difficult to kill," he pointed his sword toward Gio, who shrugged in agreement.

"You hasten toward victory and the fight hasn't even begun. I would say I'm surprised, but after fighting your brother it's clear that your family thinks very highly of themselves," Kole said amusingly.

"How about when I'm done gutting your bitch, I can pay you back for what you did to my brother!" Titus grabbed a shield.

"Oh, trust me, I would love to add another Bellator to my axe, but this life is not mine to claim. If you win, I promise no one here will harm you, but you won't win so my promise doesn't mean much." He planted a kiss on my cheek and walked back to the others to observe.

"Shall we begin?" Titus clanked the sword to his shield and charged without a word. I hadn't taken my eyes off him since they walked him out. I was ready for when he came at me. He closed the distance quickly with the shield leading his charge. He was going to try to overpower me.

I prepared for the impact, but shifted to my left, dodging the full force of his attack. He recovered quickly slashing his sword in my direction. I raised my spear in time to block his attack. Our weapons locked for position.

Koel Alexander © 2024
Raven & Fire Series

"Well would you look at that, has the useless queen learned how to defend herself?" Titus taunted me. He was trying to unnerve me, the same as before. He pushed on the sword, his strength threatening to overwhelm me as we stood in our stalemate. I called up the flame and slammed my head into his nose, forcing him to fall back.

"You bitch!" He yelled holding his arm up to his face to stop the stream of blood. He charged again slashing his sword in every direction looking for an opening, but the spear managed to parry all his attacks. Titus brought his sword down with two hands, and I barely managed to get the spear up in time to block the attack as he tried to use his strength to overpower me again.

"If all else fails, you can always thank the Gods for leading you to this moment, but let's be honest. If it wasn't for your dog over there you would already be dead." He spit in my face completely catching me by surprise. He brought his sword down even more, forcing me down to my knees. I had no way to counter the full weight of his sword. I left my guard open and he kicked me directly in the chest, sending me sliding through the dirt to the other side of the square.

I got back on my feet quickly, cursing to myself that I lost my concentration, but as I turned to return to the fight Titus pressed for another attack. I managed to dodge his sword, but the shield slammed against my head, knocking me back down to the dirt.

"Come on, Tav. Get up!" The voice sounded like Kare, but the ringing in my ear from his attack drowned out the noise.

"Why am I even entertaining this nonsense?" Titus laughed. I willed myself back to my feet, barely regaining my balance from the last strike. I swung out wide with my spear hoping to gain some ground, but he was too fast. His laughing and taunting further pushed me into anger, and I could not find my bearings.

Titus blocked my attack again as his fist collided with my jaw, knocking me to the ground once more. Before I could get back to my feet, Titus straddled me pinning my hand down under his knee. He let out a deep evil laugh as he punched me over and over, the pain of every blow sending a shockwave through me.

The Gods always reserve the cruelest test for me. I replayed watching Tiberius die in front of my face, I replayed the image of my slaughtered parents, I replayed Floria turning me over to Marcus and the flame responded to my call.

Titus stopped momentarily as the heat around us started to rise. He stopped long enough for me to grab a hold of his leg and begin to burn the flesh from his body. He screamed, releasing my hand from under his knee and frantically reaching for the burnt flesh. His eyes were swallowed with anger as he scrambled to punch me again, but I caught his fist burning more skin on his hand, as well. The fire of Mars was pulsating, moving all that anger and anguish directly into battle. Titus stumbled back clutching his hand in pain.

"No more games, you are dead!" He rushed blindly without any of his weapons looking to end the fight quickly. My vision was slowed and sharp as I moved with pure instinct, blocking his punches and countering when I had an opening.

Everything around me began to slow down. I could almost predict his strikes. His pursuit began to slow from fatigue, but I was just getting started. He exhausted himself with every missed attack, and I gained more confidence.

"Any last words before you see your father and your brother, Titus?" I asked tauntingly.

"Fuck you!" He struggled to catch his breath before rushing me yet again. Instead of waiting this time, I rushed him head-to-head. He punched me in the ribs, causing some discomfort, but the flames burned away the pain. I grabbed Titus' arm to burn him again, I could see my reflection in his eyes as fire inside me burned true. He screamed and thrashed against my grip in pain, unable to free himself. I swept out his legs from beneath him and plunged my dagger into the middle of his bicep, pinning him to the ground.

Titus writhed and screamed in pain as the gold gem on the hilt protruded from his arm. He tried to reach for the blade, but he would never be able to remove it. I rose to my feet taking a moment to enjoy the pain that Titus deserved as he yelled to Olympus. I struggled to steady my breathing as the power of Mars still burned. I was mere seconds away from my vengeance.

I looked over to Kole the same way he looked to me in his Holmgang, the last comforting reassurance that we shared. He nodded in approval. I pulled the second dagger from its holster and slowly walked over Titus. He had lost so much blood that he was barely conscious, but he needed to be awake for his departure from this world. I straddled him and slapped him across the face to get his attention. When his half-lifeless eyes looked into mine, I spoke the words that have been haunting me since that grave night.

"Witness your demise," and I plunged my dagger directly into his heart. I watched the life of my tormentor leave this world forever. The drums began to silence, the voices simmered, and for a small moment I felt the semblance of peace. I felt redemption. I felt like I could finally close the door on my underlying pain.

16 – Peace Comes At A Price - Octavia

I am finally free. Free of the demons that have been gnawing at my heels since the night of the ambush. Titus was on his way to the underworld to meet his useless, pathetic family, and live out their days in torture. As good as that felt, the job was not finished. The other traitor still breathes. No matter what I decided to do with her, dead or alive, she would never aid my peace or ease the pain from her betrayal.

Kole walked me back to the cave, hastily nursing my wounds, but I knew that Mars' fire would heal me quickly. All I need is some rest and time to clear my head.

"You fought brilliantly. I'm proud of you. Although seeing him hit you makes me want to resurrect him and kill him all over again." Kole softly touched the bruise on my cheek.

"He got what he deserves, and my brother has his justice. That is all I care about. Hopefully that pleases him."

"I know it will," he put his hand under my chin and lifted my eyes to his. "Don't ever think they aren't proud of everything you have done in their name. They believed in you then and they believe in you still." He kissed me deeply and I returned his passion in kind, even though my body ached all over.

"Do we leave for Ragnarsson tomorrow?"

"We will stop in Lundr first and summon Rollo from there, so we can all head north together," he smiled. "I would like to check on my mother before we save the world for a second time," he admitted and paused.

"What's the matter?" I asked.

"I also think it's time for Kare to come clean about what happened to her. It is unfair to keep my mother in the dark." His guilt must be eating him alive to suggest this.

"Is that your choice to make?" I questioned him.

"No, but it is my fault, and we can't keep running from the problem. It needs to be dealt with," he stated seriously.

"Are we still talking about Kare, or are you talking about something else?" His silence was clear. I had one more thing to deal with before we left, and I would get no sleep this night trying to figure out what I was going to do.

"I'll face it in the morning, Kole. Just hold me tonight."

"I would have it no other way, my love." We walked into one of the rooms together, washed off the day, and held each other as I forced myself to get some sleep.

Sleep provided no solace for the choice I was forced to make today. Dealing with the last traitor of Alexandria, my own kin. The 'flower' of my country is what my mother once called her, before blood and betrayal stained her petals. I prepared myself without thought, an empty shell going through the motions to make myself presentable.

"Are you okay, my love?" Kole walked up beside me as I finished putting on my dress. It was a deep black dress lined with grey fur stretching to the floor. My daggers sat in a holster around my back and Kole placed a fur cloak over my shoulders.

"If I'm being honest, I'm not sure how I feel. She hurt me, Kole. Deeply, but she is the only family I have left. What example would I be setting if I just sentenced her to die? What kind of queen would I be if I let this slide?"

"I want to agree with you, but you have seen what sparing an enemy has done. Kyut and Ivar are directly connected to the problem we now face. At night I wonder if I should have just ended it when I had the chance," he avoided eye contact with me.

"What are you trying to say?" I questioned him.

"You know what I'm trying to say," he stood up straight.

"You want me to kill my sister?!" My tone couldn't hide the anger in my voice.

"It may be for the best, Octavia," he contested.

"So, you charge me to do what you couldn't?" I poked him in the chest.

"I killed my father for you," he raised his voice, but I could tell he wanted to take it back immediately.

"I never asked you to!" I was so angry there was no sense in hiding it. "Fuck you, Kole!" He reached out to me, but I was on my way out before he could respond.

How dare he ask me to do that when his brother insulted me at every turn and threatened to kill me? Kole spared him easily. Why was I always the one that had to sacrifice? Why was I the one that needed to give and give and give? Fuck him and fuck the Gods. I rushed to the common room where Floria was being watched over by Cassia's men. I ordered them to release her and for everyone to clear the room. This conversation needed no audience.

I stood in this empty, cold, dark cave as Floria finally decided to acknowledge my presence.

"So, you became queen after all. Seems odd for someone who claims they never wanted it. But in true Octavia fashion you managed to get whatever you want anyway," she spoke coldly.

"Out of all the things you could say to me, that is the first thing that came to mind," I clenched my fist before I spoke again. "You have let those men poison your thoughts and turn you against me, when all I have ever done is try to get back to you. All I wanted to do was free you from them," I retorted.

"But I told you before, sister, my mind was not poisoned. Once Tiberius and our parents were killed and you were gone, I was so close to something that I thought would never be in the cards for me. I mourned all of you until I couldn't anymore. There was nothing left but for me to rule, and that pathway was clear. It was my chance, but you couldn't let me have it could you," she spit in my direction.

"I would have given up my life for you, Floria. Why don't you understand that?" Her reasoning for everything was so infuriating.

"All I understand is that you stole my kingdom. On a lighter note, you killed my bastard of a husband. For that I am grateful, but with him goes my claim to Rae, as well," she said.

"You are still thinking about ruling after everything that has happened? What in Olympus' name has happened to you? Where is the girl I knew? The one that was supposed to help me pick out the right dress. The one who told me I can be sexy and dangerous. The one that was supposed to stand by my side at my wedding!" The tears fell from my eyes. Her mood never faltered. It was a cold stare of a stranger.

"She died the night that her parents were killed and she was sold off for political gain. I am nothing to you, Octavia, so kill me or let me go, but I'm certain we will never be what we once were. Too much has happened." She put her head back down and spoke no more. Another knife in my chest, deeper than the last. Maybe Kole was right, but I would never admit it.

"If that is how you see us now, sister, then I will not fight for you any longer. I will not spill your blood, I do not want it on my conscience. Cassia! Can you come in here please?" Her blonde hair appeared around the corner. "You were the one that located my sister, I give you leave to take her back to Cosa and decide her fate," I surrendered.

"Excuse me, my queen?" she asked, clearly confused.

"You are the queen of your kingdom. I release Floria to your custody, and you can deal with her however you please. She is no longer an extension of me." I walked up to my sister and whispered one last warning to her before I sent her away for good. "I am choosing mercy, sister, but do not make me regret it. Next time I will not be so pleasant. Go and live whatever life you can salvage. Like you said, we are nothing from here on out." She said nothing as Cassia's soldiers escorted her out of the room. She didn't even look back, as I watched the last piece of my Roman life walk right out the door.

I stormed back to my room to gather my things. I needed to move on quickly or everything that I was holding on to was going to collapse, my sanity along with it.

I didn't say much to anyone as we loaded the boat to sail back to Lundr. I was conveniently avoiding my husband whenever I was able to. He could tell I was not in the mood to talk so he didn't press. We would talk again eventually, but for now, I needed some space. I was going to pretend he didn't suggest I kill my sister. Maybe some family time would put his head back in perspective.

It would be nice to see his mother again. She was so sweet and supportive of us when we got married. One thing Kole was right about is that we owe her the truth. She should know what happened to Kare. Even though this was meant to be a happy reunion before we set off again, I had no idea how she was going to take this news. We continued down the river in silence before Kole caved and called out to me.

"We should be in Lundr soon. Kare and Gio are following behind us. They should arrive the night after we get there," he explained.

We locked eyes for another beat of silence. Eventually, I nodded my head and mumbled some words of acknowledgment that could barely be heard. That was one of the most awkward exchanges we have had since the first day we met, but that is where the conversation ended.

17 – Blood Ties & Northern Skies - Kare

The closer we got to Lundr, the more I felt like I was dying all over again. I convinced my mother everything was okay after we left the wedding. I kept my distance most of the night, and I told her I would not be coming home yet. That I was still interested in traveling and learning about all the other cultures in the world. I emphasized I wouldn't be coming back home anytime soon. She was aware that vampires existed, but she had no idea that I had become one of them.

Now with everything on the line, there was no way I could hide my nature during my stay. I missed home so much more than I wanted to admit but returning was going to be bittersweet. The sunrise in Lundr was one of the best things about the city and I would never see one again.

We traveled with a small company of vampires and humans to watch over us during the day while we slept. Better to be cautious with the spirit on the loose. Gio had been hammering that into our heads for months. Veronica traveled with us mostly in silence, completely ignoring my presence unless I was giving an order. I could care less as long as she followed the order, the silence made no difference to me.

We haven't had issues since our altercation in the cave, but I still did not trust her. Her passing sneer made it clear that she still harbored a dislike for me. She still didn't believe I was one of them. There is nothing I could do to prove otherwise.

I thought about Gio kissing me, then realized that I had kissed him back just as fiercely. Guilt soon followed, because if any of them found out what happened in his room they would start believing the lies.

I felt a quick flutter in my stomach thinking about his hands sliding across my skin as the kiss replayed over and over. Did that make Veronica's claims true? Was Gio only pursuing me because he knew that my brother was in power? Was he pursuing me? Is that why he saved me in the first place? I hope no one can see me panicking. *Gods, Kare, get out of your head.*

"I don't think I've ever seen you so worried since I've known you." Jordan appeared behind me. I was glad he decided to come. I needed someone I could talk to that wasn't Gio.

"I'm good, just thinking about going home. It's been so long and so much has happened," I answered.

"Are you worried about something?" he asked.

"Besides telling my mom that I am an immortal who drinks blood to sustain myself, I can influence mortals against their will, I'm stronger and faster than I could have ever dreamed., and apparently the blood lust has the potential to lead me to the point of murder?" I shrugged.

"Okay, I can see how that can be complicated. How much further until we get there?"

"Not too much further. We should be there by tomorrow night." We could probably reach the city tonight, but then I would have to sit around and wait to talk to my mother once the sun went down. I looked back at Gio. He wasn't too far behind us.

"Why do you keep staring at him?" Jordan asked.

"What are you talking about? I'm not staring at him," I responded, but Jordan was not convinced at all. He grabbed me by my arm and pulled me close so only I could hear him.

"Something happened between you two, didn't it?" Jordan whispered. My body tensed in alarm. I couldn't be that obvious. How the hell could he know without me even saying a word? I grabbed Jordan and dashed him off the trail to make sure no one was listening.

"Holy Olympus! Something did happen, didn't it?" He pressed for information.

"Jordan, listen to me. Nothing happened," I stressed. His face curled in disbelief, and he paused waiting for me to finally speak the truth.

"Whenever you're ready to tell the truth we can go back and join the others. You have been acting weird ever since we left. Something definitely happened," he reaffirmed, crossed his arms and waited.

"Okay fine, something happened, but you must promise not to tell anyone. I don't need anyone hating me any more than they already do," I pleaded with him.

"You know I would never tell. I'm just glad I was right. Now, let's talk details," he rubbed his hands together.

"That's not going to happen," I smiled and zipped us back to the group. We should be getting ready to find a place to camp pretty soon. Kole and Octavia should already be in the city, hopefully softening up my mother a little bit.

"Have the others found another place to sleep today?" I asked.

"Yes, they are preparing the cave right now. It's going to be a tight fit tonight," Jordan said with a smirk.

"Sounds like fun," I replied sarcastically. "How has Veronica been treating you? I know she's the one that attacked you even if you won't say it." He put his head down.

"You won't tell me your secret so I'm going to keep this to myself. I had a disagreement and, as you can see, sometimes we get out of hand. I will be okay, you do not need to worry about me."

"I know I don't, but I hate bullies, and that is what she is," I practically growled.

"I think she is just jealous," he replied.

"Clearly, but that is not my concern. I am here now and I'm not going anywhere. She has to get used to it or we will find ourselves in the same place we were in the Delphi caves, and I may not be so easy next time." I playfully flashed my fangs.

"You're scary when you're serious," he laughed. I pushed him on the shoulder as we headed inside the cave.

I locked eyes quickly with my maker as I walked in. I cannot explain why but ever since the kiss I've been avoiding

Gio. I don't know why, but I have to sort out my feelings about what happened.

Octavia catching us did not help the situation at all, torturing us even more by forcing us to tell Kole. I have no idea how it will play out, but I'd guess he won't respond positively. I walked past Veronica expecting to hear something under her breath, but all she gave me was the usual scowl, which is fine by me.

Gio was sitting in the back of the cave in his own space, as usual. He nodded to me as I walked by. I tried not to engage with him at the moment. I had to update everyone on what we were doing next. I stood in the front waiting to get everyone's attention.

"Alright, we are only about half a day out from Lundr. The sun is coming up so we will camp for the day and continue at sunset." The rest of the people murmured in the background, but it seemed like the message was delivered.

"What a gracious speech," his relaxed tone slipped down my bones.

"I'm just glad everyone listened." I turned to find Gio directly behind me, letting his smile peel past his fangs.

"Are you excited to return home?" he asked genuinely.

"I have mixed feelings. I'm more terrified of how my mother will take the news," I admitted as he passed me a cup. I could smell what was in it before I looked.

"Why wouldn't she understand? She doesn't strike me as someone who would hold this against you."

"She isn't, but I'm still wrapping my head around the fact that I am going to outlive everyone I've ever known or that she will never see me have children of my own. How do you even explain something like that?"

"That's fair, but give her some credit. I think she may surprise you." He makes some good points, but I have a hard time believing will be as easy as he was making it out to be. Would I be able to convince her that I am still me? I'm still the proud Norse woman she raised, and this is still my home.

This very important, nerve-wracking conversation with my mother isn't the only thing weighing on my mind... I still needed to find time to tell my brother that I kissed Gio, or he kissed me. I didn't even know how I was going to word it.

Gio placed his hand gently on my shoulder, and it took everything in my body to not zip across the cave. I didn't want to make this more complicated, but there was a comfort in knowing that I had him in my corner. Unfortunately, all my focus had to be on what I was going to say tomorrow.

"I'm going to try to get some sleep," I said, then quickly got up and moved to the other side of the cave before he could respond. I didn't even look back to see his expression.

"Wake up Kare, we are ready to move." Jordan was shaking me on the shoulder harder than was necessary.

"Okay, no need to shake my brain, Jordan. Make sure everyone else is up so we can move on." I tried to get myself together. Being a vampire had its perks. I always looked the same, but I was looking forward to a nice warm bath.

The moon was full, and the breeze felt so familiar. This was home to me. A short walk over the clearing and I could already see the torches from outside the gates. Lundr was just as glorious as I left it. Gio appeared next to me. He had an annoying knack for sneaking up on me.

"Wow. I didn't want to believe the Norse, but this place is magnificent. No wonder you are such a proud people," he said genuinely.

"You haven't seen anything yet, wait until you see us party," I smirked.

"That sounds like something I need to be a part of," his tone caught my attention. I could see the boats from the top of the hill. Kole had already arrived, which means that maybe I could slip in without being noticed. He has always been the golden child of the country.

We reached the front gates but were stopped by the guards. I removed my hood and showed my face, and the guards moved aside with no issue. I wasn't queen, but I still had some pull around here. The market was booming with the same energy that I was used to. Shopkeepers yelled greetings to me as I walked through with Gio and the other vampires. Treating me like nothing had changed at all.

"The princess has returned!" The crowd began to chant sending a redness to my cheeks.

"I see they haven't forgotten about their beloved princess," Gio joked. I sent him a death glare. We continued up through the market.

"How will we find your brother and the others?" Jordan asked.

"They only go to one place during times like this," I explained.

The longhouse was surrounded by torches illuminating the night. Warriors were outside drinking, singing songs and enjoying themselves, clamoring about the king's return. I knew my mother would throw a feast as soon as she heard all of us were coming back.

"This is a longhouse?" Jordan couldn't hide the wonder in his eyes. "This is unbelievable. If this is where you used to live, why did you decide to come stay in the Delphi cave with us?" he asked. The other vampires stared at him registering the insult.

"Yes, this is a longhouse. I know the Roman stories don't do it justice, you have to see it yourself to believe it. Let's go inside and find out if my mother is as accepting as Gio suggests." I took a deep breath as I entered.

We pushed past the curtains and walked inside. Silk fabric draped down the pillars, runes of celebration and protection carved into any piece of wood you can see.

The ceremonial fire burned high in the middle of the room. Guests were throwing offerings into the fire to ask the Gods for favor. A custom that seemed beyond us at this point. If they only knew that no one was listening. Gio turned back and told the others to make themselves comfortable but stay out of trouble. No need to agitate anyone for no reason. He and I made our way up to the front to join Kole, Octavia, and my mother.

They were deep in conversation, but as soon as my mother saw me, she jumped up off her throne and wrapped her arms around me. This was going to be way more difficult than I expected.

At least I had Kole and Octavia here to back me up. We have all been withholding the truth from her for months. I know it wasn't fair, but I was not ready for her to know. Unfortunately, the time for secrets was over. She had the right to know why I was spending all my time away from home.

18 – Is This A Rift? - Kole

Kare walked into the longhouse with Gio right behind her. My mother was ecstatic to see her. It didn't take her long to bounce out of her seat and squeeze the life out of her. We have been waiting for her and Gio to arrive, but we spent most of the time letting my mother know everything we went through in Midselium, and how once again the Gods ask for our assistance.

Delphi was making all our lives miserable, there was no way we could let her get away this time. But first, we needed to get Rollo and head up north to figure out what Ivar has to do with any of this.

Octavia hadn't said much to me since the cave or the boat ride here. Whatever rift between us that existed was still there. I may have crossed the line suggesting she just get rid of Floria, but if I had been brave enough to do what needed to be done maybe we wouldn't be in the situation we were in now. I didn't fight my father for her specifically. Replaying our conversation in my head, I wish I could take my words back. It was not fair to place that blame on her shoulders, especially because I didn't mean it. Odin set me on that path knowing where he wanted it to go. My father's death at my hands had nothing to do with her. I hope she knew that, but I had a feeling I would be paying for this for a while.

My mother finally let Kare go so she could come up and greet the rest of us.

"Glad you guys made it safely. How was the journey?" I asked.

"It was great, and I must say your country is a marvel of its own. I wonder what it looks like during the day," Gio's mouth curved in a devilish grin. This newfound sense of humor was so weird, but it was better than the miserable vampire I met in the Delphi caves. He must have decided to take Selene's advice.

"Thank you, Gio. You are free to venture wherever you please. I'm sure Kare will be an incredible guide for you." I motioned for them to join us.

My mother exclaimed, "I'm so happy that you are back home, my daughter. This place has not been the same without you. Your room is exactly the same, I forbid anyone to touch it or change it. Go and clean yourself up so you can get more comfortable." I watched Kare's face tense up. Whatever bravery she marched in here with was withering away.

"Mother, how is the construction of the dome coming? The vampires will need a place to stay during the day. I had hoped it would be complete already," I asked. Kare looked at me with a great sigh of relief for diverting the attention from her.

"It is almost complete, maybe another day or so. The structure is safe enough for them to stay in, but it will take time for us to gather everything that is needed."

"A place to lay our heads is more than okay for us right now. Thank you for your hospitality, Astrid," Gio gave a slight bow.

"The pleasure is all mine. Now all of you go and wash, and then come back to join the feast," she smiled.

"You think she is going to tell her tonight? I can't stand lying to her face for much longer," Octavia looked nervous.

"I honestly don't think she will have a choice. What other reason would she have for never being around during the day while we are here? I just hope my mother is ready for the news."

"I don't think anyone is ready for that news, but if anyone could handle it, it would be her." She smiled at me for comfort. I reached out to grab her hand. I just needed to reassure myself that we were in a good place. She didn't retreat from my gesture, so that was a start.

"Listen Octavia, about what I said back in the cave," I started to go into the apology I have been preparing for days.

"No need to explain yourself, Kole," she interrupted coldly. "This is not the time to deal with that mess. And you made yourself perfectly clear." That was not the reassurance I was looking for, but after what I said I'd be lucky if she was ever warm toward me again.

All of this has been building since our honeymoon. It was the first time since we met in the woods that we were literally at each other's throats. Prior to Midselium, we were perfect, nothing was able to knock us out of sync... but now I was having such a hard time getting us back to that place.

My parents would always tell me a relationship is never perfect, but I had something that was as close as it could get. Now, because of my big mouth, I put it all in jeopardy. I don't even know where it came from. The idea that she would ever be able to kill Floria was crazy. I stood in front of my people being ridiculed and disrespected by my brother my first five minutes as King, and yet I still spared his life. The guilt pressed heavily on my mind trying to figure out what triggered me to say something that I knew would hurt the woman I had vowed to never hurt.

"I know it is not the time but," she raised her hand to stop me from speaking, and I decided to relent for now anyway. We took my mother's advice and went back to our room to relax before the feast.

The first time we stayed in Lundr it was in my tiny room, but now my mother has given us the royal quarters she and my father once called theirs. The room itself almost doubled the size of mine with a view of the docks. The bed had more room than two people would ever need. Silk lined the furniture and the pillars of the bed, a dining table in the middle of the room was topped with food and drink. I was starting to wonder why they ever left their chambers in the first place.

Octavia walked in slowly admiring the royal space. She turned and headed to the bathroom, and I followed. A nozzle poked out of the back wall, which I assumed was connected to a well for fresh water, and a bathtub for two sat in the center of the room. A pyre for a fire sat in the corner ready to heat the water when the time came. The tables lined with candles surrounded it, bringing the full focus to the gigantic tub.

"Does this pump out fresh water?" Octavia asked while examining the nozzle.

"I believe it does. I want to point out that no one else in Lundr has such a thing." I walked over to the tub in awe of what would now be mine. But without Octavia to share it with, none of this really meant anything to me.

"I guess this is what it means to be royalty as a Norse," she joked.

"This is royalty even I am not accustomed to," I responded happily to see that amidst our issues we could still joke around. I walked back into the bedroom and poured myself a cup of ale, and another just in case Octavia wanted one. I sat and waited for her to come back to join me.

All I could hear from the bathroom was the water spilling out of the nozzle into a bucket. Was she really going to enjoy that giant bathtub without me? It almost felt like an insult. I was in no position to press so I sat down patiently waiting for her. It felt like I waited an eternity, but she finally emerged from the bathroom in a sheer silk slip that cut off right above her knees, rubbing the water from her hair.

I gulped down my ale, almost choking to death from my own surprise. Our eyes met but she said nothing, just walked over to the table and grabbed the ale I poured for her. She sat in the chair next to me and folded her legs to show me everything that I could not have, unless I had something very good to say.

Her hair fell over her shoulders, messy and enticing. The slip rode up when she sat down right at the curve of her hips, pulling my focus where she wanted it. She had played this game with me on our honeymoon in a much more playful manner, but now, I couldn't understand her motives. Was this the same game or was I being punished? She finally broke our silence.

"It feels great to have a proper bath again. I will have to thank your mother twice over for these accommodations," she sipped her ale while glancing over the rim of the cup at me.

"I will have to thank her, as well. This is more than I ever expected," I agreed, figured I should play nice and see where that could get me.

"Well, you are the king. The most powerful man in all the land, correct?" I wasn't sure if she was taunting me or not. "The descendent of the king of the Norse, the master of wisdom." I could see where this was going, and it wasn't good. "The decider of who gets to live and die, as long as it is on your terms," she spit the words with venom as she slammed her cup to the table. That was a clear sign that play time was over.

"Are you going to allow me to speak or is there more things you want to get off your chest?" I asked lowly. Her face filled with rage, but I don't know how long she expected me to put up with her taking jabs at me.

"Are you fucking kidding me, Kole? You think I'm saying these things because I want to hurt your feelings? For someone who is supposed to be so smart, you can be incredibly stupid," she yelled.

"Then stop speaking in code and tell me what your problem is so I can fix it." I was growing impatient. I had no idea what I was supposed to say.

Koel Alexander © 2024
Raven & Fire Series

"I don't want you to fix the problem, I want you to understand why I am angry. I want you to show me that you are the man that knows me inside out," she stressed.

"I do understand!" I yelled frustrated.

"Do you?" Her hands began to glow faintly. I was speechless. Everything that I said seemed to set her off. I opted to just stay quiet.

"The great King Kole, speechless," she taunted as she poured more ale.

"From the first day I met you, I knew you were special, as much as I hate to admit it. The Gods will say it was by design, that I was drawn to you because of a purpose, but we both know what was real. We sat around that campfire after you freed me and something clicked. I can't explain it, but I know you felt it too. When you told me the story of Odin, I had my suspicions that you could be manipulating me, and yet I went with you willingly, anyway. After everything that we have been through, you showed me that you were the opposite of what I suspected. You weren't this greedy, ambitious man looking for power and glory. You took on the burden of myself and others, even when we didn't ask, which is the most selfless thing you could do. The Gods blessed you with immense power, but there is one thing I have always known about you, Kole. You are not cruel!" Her words pierced me like she had been waiting to release them for some time now.

"For you to tell me to kill my sister, just to be done with it, was cruel and I have never seen that from you. I thought more of you than the world itself, and in that instant, you caused me to question the man that I thought I knew," she was face to face with me, tears burning her eyes, which forced the tears to run from mine.

"I...I don't know what to say," I forced out the words.

"I only want you to understand," she placed her hands on my chest.

"Everything that I have done has been to keep you and the others safe. You have said so yourself. Why is it that we are the only ones who must sacrifice? Always giving and never taking. The weight of the crown is unyielding, Octavia, and all of it falls on my shoulders," I didn't realize I was raising my voice. All I could feel was the darkness echoing in my voice.

"The kingdom, my sister, you, and now Rollo could be in danger. All because of the decisions I have made. So yes, I said the words, but I understand how it hurt you and I promise to never hurt you again." I grabbed her hands. "The words were to ease some of my own guilt... A small part of me was hoping that you would be stronger than me. I couldn't kill Kyut when I should have, but you are far braver than I will ever be," I confessed.

"That's the reason you have us. We all appreciate everything you have done, but you can't go at this alone. Think about what the others have endured. Think about all they have lost in the process. Are we not owed that respect? Did we not fight next to you while the weight of the world threatened to flatten us all?" She searched me for an answer.

"You all are the best things that has ever happened to me, and even though I can see what most cannot, somehow I still overlooked this." I rubbed my palm against her cheek as the

Koel Alexander © 2024
Raven & Fire Series

fire danced behind her eyes. "I love you, Octavia Alexsson," I made sure to sound out her new name.

"Don't start talking all nice to me, I'm still mad at you," she smiled. "And don't think you're getting lucky tonight, I plan on going right to sleep," she flashed a grin as she walked back to the bed, making sure I could see every angle of her body the slip did not cover.

"I would never assume such things from a lady," I removed my clothes and followed behind her. Though we did not resolve our disagreement completely, I went to bed finally understanding how she felt. I moved closer to her, so our bodies were pressed against each other. My hand may have drifted on the edges of the slip, sliding along the fine line of her curves before her hand stopped the progress of mine.

"I meant it, Kole. You're going to have to try harder than that. Goodnight."

"Goodnight Octavia." I smiled and tried to find some sleep in the mess of my thoughts.

19 – Your Only Daughter - Kare

The dome was bare, but we had all the necessities that we needed. There were places to wash and change, if it was needed, and areas to give us some privacy. Vampires didn't really need to bathe, but no one liked to walk around filthy. No matter how warm, cold, or wet I got, my hair would always return to its same bouncy curls. One of the many perks of my transformation.

The others grabbed furs and made themselves comfortable while we prepared for what the next day would bring us. I was not going to be able to avoid my mother for the entire day, so this would be the time I would have to explain what happened to me.

"Battle in your mind winning again?" Gio questioned.

"Always."

"I will not pretend to know what it is like to tell your loved ones what has become of you. It is something I never had to do," he spoke softly.

"What do you think she will say?"

"I honestly have no idea," he admitted. That answer did not help at all. What if my mother just renounced me? What if she didn't believe I was her daughter, just some demon sent here by the Gods to further her torment?

"Kare, you're doing it again." Gio sprung me out of the prison in my mind.

"Do you think I could try to influence her, to take the news a little better?" I asked him.

"Your mother is of royal blood, her mind is most likely too strong to be swayed by the influence. I would advise against it," he said sternly.

"So, you're saying that I'm stronger than the others, but this I still cannot do. Thanks for the help, my powerful mentor." He laughed, only further annoying me.

"In all seriousness, you don't want your mother to hear the news under the influence. It is her right to know what has become of her only daughter. Don't be afraid, whatever her reaction is I'll be here." His hand gently slid down the side of my arm, driving my senses crazy. I was dialed to one hundred all the time, but he managed to push me past that. I pulled away, still not sure of how I felt.

"If you want to keep touching me that way, you have something you need to tell my brother," I smiled.

"I will tell him what happened between us when you tell me how you felt about it," he answered cheekily, his fangs appearing over his grin. I wasn't sure how I felt about it. I know how my body felt. The heat, the rush, and the insatiable need for more of it, before Octavia forced us apart. If I wasn't a vampire my face would have turned red from how embarrassed I was.

"How about I deal with my mother first and then deal with you afterward?" I suggested.

"Only if you promise to be rough," he laughed as he got up to clear the others out of the dome so that I could bring my mother here to deliver this impossible news.

"I think I'm ready," I declared, not at all sounding convincing.

"You should eat first, Kare," he sounded concerned. I ignored him, even though I knew he was right.

"Send for my mother, my brother and Octavia," I requested.

I could hear my heart hammering in my chest as the time dragged on. I felt like I could barely hold myself up, everything was crashing in on me at once. Octavia and Kole had arrived quickly. Now we waited for our mother, and she was taking her sweet time. I have never been so nervous, the anticipation felt like dying all over again.

"Kare, are you okay?" Octavia asked. "You don't look too well."

"That is because she has been up this whole time, and she has not eaten." Gio emerged from behind them with a cup in his hand. I could smell the warmth in the blood without turning to look at him.

"Why would you not eat?" Kole asked.

"I don't know, I didn't feel like it. It's bad enough I must tell her that I am an immortal, blood-drinking hunter. I figured that message was better delivered without the stench of blood on me," I snapped, losing the grip on how I was feeling.

"You are only going to get more volatile as time passes. Is this really when you should test how long you can go without drinking?" He held out the cup to me.

"Shut up, Gio!" I retorted.

"I promised Kole I would protect you and show you our way. Now, if you want to lose yourself in bloodlust and hurt the people you care about because you are too stubborn to feed yourself, then be my guest," he sounded amused.

"Gio, is that really helping?" Octavia interrupted.

"It's not about helping. I have made sure she has been fed regularly. She has no idea how strong the pull is when it is not taken care of. So that leaves two options. Drink now and do this the right way, or don't drink and I will be pulling you off your mother's dead body, and you will have to live with what you have done for an eternity." He shrugged.

"You really are an asshole," Octavia yelled.

"I can only be me, my queen," Gio said.

"Kare, I understand how you feel, but we need to make sure mom is okay. It is going to be hard enough for her to stomach what is happening, I don't want you to have to worry about hurting her." Kole had the cup in his hand next to me. His eyes begging me to do this. He was only looking out for me, and

I was happy to have my big brother there. I grabbed the cup and downed the blood, and it immediately took the edge off my nerves. The others were staring at me like they had seen a ghost.

"What are you staring at?" I asked swirling my tongue across my teeth.

"It is just almost unreal. Your color came back instantly. Even your hair has become fuller." Octavia was speaking as if it was something impossible, but I couldn't argue with the results because I felt so much better. The effects did not last long because I turned to see my mother walking in and we all got silent.

"Sorry for my tardiness, I have been trying to make sure that the furniture would be delivered to the dome in time for our guests. What kind of kingdom would we be if we let them sleep on the ground during their stay?" My mother walked in smiling.

"Thank you so much, your majesty. Your hospitality is most gracious." Gio was bowing behind us all. I really wish he would stop talking. I could feel my heart pounding in my ears again. How are you supposed to even say what I need to say? Hey, mom, remember when I convinced you to let me get on the boat with my brother to sail into certain danger? Well let's just say it didn't go as planned. This was so much easier when I practiced it in my head on the way here.

"Why is everyone so quiet?" She stood waiting for anyone to say something. The words just would not come out. "What is going on?" she asked concernedly. Still, no one said anything.

Koel Alexander © 2024
Raven & Fire Series

"Mother…listen," Kole stepped up. "There is something that we need to tell you and we just haven't had the right time to do so."

"Kole, no. I must be the one to tell her. I can't run from it anymore. I have to face it," I interrupted.

"Can someone please tell me what in Odin's name is going on?" There was wariness in her voice.

"There are parts of the story involving our journey in Alexandria that we did not tell you." My voice was shaking as I spoke.

"Parts of the journey?" She questioned. "This is not making any sense."

"After our battle with Marcus, the spirit Delphi intervened," I was stumbling through my words.

"Yes, I know you've told me that part. Can we get to the part that you all have left out?" She scanned all our faces in the room, making her disappointment obvious.

"Kole made the deal with Delphi to save the vampires as you know, and that was supposed to be the end." I choked on the words as I was speaking.

"Go on," she urged.

"The battle was over, and in the midst of all the commotion, Gio separated from the group to leave the arena. We thought we had taken care of everyone, but a soldier tried to ambush him and I jumped in front of him…" I could barely finish the statement, the realization of what I was about to say had sewn my mouth shut.

"Are you telling me you were wounded? I know I can come off as a little uptight. Surely, I'm overprotective but none of you needed to spare me the details of Kare being wounded in battle. By all means, she is still here, so thank the Gods for that." She said with a smile.

"That is not all, mother." Kole nodded to me to continue.

"What else could there be?" She looked even more confused.

"Yes, I was wounded, but far worse than it appears. I was on the arena floor bleeding out of my stomach, wondering if I was ever going to see another day," the emotions were building but I couldn't stop now, or I would never get through this. "I remember Kole holding me, crying and screaming for me to stay with him, but I was too weak to respond. I did not want to leave him, but I felt the Valkyries pulling me to Valhalla."

I glanced up at my mother to gauge how she was feeling but her face was stone. Likely sorting out everything that I was saying. I waited to see if she was going to speak but she remained silent, so I continued with my story. I haven't been able to explain to anyone exactly what happened to me that night.

"I felt myself slip away into the abyss. I wasn't falling for long because an excruciating pain sprung me out of the darkness. The venom spread through my body, ripping apart everything in its path. I have never felt this type of pain and I was not sure if I could endure it," I turned to my brother.

I could remember him screaming and asking why I was in so much pain. I wanted to answer his calls, but the pain crippled me completely.

"Kare? What are you trying to tell me? I don't understand," her voice quavered with her reply.

"Let me finish, mom," I took a deep sigh. "The pain settled to a light hum and plunged me back into the darkness. I was in a state of nothingness. No sound, no smell, just pitch black. It was maddening. I thought maybe the Gods changed their minds about me. Maybe they were punishing me for protecting a vampire. My last act was an honorable one and I had died in battle as all Norse dream to, but maybe that wasn't suitable for Valhalla."

"Are you telling me that you…. are you telling me that you died that night?" Her stone expression began to break down as she fought back against her tears.

"Technically, yes, your majesty. She did." Gio added from behind everyone.

"Gio, shut up!" Octavia snapped. Silence ensued until I continued.

"The darkness was frightening, but then a bright light appeared in front of me, as tall as the heavens themselves. I could see giant majestic doors parting, inviting me into the great plains to see all of our people." I put my head down and smiled as I remembered what it looked like.

"You saw Valhalla?!" I could hear the surprise in Kole's voice.

"Yes, brother. I saw it as clear as I see you now." I turned to him.

"Did you…. did you see him? Did you see father?" The pain in his expression was enough to break me.

"I saw him standing at the gates. He was smiling, waving at me to join him, and I could not wait to be reunited with him."

"Kare?" My mother spoke my name as the tears rolled down her eyes. "You saw him?" She choked the words. "Did he look well?"

"Of course he did, mother. I was inches from the gate before something snatched me back like a rope was tied around my waist. I reached for him as I was being pulled away, calling his name, but he was not shocked I was leaving. He waved goodbye like he knew this was meant to happen.

I woke up in bed with an unbelievable hunger in the pit of my stomach. Something that I still can't describe with words. Kole and Gio's voices echoed in the room as I tried to make sense of my surroundings. I came back not as the girl you knew me as before, but as this."

I turned back to my mother and flashed her the long fangs gifted to me when I became one of Gio's hunters. She jumped back in surprise before placing her hands over her mouth in disbelief.

"Kare... you are...."

"Yes, mother. I am a vampire."

20 – I'm Not Mad I'm Disappointed - Kole

My mother was speechless, and I was just as lost. She gave us bits and pieces of what had occurred during her transformation, and I always wondered what she had seen in her journey between life and death, but she never confirmed it. Kare had made it to the gates, and she saw my father.

If anyone deserved to be there, it was him. No one served the Gods with more reverence than him. I was somewhat envious that Kare would always have that memory but knowing that it is hers alone for an eternity was comforting. What I would give to see his face one more time and tell him how sorry I was. My mother had taken a seat, her face cradled in her hands catching her tears.

"Mother, I'm sorry we didn't tell you, but we felt that it wasn't our secret to tell." I tried to comfort her. She looked up at me with fury in her eyes.

"I told you to protect her, Kole. You were supposed to protect her!" she yelled. The words pierced my heart.

"I know mother, I know," the tears started to flow from my eyes. "I tried. I tried to protect everyone, but this was the only way to make sure I did not lose her forever. I could not return home to face you if she was not still in this world." I pleaded for her to understand. She turned her rage to everyone else.

"All of you lied to me! Kept this from me!" She was furious. "What have I done to garnish such secrecy?" I had no answers for her, and I welcomed all her words because it is what I felt I deserved.

"You!" she pointed to me. "My own son! I stood by you after the Gods tricked you into the fight with your father. I watched as he did his duty to his beliefs and supported all of you in such an endeavor. I watched as the Gods planned to strip me of either the love of my life or my first-born son. I supported you when sent your brother to the mountains to live out his days in misery. And for you all to keep me in the dark when it comes to the only child I had left to protect is an insult, and I will take it as such." She was making her way out of the room.

"Astrid, please!" Octavia reached out to her. My mother turned back to us all, but she didn't say any words. Her eyes scanned the room before settling them back on my sister.

"Kare, my dear, I am so sorry for everything that you have been through. I'm sorry that you felt that you couldn't tell me until now. It will take some time to adjust to the new life, but I am open to learning." Kare looked up in surprise. "From now on, don't you ever think that I would love you any less. Do you understand me?"

"Yes, Mother," they shared a long embrace while the rest of us stood completely still in silence.

"Mother?" I tried to reach out to her one more time before she stormed out.

"Kole, not right now. I need some time alone." She released my sister and gave us one more sneer before she made her way out of the dome. I had no words for what had just happened, and I could not predict the amount of damage we have done by not being honest with her.

"Well, that went as good as it could have, I guess," Gio said.

"Odin's beard, Gio, please shut up for once." I know it wasn't his fault, but trying to work through my emotions and deal with his comments was taking up too much space in my brain. No one blamed her for the reaction, but the most important thing is that she directed all of that disappointment toward me and Octavia. We had every opportunity to tell her, but my sister was not ready. If that is another burden I have to take on, then so be it. Either way, it does not make it hurt any less.

"I can see you are already doing that thing you do," Octavia spoke from behind me.

"I'm doing no such thing," I smiled.

"Bullshit. We all bear this deception. I sat with her on my wedding day and, throughout all the kindness that she has shown me, I lied to her. All of it to protect Kare, but still she has the right to be upset."

"I know she does, and I told you I'm not taking it all. This is just as much your fault as it is mine," I said playfully.

"Oh, is that right?"

"That is right, my love." I wrapped my arms around her waist and pulled her close to me. The result wasn't what I wanted, but it felt like a weight had been lifted off all our shoulders. Secrets had a way of becoming heavier the longer you hold them.

"Don't get too comfortable, I'm still mad at you," a tiny grin stretched across her face.

"I am not so sure about that. It doesn't feel like you're mad at me," my hands ran down her back stopping right before the small of her back.

I wanted to see how far she was going to let me push this. I brought my face down to hers as close as I could get without my lips touching hers and I smiled. She didn't say anything but the flicker of flame in her eyes was telling me what I needed to hear. I tightened my grip on her waist and she let out a tiny gasp, which drove me crazy.

I could get lost in this woman every second of every day. I know she wanted to maintain the illusion of being mad at me, but I could feel the pull from her. I could feel the heat rising inside her the same way it did when we touched. All I needed to do was wait and not say anything to dig a hole for myself further.

"You guys mind not doing that directly in front of me," Kare interrupted us as we broke apart. I made sure my gaze never strayed. I wanted her to know that this was not over.

Koel Alexander © 2024
Raven & Fire Series

"Sorry, Kare, your brother and I have a lot going on. Marriage isn't as easy as it looks," she glanced back toward me.

"Looks like everything is falling right into place. You both have that look on your faces," she remarked nonchalantly.

"We do not have a look!" Octavia exclaimed embarrassingly.

"Oh, trust me, you two definitely have a look," Gio chimed in.

"Bullshit." I smiled. "Anyway, I'm glad that this was partially a success. Mother will move past this, just give her some time. A lot is happening very fast, but let's all get some rest, and we can pick this back up tomorrow." Everyone nodded and I led the way out of the dome back to the royal quarters.

Octavia was following behind me. As we rounded the corner on the way back to our room, still feeling the pull and need for her touch, I stopped short. She ran into me, almost tripping us both.

"Is there a reason why you stopped?" she asked.

"I'm not sure yet. What happens next will determine if the reason was a good one or not." I turned and pinned her against the wall.

"You have my attention," she smirked.

"Do I?"

"Yes, you do." My hands were pressed against her wrists, keeping them in place. I leaned in so close, feeding off her anticipation as she bit on her bottom lip.

"You still mad at me?" I asked again.

"Yes," she answered as her breathing got heavier. My head moved past her lips down to her neck tracing lightly over the line of her collarbone. She tried to lean her body against mine, but she couldn't move with my hands still holding her in place against the wall.

"Why are you teasing me?" She forced out the words over her breathing.

"Are you still mad at me?" I whispered into her ear. She didn't say anything, so I guess the answer was the same. I released one of her hands and she instantly grabbed me and pulled me closer.

Her mouth was on mine as I predicted, our tongues dancing in rhythm as she pulled me even closer.

"I think that answers my question." I smiled as I broke away for a second. "Are you still mad at me?" I asked again not really caring about the answer, but this was way more entertaining.

"If I say yes, do I get more?" She knew exactly how to say it to drive me crazy. I didn't have a clever response for that. I let her go as she led me into the massive bedroom, but I didn't see anything but her. I had to have her. It did not take long for me to realize that I was no longer in control of this situation.

Octavia had a way of making me feel like I was the one in charge. Everything about her made my body rush. She kept walking across the room, slowly showcasing every curve, every part of her that I wanted, as she slipped out of the dress she was wearing.

She walked over to the fireplace and bent over to add more wood, without breaking eye contact, as the sheer gown she was wearing rode up exactly the way she wanted it to. She didn't need to tease me anymore to make her point. I walked over and pinned her hands against the wall once again, placing myself behind her. A sultry moan passed her lips as she felt my body press against hers, just as she planned.

"If I say I'm still mad, do I get more?" she asked with that smirk she knows I love. Before I could answer, she arched her back and moved her hips slowly against me. I pushed back against her, showing her I was not going to relent until I wanted to. "I think I have my answer," she smiled and moved her hips faster, making it impossible for me not to take her right here and now.

"Okay, my queen. How about we give you some more? Put both your hands on the wall." She followed my instruction. I took a small step back, trailing my hands down her body, from her wrists to the small of her back. I rubbed her waist slowly, working her up into a state, her small moans and gasps filling the room. Then, my palm landed firmly on her ass, the sound of the slap ringing out and forcing her to let out a much louder, lustful moan.

"More, Kole... please more," she begged. My one palm landed firmly repeatedly, as I prepared myself to enter my own personal Valhalla., Finally, relieving us both, I entered her. Slowly at first, then I picked up the pace, and she followed my lead as we both drowned ourselves in the pleasure. She pushed back off the wall, willing me to go deeper and harder. I grabbed her and pulled her body close to me, kissing her, our moans swallowed between us lost in the embrace.

I reached around the front and rubbed her center as I thrust harder and faster until we both crashed into the climax. Our breathing was heavy, but we kissed passionately in front of the fire, giving me hope that no matter what we were going through this would always be right.

The next day we walked into the longhouse and I stopped at the steps, staring at the throne that technically I earned. Regardless, I would never be okay with the way I had to take it. Octavia's hand brushed the back of my shoulder. A sign of comfort and support.

"You think you will ever be used to that being your seat?" she asked.

"No, it never will. But this isn't our home anymore. What we built outside of Midselium is our home," I said confidently.

"We should come up with a name, it feels so incomplete when we talk about it," she had a point.

"You're right, but the name wasn't important. Making you my wife was." She practically rolled her eyes to the smirk on my face.

"And now that I am and will be forever, it needs a name," she urged.

"Let's save the world again first, then we can worry about the name."

"Deal." I sat down on the throne, and Octavia sat in my mother's seat to my left.

The longhouse was empty, which I knew would not last long. In no time Lundr would be awake. Rollo should have been here by now. I sent word days ago for him to meet us in Lundr so we could head up to the mountains together. I figured he was traveling with Marcella so he would have to find shelter during the day, but it should not have taken this long.

The curtain opened and my mother was making her way up to the throne. Her face was stone, no longer the inviting expression I was used to from her. Our deception must have still been fresh on her mind. She stopped just short of the throne and gave us both a slight bow.

"Blessaour mother, you know there is no need to bow."

"Just because we are family does not mean respect shouldn't be paid. We need to set an example for everyone," she said dismissively.

"I understand."

Cassia walked in behind my mother, and Floria followed. I grabbed Octavia's hand knowing that her sister's presence was always an open wound.

"Blessaour Cassia, I hope the trip wasn't too bad." I had to say something to cut the tension.

"It was fine, your majesty." She leaned, a slight bow to us both. "Octavia, good to see you."

"You, as well. I see you have decided to make some use of my sister," she gestured toward Floria.

"She has her use for now, and when I head back to Alexandria, she is going to help me understand the country. The loyalists of Marcus have scattered, but the traitors still slither underneath the surface." She looked back at Floria.

"I have no doubt you can be the one to restore Alexandria to its former glory. I only tell you to be careful with whom you trust." Her eyes were pinned on her sister. Floria stepped forward like she was intending to speak, but she reconsidered and remained silent.

"So, now we are just waiting for Rollo, which is not unusual." I waved to a servant to pour me some ale while I wait. My mother walked over to me slowly.

"Well, unfortunately son, I have some news on Rollo." I stopped drinking immediately to make sure I heard her correctly.

"Are we too late? Did something happen?" I asked concerned.

"I'm not sure, but I got a letter from his mother this morning."

"And?" I asked impatiently.

She handed me the letter and I read it as quickly as I have ever read anything in my life. I looked up at Octavia, and she could see the contents of the letter was not what I wanted to hear. It was written all over my face.

"What Kole? What does it say?" Octavia asked quickly.

"Rollo….. He has already left for the mountains days ago. His mother writes that he left in a hurry and she hasn't heard from him since." I crumbled the parchment in my hand.

"I don't understand. Why would he leave?" Octavia asked.

"I have no idea. His mother writes that she delivered the letter, but for some reason, he still ran off on his own."

"This is not good," she said.

"No, it is not." I could feel the darkness trembling under my skin.

Koel Alexander © 2024
Raven & Fire Series

"Calm down, my love." Octavia placed her hand over mine. "We are going to find him. Don't worry. Besides, he can take care of himself." There was no time to waste. Whatever made Rollo leave right away must have been important, and now we had to move quickly to catch up. I was not happy about rushing into the unknown, but at this point what choice did I have?

"With Rollo possibly already in the mountains, we need to make our way there immediately. I know we wanted to plan properly with all of us here, but that will not be an option now." I stood up in front of everyone.

"What do you have in mind? You want us to run up there with no idea what is waiting for us?" Cassia asked.

"You are going to return to Alexandria. Take Floria with you and clean out the Marcus loyalists. Gather all the men you have that you trust. After we find the artifact, I have a feeling we are going to need all the help we can get when it comes time to trapping Delphi."

"You want me to run back home and pretend that a fight isn't happening?" She moved forward, clearly insulted.

"I would hardly consider gathering the very army we are going to need to win pretending, Cassia," Octavia intervened. "We saw what Delphi was capable of in the arena. If she knows there is even a chance that we can get rid of her, I'm sure she will be coming with everything she's got." The blonde queen contemplated a retort, but I think she was finally starting to see that her objective was important to our task.

"Fine, you two go and save pretty eyes, and I'll make sure we have what we need when we get the word." She was turning to walk out, ready to do her part.

"Make sure if you're going to keep her around you put her to work," Octavia called out, speaking about Floria as the two made their way out.

"Mother, will you have the company prepare the boats, and when Kare and Gio wake, tell them where we have gone? Gio will know what to do after that," I spoke quickly.

"Will do, my king," she bowed and walked out of the longhouse. She said nothing more and nothing less. That hurt more than I could say, but my feelings weren't important right now.

"You ready, my queen?" I rose from my seat and reached for her hand.

"Another mission, more unknown mysteries, and obtuse riddles... of course, I'm ready." She grabbed her daggers and holstered them. "Look on the bright side. I get to be the one that saves his ass this time."

21 – Monster A Monster - Rollo

The icy chill from the mountain ripped through the furs I was wearing. It felt like I was wearing nothing at all. Marcella didn't seem to mind how cold it had gotten. I knew there was a reason why I never visited this Gods-forsaken place. We had been hiking up this path for a few days and we have yet to run into a single person. How could a whole kingdom feel this barren?

The thick clouds completely covered the night sky. The higher we climbed the more the air began to thin, making it harder to breathe. I clenched my hands in my furs, pulling them closer to my body searching for any kind of warmth. We shouldn't be too far from gates by now… but where the hell were all the people?

This place was absent of life, completely void of an identity. How could anyone even stand being here? What the hell did Kyut and Ivar manage to turn this place into? Marcella and I eventually passed slowly through the gates before following the path that would lead us to the main longhouse.

Like most villages, we needed to walk through the market first. Most Norse cities all had the same setup. Since the first time we arrived, we ran into some people.

They walked around somber in expression, as if their souls were missing. Nothing like the market in my home or in Lundr. This was nothing like anything I'd ever seen, honestly. Most of the time the kingdom worked in a sort of unison, but everything here seemed to be in a state of limbo. Like this place was just left to feed on itself.

"What a miserable place to live, and this is coming from a girl that is used to living in caves," Marcella remarked.

"I haven't been here since I was a boy, but I know for a fact it was never like this," I reminisced and looked around in confusion.

There was muffled chatter as the people conducted business, or whatever semblance of business this was anyway. The way everyone was dressed, you could tell there wasn't a lot of currency being passed around. Someone had to know what sucked the entire essence out of this place.

A small slender woman passed in front of us heading toward the longhouse. She seemed to be moving quickly, purposedly to reach her destination before Marcella and I stopped her. I kept my hood down not risking having my presence discovered.

"Excuse me, miss, can I ask you for some assistance?" Her facial expression told me she had no intention of listening to anything I had to say. She didn't even stop to look my way, she just kept walking. Marcella dashed into her path in the blink of an eye and stopped her in her tracks, once again. The woman jumped back in surprise.

"What the hell do you want?" she snapped. Marcella smiled, likely holding in her frustration.

"We do not want to take up too much of your time, we just had a few questions," she said politely.

"I have nothing to say, aside from the fact I do not know who the hell you are," she snarked, trying to dismiss us again.

"It will only take a second, miss," I pleaded. The woman continued to ignore me and pushed pass us once more. Marcella stepped in her path again, this time capturing her gaze. The woman's shoulders relaxed as her eyes fell in line with Marcella's.

"There is no need to hurry, we just want to ask you a few questions," her voice was low and soothing, with almost a hint of a subtle command. I could feel her words pushing onto me, scrapping the barrier of mind. It was something I never noticed up until this point. I shook my head and repelled the feeling. Marcella continued to speak softly.

"I was told this place used to be beautiful. Can you tell me what happened here?" In a trance, the woman began to speak without resistance.

"Ever since the exiled princes' were sent here, the city suffers." Marcella looked at me, waiting for my cue. I nodded for her to continue. I don't know what she is doing, but if it was going to get me some information, then she could have at it.

"Where are all of the people?" she asked.

"The streets used to be full of people. I would not say this was a popular place, but it was never as barren as it is now." The woman's voice was methodical.

"Why did everyone leave?" Marcella asked, coercing the answers from the woman further. With every question, I felt the slight tingle of her reach brushing my mind.

"The beast!" She exclaimed her eyes widened in fear.

"What beast?" I interrupted.

"His eyes light up the night and his fangs can tear through the fabrics of the Gods themselves." Marcella and I took a second to remember what we encountered in the woods. There was no way that this was a coincidence. You could see the fear as the woman spoke about the beast that lurks around the city.

"Where is the exiled prince?" I asked. It was time to figure out what the hell Ivar and Kyut were up to, and why they have allowed a beast to run wild in a kingdom that was their responsibility.

"He lives in the longhouse at the top of the hill. He is rarely seen, only by the people that he trusts."

"Thank you for answering our questions. Now gather your things and get somewhere safe," Marcella said to the woman slowly, in a low convincing tone. The woman nodded and walked away as if the conversation never happened. I watched her walk away before turning to Marcella, looking for some sort of explanation as to what just happened.

"How the hell did you do that? Was that some kind of mind trick?" I asked not sure if I wanted to know.

Koel Alexander © 2024
Raven & Fire Series

"No, Rollo. I do not do mind tricks. Let's just call it a perk of being cursed," she murmured.

"But how?" I remained curious.

"Another skill acquired from the huntress. I am able to influence humans, especially those with a weak mind," she spoke so nonchalantly.

"That seems like it could come in handy when you need it." I think I might be jealous.

"Of course, it does," she smiled.

"Have you ever used that on me?" She seemed offended at the question at first, but that sentiment disappeared just as quickly as it presented itself.

"Do you think I have used it on you?" she retorted.

"I wouldn't consider myself weak-minded, and I have never felt that push coming from you before today, so I'm going to assume that you haven't."

"My influence does not work on those with royal blood, even more so since you have been blessed by your Gods. Sorry to break it to you, King Rollo, but your feelings toward me, however strong they are, completely belong to you," she smirked.

"Good to know," I smiled. "Now how about we go up to the castle and pay these two troublemakers a visit? Time to figure out just what the hell is going on."

The longhouse was in worse shape than the market below. It was dark and cold as we pushed through the front curtains. The wolf banners were filthy, covered in layers of dirt. Why hasn't anyone been cleaning here? It felt like it had been abandoned for some time. How the hell could anyone live this way voluntarily?

As much as I hated Halfdan, I know he never lived like this. He was a snake and a traitor, but this was ridiculous. We ventured further into the longhouse, peaking around the corner to find a fire lit in the center of the room, struggling to keep itself alight. Ivar was sitting on the throne. His eyes trained on me through the fire with a scowl that could burn a hole directly through my skull.

"Here ye! Here ye! The great Rollo Thordsson has decided to grace us with his presence. Hide the drinks and the women, we should all be lucky to be in the same room with the blessed son of Thor," he clapped his hands slowly, the sound echoing inside this empty room. We walked around the fire heading toward the front of the throne. Ivar adjusted himself in his seat to address us.

"Ivar, you have not been answering any of the letters from Lundr. I would say we were worried, but that would make me a liar."

"You always thought you were better than me, Rollo. Now, even as I sit on a throne, you mock me," Ivar snarled.

"I find it hard to take you seriously, considering how you've maintained this place." I gestured to the condition of the longhouse. "And if I'm not mistaken, King Kole stripped you of your kingdom. Why are you on the throne and not Kyut?"

"This is my home, you brain-dead soldier! Do you really think I would let anyone else sit on my father's seat? Do you think I would let an Alexsson sit on my father's seat after what you all did to him?" he exclaimed angrily.

"Do you really want to talk about fathers, Ivar? You really want to go there?!" I could feel the power brushing against my hands as I stepped forward, but Marcella leaned against me to hold me back. Ivar rested himself in his chair and waved his hand.

A man came through the curtains behind him, dressed in the same raven armor as my best friend. He was noticeably taller, and he managed to fill out since the last time I saw him. He was no longer the little kid that I remember. Time up here, if anything, had turned him into a soldier. Visually, anyway. Kyut made his way to the front of the throne and stood between us and Ivar.

"Good to see you, Rollo. It has been a long time." His voice was even deeper than before.

"That it has. I wish it could be under better circumstances, and preferably somewhere cleaner." I wiped the dust off a table next to me.

"Well, your best friend is the one who sent me here as a punishment for telling the truth. How is my brother, anyway? Still choosing himself over everyone else?" he drawled sarcastically.

"That is not what happened, Kyut. You were out of line. Your brother spared you and Ivar when others would not have done the same," I chastised. "You are supposed to be on the throne, as ordered by your brother. Can you explain why you aren't?" I crossed my arms over my chest.

"I did not want it then, and I do not want it now. What I want is for my brother to pay for destroying my family." He paced slowly, and I dropped my hands to hover over the hilt of my hammer. "Kole told everyone the Gods put him on this path. Would it be hard to believe that the Gods also had plans for Ivar and I?"

"That does not surprise me at all. Odin is the only reason that Ivar is still breathing," I retorted.

"Remind me to say a prayer and thank him for that," Ivar interrupted.

Power was in the air, pushing and pulling for control. I'm not sure who it was coming from, but it was something that I have never felt from either of them. Something was different, but I could not figure out what it was. The longer we stood here, we would just keep talking in circles.

"Kole believed he was the only one set on a path to destiny, but I'm living proof that he was wrong. He hides his guilt and shame behind the notion of doing me a favor. He perpetuates the image of a benevolent leader by showing me mercy. He cannot fool us. We know this is a punishment for speaking the truth. We know he just wanted to take the crown and be able to keep his pet in peace. Fear not, Rollo, his arrogance is my blessing." He sounded almost delusional.

"Kyut, as much as I would love to listen to the story of your destiny, I have things I need to do, and you both are wasting my time." My annoyance was evident in my tone.

"See that is just it, Rollo. This is not a waste of time. It's something that you are going to want to hear, and I pray you listen carefully. I know that isn't your strong suit," Ivar interrupted again.

Koel Alexander © 2024
Raven & Fire Series

Kyut continued, "My time here was miserable as I was recovering physically and mentally. Unwillingly, I honored the terms of my exile. Upon my arrival, Ivar and I spoke. I assured him I wanted nothing to do with running his kingdom. I retreated into the woods where I trained every day until I couldn't feel my limbs, and at night resorted to trying to drink myself to death. Replaying the embarrassment of being sent away from the only home I have ever known, over and over. Praying for the day that I ran into you both, or the day that I died." He tensed as he spoke, and I felt the nudge of power again. Was that coming from him?

"Words of your exploits out in the east reached all our ears, killing the Roman king, and gaining more power and control over this world. It infuriated me. Why must I be in the shadow of my traitorous brother and his stupid best friend? Am I not of royal blood, as well? I cursed our Gods for not helping me. I rebuked and pushed them away, locking myself off from them completely. If Odin didn't see me as worthy, then fuck the Aesir," he snapped.

"And then, everything changed," Ivar spoke up from behind him.

"It came to me in a dream. A spirit older than our Gods promising to help me enact revenge, not only on my brother but the Gods who have turned their backs on me." My eyes widened in surprise because I had an idea of what visited Kyut in this dream. Maybe this was worse than I feared. "It seems that my brother can't help but offend anyone he comes across, and his latest slight will be his downfall." Kyut smiled.

"Are you talking about Delphi?" Marcella asked.

"I'm not the least bit surprised you are smarter than him," Kyut sneered.

"She is only smart because she has been alive longer than the information. I did not forget that your master tied me up and held me hostage before giving me up as a prisoner," Ivar spit toward her.

"In hindsight, it was the right choice, don't you think?" she answered.

"We are happy that the lack of reports has led you here, because now it is time for me to get the revenge that I have been working toward. With the help of the spirit, I will have my revenge on you, Kole, and the Gods that have spurned us both," Ivar yelled.

"She is just using you both. Do you not realize that?" I asked. The power went from a nudge to a push. It was like a boulder was trying to lay its weight on me. It felt massive compared to just moments ago. The force of it made me take a step back.

"No, Rollo. She has given me what I need to make sure I come out victorious. The Gods have done nothing but use us all, and frankly, I am tired of it. So, if her plan is to foil their plans, then I will happily be her vessel to do so." What was he talking about her vessel? It did not make any sense, what could she have given them to make them so sure of their victory? Marcella's eyes shot to Ivar, and she grabbed my arm so tight I felt a jolt of pain under her grip.

"What is it?"

She tilted her nose to the sky, sniffing continuously, trying to pinpoint a scent.

"It's here," she said lowly. "The beast, I'll never forget that smell. It's here."

"Right now?!" I said intently. She nodded as we tried to assess our surroundings to be prepared.

"Kyut, Ivar. We need to get ready now. It's coming." I grabbed my hammer, summoning up the lightning to the surface.

"Poor Rollo," Ivar laughed. "You really don't know anything, do you? The beast is not coming, it's already here." His voice went deep and carnal. He raised himself up off the throne. I swear he seemed to be taller than I remember.

"Add this to the list of things that are Kole's fault," he yelled, as his teeth turned into fangs and those bright terrifying eyes that I saw in the woods replaced his own.

"What the fuck?!" I screamed.

"Another deal and more consequences," Kyut spoke as Ivar huddled over in pain, his bones breaking to replace the new ones.

"What in Thor's name have you done?" I could not believe what I was seeing.

"What I have done doesn't matter. Just know that we are so happy you are here, and you will remain here until my brother comes to rescue you." Kyut reached for his axe as the beast stalked behind him, its bright eyes trained directly on us. "One king with a Roman whore and another king with a dead one. How scary it is for the advancement of our people," Kyut's grin was maniacal.

Before I could respond, the beast surged past Kyut straight toward me. Marcella intercepted his advance quickly and knocked him back before he regained his footing to charge at me again.

Kyut attacked while I was occupied with making sure that Marcella was okay. He was so much faster and stronger than I remember. His strikes were more precise as he swung his axe with no remorse, just anger and hatred.

Delphi has poisoned his thoughts, and now it is all that fuels him. I called on the power of my own to parry his attacks. I did not want to hurt him, but there was no way I was going to let him kill me. Marcella and Ivar wrestled around the longhouse like two rabid animals, destroying everything in their path.

"Don't worry about her, you should be focused on me," Kyut implored. He closed his eyes and took a deep breath. I could feel the darkness building inside of him. A similar darkness that I feel when I'm around Kole, but this felt sinister. Kyut opened his eyes and they were pitch black

"Let's even the odds a little, Rollo," he pressed again faster this time. His strikes knocked me back, and I started to lose ground. I raised my hammer to block his axe. The block left me an opening to counter. It wouldn't be a killing blow, but it would hurt him enough so that I could help Marcella.

I landed a punch to the chest with my left, the force knocking him back a little. I aimed for his head with my right before something stopped my arm mid-strike. I looked toward Kyut and his eyes were pitch black holding my fist in place. His

Koel Alexander © 2024
Raven & Fire Series

power had finally manifested. He had the same abilities as his father Styr.

"Not the only one that is chosen, huh Rollo?" He sneered before he punched me so hard in the jaw that my ears were ringing as I slid across the longhouse.

He caught me completely off guard. He always had the potential to be a skilled fighter, but he was always just Kole's little brother. I never once saw him as a threat. Now that his powers have manifested, this was not going to be a walk in the park.

"So, you have finally tapped into your powers," I implied, wiping the blood from my mouth.

"It's only right that I am granted the same abilities as my father. The father that was taken from me because my brother fell for a pair of pretty eyes," he snarled.

"You really think that is what this is? Your brother never even wanted this, and if you could see him, you would know he is tormented every day for what he had to do to your father. Instead of talking to him like a man, you wallow in your pity and jealousy like a small child." I rose to my feet.

"Enough! Rollo, nothing you say will change my mind. Whatever my reasons are, they are my own, and there is nothing like vengeance to put things in perspective." He charged quickly and tackled me to the ground. He reached for my throat to choke me, but I countered with an elbow to his face to get him off me. Marcella and the beast still wrestled around the room, slashing and clawing at a speed my eyes could not keep up with.

Kyut wiped the blood from his nose and attacked again. He was sharper than he was before, but he lacked the experience and focus. His thirst for blood was distracting him. He swung his axe recklessly trying to hack my head off. The look on his face was frightening. He was completely lost in rage.

I blocked his attacks with my hammer and shot the lightning from my hands in his direction. He raised his hands, stopping the element right before it struck him. I could only stare in amazement. This was a skill I wasn't even sure that his father had.

"The cute tricks won't save you, Rollo," he snarled.

I ignored the insult, loaded up my hammer and threw it directly at his head before he could recover. He had to break his concentration to dodge it just long enough for me to rush him. I barreled into his chest, driving him to the ground. I pinned him to ground with my axe to his throat.

"Yield Kyut! Before you make me do something I will regret," I screamed. I did not want to be the one to spill his blood, but I would do it if he forced me.

"The mighty Rollo has gone soft. Go ahead, send me to my fate like you did Halfdan, or can you not do anything without the say-so of my brother?" he taunted.

"Shut up Kyut and yield!" I commanded.

"I will not yield, and you are going to let me go either way," he laughed.

"And why would I do that?" I pressed the axe deeper into his throat and he smiled even more. He motioned for me to check out what was behind me.

My adrenaline was running so high from the fight with him that I didn't even notice that the noise had come to a stop. The beast had Marcella pinned to the ground. Blood was rushing from her wounds, the giant claw marks leaving her skin raw and exposed. The beast hovered over her neck, threatening to end it all.

"You see. You are going to let me go, and you both will yield, or she dies," he said sinisterly. I contemplated what I could do next, but I could not risk Marcella's life. I slowly lifted the axe off Kyut, realizing that I was out of options.

The beast started to convulse as it returned to normal size. Ivar stood in place of the beast.

The transformation was just as unbelievable as the first time I had seen it. Ivar emerged in front of us, completely nude with the same evil smirk on his face. He tossed Marcella to my feet like she weighed no more than a blade of grass. I instinctively dropped down to console her. She was breathing but her breaths were shallow and ragged.

"Now I will find somewhere to put you both, because I'm sure Kole will be on his way shortly, exactly as I planned." He walked back to his throne and sat down.

22 – A Painful Existence - Kare

"You're coming along faster than any other vampire I have ever made. Your hunger is basically already under control. You move as if you are twice your age, and your compulsion is almost masterful." Gio spoke confidently about my progress.

"You say that like you are surprised," I snarked.

"I say that to acknowledge my exceptional intelligence. Clearly my intuition about you was spot on, so give me the victory lap, my flower. You are even more than I could have ever expected," Gio divulged.

He was laying the flattery on pretty thick today. Even in the face of undisclosed danger, he was showering me with compliments. I glanced over to the other vampires making themselves somewhat comfortable in this tiny cave. I really hope they weren't eavesdropping on our convo. I knew it wasn't true, but I still did not want to be seen as the master's pet project. I didn't pick up on any wandering eyes, so I must be in the clear for now.

We are traveling north to figure out why Rollo would just leave without us. Kole and Octavia were going to head to Ragnarsson first to see if they could find the reason why he would ignore the letter and just run off.

I was finally going to see Kyut again, although the last time we saw each other was less than pleasant. I harbored some guilt for technically choosing Kole over him, but the things he said were just too hateful for me to agree with.

My father believed he was doing the right thing, so we should have been there to support Kole no matter what. I lost a parent as well, but I did not think to blame him or Tav for what happened. When I saw my father, joyful and happy at the gates of Valhalla, I knew that he had forgiven Kole. So, if he could forgive, then so could I.

Ivar, on the other hand… if I could end him myself for what he has put everyone through, I swear that I would. I would never forgive him and Halfdan for coming back home and lying to us all. They made me mourn my brother and Rollo, all so they could try to turn our city against us. Trapped us for weeks, not knowing if either of them was going to come back to me. He deserved so much worse than he got.

Either way, we needed to push on. The options to camp during the day were getting slimmer, so the mood was not exactly enthusiastic. We were all on top of each other. Jordan was huddled on one side with his friends, who didn't seem to mind being cramped. Veronica sat with her legs crossed on the other side of the cave. Her eyes never left mine, which was normal ever since we left Delphi. She was a caged snake waiting to strike, and I would be ready for whenever she felt the need to make her move.

We wouldn't be here too long, but there's no sense in wasting a good day's rest. Especially since we have no idea what we are walking into. Before I lay down for the day, I plan to go over more vampire history with Gio to distract myself.

I sit down close to him to try to keep some of the conversation as private as possible. These lessons were especially interesting. He was so focused when we spoke, like nothing else existed. So much attention to detail, but the fact that he always seemed to lose his shirt somewhere during the lessons was more than distracting for me.

Hundreds of years, and I was just scratching the surface of what this life could offer me. While there was a sense of wonder about what to expect, I imagined there was a much darker side of being immortal that I needed to prepare for.

"You managed to tell me all the good things about being a vampire, but it can't all be good. If I'm going to survive and live, I need to know all of it." I forced my eyes to the floor so they would stop wandering to his chest.

"There is a dark side to everything, princess. Being one of us is a constant wave of darkness, and it exists forever. There is no need in sheltering you from things that will inevitably affect you," he said calmly. "Being a vampire can be one's best accomplishment or worst nightmare. We exist to live somewhere in the middle. A reminder of ultimate death and a figure of everlasting life. As I told you before, who you were in your previous life will dictate some of your actions after the turn, but do not underestimate time and trauma, my flower. It can be an insurmountable adversary if left unchecked."

"What do you mean?" I asked curiously.

"You remember what it was like when we first met. The time mixed with my need for vengeance soured the once adventurous soul that I was before I turned. Add onto that the unresolved issue of past transgressions... it led me down a path of violence and survival. A life that I never want for you, my flower," he smirked, but a sadness lined his eyes.

"But I have come to terms with my transformation. I made the choice, and it was the right thing to do. I would do the same thing all over again if I could," I emphasized.

"And that is why I believe in you, but you are very young in this new life. You have so much road ahead of you." His eyes burned with passion.

"Is that why Veronica is such a bitch?" I smiled knowing that she could hear me. Gio did not speak but a low chuckle came from his chest.

"I see that Norse blood still runs through you," he drawled. I thought about my brothers and how they inadvertently molded me. I thought about my mother, who was the strongest person I have ever met. Nothing would change that, dead or alive. I would always be Norse.

"On a serious note, there are things that will eventually weigh on you. If you refuse to come to terms with them," his eyes drifted back to the ground signaling an uncomfortable topic was coming.

"Like what?" I pressed further.

"There are things you will never have in this life, my flower." My stomach dropped as he said it. I had an idea, but maybe hearing it would increase the severity of what was waiting for me in the future. "Let's start with what we know. The sun will become foreign to you, if you haven't already noticed. Restricting you to only darkness, and it may not seem like much now, but it will take a toll on your mind eventually." He leaned closer to me. "You will never experience the joy of having children," he grimaced and paused, letting the words sink in.

I returned his gaze, but I did not really have much to say. I had never pondered having children. I always figured I had more time, but now that was not the case. Then again, I should've guessed as much. I didn't see any vampire children running around.

"Will you have companions? Yes. If they are lucky enough to remain in your presence," he smiled. "But as it stands, I am the only one who can create other vampires."

"So technically, you have children?"

"You could say that, but I imagine it not being the same as watching a human grow from a babe to an adult."

"You're probably right," I admitted.

"You have already felt the persecution of being what you are from others, though I hold some of that blame myself for how I have conducted myself over the last couple of centuries," he spoke curtly.

Octavia and I were on much better terms, but her outburst in Alexandria was something I could never forget. Someone so close to me. Someone that I looked up to thought that everything about me had changed and that I was capable of hurting people for no reason. I forgave her but the pain was still there.

Maybe Gio was right. I had an eternity to dwell on that incident. What if as time went on it grew into something more? What if it grew into something rageful? Gio was still talking, but I managed to let my mind wander for a moment.

"Are you listening, Kare?" He nudged me to get my attention.

"I'm sorry, what were you saying?"

"The last thing I need to share with you will be the hardest for you to accept." He seemed hesitant to continue.

"Why is that?"

"Because of the life you came from. A life of family and support and love. These are the hardest vampires to transition. You will begin to crave that familiar feeling that your old life provided." He grabbed my hands brushing his thumbs over my skin. "The people around you will grow old, moving on with their lives. Having children, who will grow old together. As the generations pass, you will remain the same." He searched my face, checking to ensure the reality of my situation has truly sunken in. It seems he's also searching for any sign of regret in my eyes.

"Immortality," I murmured.

"Yes, the greatest gift, but also the most difficult test. More vampires succumb to the stress of immortality after they have beaten the bloodlust. The difference is you can find blood whenever you please. Your food source is something you can control, but time is happening all around us. It is constant and uncontrollable. Nothing in this world can stop the passing of it."

This was always a reality for me, but hearing it made all the difference. My skin crawled with anticipation, but I was not sure I wanted to hear more.

"Kole, Octavia, Rollo, your mother, your kingdom. All of them will age and grow, and you will be here for it all. You will have to say goodbye to your family repeatedly until your heart stops beating, which will never naturally happen. Reliving the loss all while accepting the fact that we are permanent and everyone else's journey comes to an end."

"That's enough, Gio," I implored, suddenly feeling uncomfortable.

"Your brother's children, Rollo's children."

"Enough, Gio."

"Everyone you have ever known," he continued.

"Gio, enough!" I felt the pang of anger edging my body to release my fangs.

"Over and over," he pressed.

"I said enough, Gio!"

I lunged at him quickly, my hands around his neck and my fangs fully extended, same as his. The other vampires reacted almost instantly. All of them were ready to rip me apart for putting hands on our master. I held him in place preparing the punch that he so very much deserved, but then he spoke softly as he motioned for them to stay put.

"And you, my flower, will have to mourn them all." I only felt the blood pumping, urging me to do what a predator does and snuff out the threat. I released him and retreated to another area in the cave. Maybe I was not prepared for as much of the truth as I thought. Veronica and her crew snickered in the corner as I moved past the others to situate myself.

All I wanted to do was run outside and clear my head, but the sun was up, and for the first time I felt the crippling words of my maker reminding me that the sunlight has me imprisoned. Forced to sit here and contend with the harsh truth of my everlasting future.

23 – Got That Dog In Em - Octavia

It didn't seem right arriving in Ragnarsson and not having Rollo here to greet us. I know he hated being away from home for so long. Nothing could explain why he would leave so suddenly, especially after we sent the message that we were coming. What would make him just ignore the letter and leave?

The land was so peaceful here. The more places I visit in Najora, the more I understand why the Norse look down on Gracia. How could a land be so enchanting no matter which part of it I explored? It had some resemblance to Cosa, but I hadn't been there since I was a child so I didn't have much to compare it to.

The water was blue and vibrant. The air smelled clean, and the breeze was at the perfect temperature. It wasn't as loud and rambunctious as its king. It was almost the opposite. Just a model of comfort and tranquility.

Rollo's mother greeted us on the dock. You could tell from the stress on her face that she was just as worried as we were. This whole thing was getting stranger by the moment. Rollo wasn't necessarily patient, but it wasn't like him to try to get himself hurt on purpose.

"I just don't understand it. Why would he just pack up and go right after I told him to wait for us in my letter?" Kole asked anxiously.

"I'm not sure, I just know that he was certain that he needed to leave right away. Something about needing to get up north as soon as possible. He made it seem like it was more important than anything," his mother explained, stress and worry practically seeping from her pores. Rollo's sister appeared from behind her quickly.

"He took Marcella with him. Did you know she was a vampire? How cool is that?" she interrupted.

"It's the coolest thing ever," he said sarcastically, glancing back at me. "Can we get back on track here?" Kole insisted.

"Did he even get Kole's message?" I asked.

"Of course, it was hand-delivered to him. We assumed he read it right away, but who knows what goes on in my brother's empty head," she joked, though it wasn't the best time for it.

None of this made sense. We had to be missing something. Nevertheless, we needed to get to him fast. Between the curse and Delphi and everything else, I would never forgive myself if Rollo managed to get hurt because we didn't act fast enough.

"Thank you for all the information, but it would be best if we didn't waste any more time. If we have any chance of finding him, we need to leave immediately." Kole gave a slight bow and returned to the boats to retrieve everything that we would need to bring with us up north.

Kole insured me that this trip up north would not be as pleasant as my other adventures in Najora. Hours into the hike, he was correct. Everything that I enjoyed about the Norse country was noticeably absent on our ascent. Not to mention it was so cold that you could probably hear my teeth clattering in Olympus. It was loud enough for Kole to give me his extra fur, which didn't completely warm me up but it was a step in the right direction.

The cold didn't seem to bother him much. I watched him closely, as he tried to keep his composure for his best friend. I wanted to believe that we were in a better place, but there was an invisible wedge between us that we needed to fix. However, every time we tried to broach the subject, someone or something needed to be saved. Exhausting is an understatement for how our never-ending responsibilities make me feel, but maybe this is what ruling is all about. Your work is never finished, and people will always need you.

"You're worried. I can feel it," Kole remarked, startling me.

"You're one to talk," I responded. He smiled and put his head down.

"I am worried, honestly. I'm worried about Rollo, I'm worried about you, I'm worried about Kare. I'm worried about my kingdom," his tone was somber, a sentiment that went straight to my heart.

"I'm worried about them all, too." I grabbed him to stop him from walking too fast ahead of me. "But we are a team. Me and you, always. What you endure, I endure and that is not going to change. Do you understand?" I asked, anxiously waiting for his response.

"I understand, my love." He smiled at me, softening me in a way only he could.

"Now, keep me warm, because it is ridiculous how cold it is. Tell me we are close, at least."

"We are close. We should be reaching the gates by daybreak. The vampires should be making camp nearby. We are going to have to go in without them."

"Do you think that is a good idea? Shouldn't we have all hands-on deck?" I asked.

"I would love to have all hands on-deck, but that would mean we would need to wait all the way until nightfall. I'm not willing to spend another moment waiting to find out what happened to Rollo." He made a valid point. Neither one of us liked the idea of going in blind, but time was not on our side, as usual.

"Why didn't we just sail up the river in the boat to get there? It would have saved me all the pain in my feet and we could have carried more supplies," I complained, finally sounding like the pampered queen I should be, even if I'm nothing of the sort.

"Only Odin knows what is waiting for us up there. This way, our approach is quiet and covert. Showing up on a boat immediately alerts to our arrival, not ideal if we are trying to assess whatever situation we are walking into first. The land does not lend us much advantage, but at least we can move quickly if something was to go wrong." My husband, the tactician. I gave up asking more questions and decided I would just be ready for anything.

The reunion with Kyut would be an aggressive one. I grabbed the hilt of my dagger on instinct. It brought a wave of comfort, then I reached for the gold arm ring that Kole placed on me at our wedding. The symbol of our love and union, but I swear if I didn't get somewhere warm soon, I was going to lose a couple of fingers and toes.

The cold was not distracting me enough to ignore that Kole and I were still walking on eggshells around each other. Maybe this is what his mother was talking about on the day of our wedding. Marriage is not nearly as easy as I thought it would be, but something in you just knows that you will get there, even if you have no idea how.

After a couple more hours of hiking, we could see the sun coming up over the mountain that revealed a city in even worse shape than Alexandria was when I returned home.

The gates were barely standing, far from keeping anyone out, and even further from being welcoming. The people inside the market roamed around like lifeless souls, scrapping for anything that could keep them going until the next day. Men and women begged on the road for food and clothes. Children ran around with ripped clothing and skin attached to their bones as if they have barely eaten. What in the world had happened here? I knew Kyut and Ivar wouldn't be the best rulers, but to even let themselves live this way is extreme.

"What the hell is going on here?" I asked.

"Honestly Octavia, I have no idea, but this is not what I was expecting." Patrons walked past us as we traveled through the market, barely acknowledging our presence. As if they were ghosts focused on the afterlife.

I tried to politely stop a woman to inquire about what's transpired, but the more I tried, the more they ignored me. Finally, Kole grabbed a man shuffling through the market and demanded he tell us what the hell was going on here.

"Where is Kyut?" He shook the man as he spoke.

"Kyut is only second to our king, and even lower than the beast," the man mumbled quietly, as if he didn't want to speak the words into existence.

What beast? I could feel the pulsating push of darkness coming off Kole. His patience was waning, but the man could only be talking about one other person, who was specifically not meant to be the master of this place. Kole grabbed the man by his collar and pulled him closer.

"Where is Ivar?" he snarled as the darkness shifted the air all around us.

"The master waits for you up at the longhouse, King Kole," a dark grin stretched across his face. "The longhouse is at the top of the hill. I pray that you fare better than the last King that made his way through here," the man laughed in Kole's face.

"What the hell did he do with the last King?" Kole was screaming frantically, as the man just continued to laugh as if he was playing a sick game. I reached for Kole's arm instinctively. I did not want him to hurt the man out of anger.

"Kole, we need to go now!" I said purposefully. "Whatever Ivar has done is done. Whatever he is planning to do next, we can't stand around and wait for it to happen. We need to move now." Kole threw the man to the side he landed in the dirt. No one reacted at all, they just kept walking, keeping their business to themselves. This place gave me the fucking creeps.

"Fucking Odin!" Kole screamed as we marched toward the top of the hill. "He should have just let him die. Why would he need him alive if it was always going to lead to this? What is the meaning to all of this? Why would Odin make our journey more difficult? I don't understand it," the frustration was beaming off his brow.

"When have we ever understood the Gods and their games?" I asked, not necessarily looking for an answer.

"I swear if he has hurt Rollo, I'm going to kill him, no matter the consequences. Odin saved him once, but he is not here to save him again." He only looked straight ahead as he spoke, the darkness still pushing the air around us. We would all sleep a little better at night if Ivar wasn't alive.

I didn't think anything could look as dark and depressing as the market, but the longhouse proved me wrong. How could anyone stomach living this way? We walked through the entrance, our instincts willing us to keep our hands near our weapons. There was no telling what we could be walking into.

Outside of our altercation in Lundr, I didn't really get to talk to Kyut much. I knew nothing about the man that was supposed to be my brother-in-law.

Kare and Kole are still family, so how far would Kyut take this? Would he go as far as to set an actual ambush for his brother? I know Ivar had no problem doing it, but killing your kin was different.

The tables were covered with bowls of food wasting away on the tables. Smashed plates and cups were scattered all over the floor. If there was a feast here at some point, the days of celebrating have surely passed.

"This place is disgusting," I complained, as I was gingerly watching my every step to avoid the mess that is this longhouse.

"Everything about this makes no sense to me. Even if this was a punishment, why would you willingly live in filth?" Kole asked himself.

A noise coming from the front of the longhouse jolted our attention. My knuckles gripped tightly on the hilt of my daggers as I turned and came face-to-face with the man I embarrassed in the square.

Kyut looked the same, but he had grown in stature and muscle. The rest of the city appeared to be starving, but he managed to keep himself in great shape. Kole's shoulders tensed as his brother's evil glare pierced us both as we walked toward the throne. Neither were willing to break the gaze or the silence.

I wanted to interrupt, but this felt like something Kole wanted to handle himself. Family was so complicated. I'm sure he harbored love for his brother still, but like myself, the deception and betrayal are unbearable weights that no one can carry easily. Forgiveness seems less like relief and more like defeat after experiencing what we have.

The silence was deafening. Someone had better say something because this was starting to get awkward. The sun peaked through the holes in the roof of the longhouse. Kyut finally spoke.

"Brother," was all he said, a sly smirk stretched along the corner of his mouth.

"Brother," Kole returned the sentiment, with not a hint of kindness in his voice.

"It took you long enough. I figured you would come running when you heard your precious Rollo was here." He laughed and Kole tensed even more as the darkness simmered inside him.

"I'm here now. So where is he?" Kole asked calmly but sternly.

"He is comfortable, as is his new vampire pet. Which is very interesting might I add. The fact that something like that exists, and here I thought I had seen it all," he said playfully.

He obviously had no idea that Kare was now one of them. But at least we know they are both alive.

"Do you know how hard it was to find a place where no sunlight can get in? Though, I'm curious… Do you know what happens to vampires when sunlight hits their skin? I assure you, it is fascinating." The smile that he gave this time was infuriating, I could not ignore it.

"What did you do Kyut?" I yelled.

Koel Alexander © 2024
Raven & Fire Series

"That is none of your concern...queen," he dismissed me almost immediately. He spit the last word out, clearly still bitter about my place in Kole's life.

"Enough, Kyut. We have more important things to deal with right now. Give me Rollo and Marcella, and I'll think about showing you mercy, although I am running short on that right about now." Kole stepped forward, his hand resting on his axe.

"Don't worry, brother, we will get to that. First, you need to present yourself before the king. Isn't it customary that you speak to him before you start making demands in his kingdom?" Kole and I exchanged a glance looking completely confused.

"There is no King here. You were told to look over this city and Ivar was to advise you. Once again, you spit in my face when I am the only reason you are still breathing." The darkness pulsed once again, this time much more volatile.

A figure walked into the room from behind Kyut. Ivar came into view, calm and collected, far from the beaten and shackled man I saw in Lundr. He seemed very much in control, but his eyes were holding something vicious and feral inside.

"You really thought I was going to let someone else sit on my father's throne? You might be more of a righteous asshole than I thought." He walked around and sat on his throne as Kyut took a step down in front, almost guarding Ivar from us both.

"I thought I made my request quite clear. You are also a product of my compassion, and now both of you stand before me keeping another king hostage and directly defying my orders." Kole's tone growing more exasperated.

"You make no orders here, Odin's pet!" Ivar screamed his eye color shifted with his anger but disappeared in an instant. "Your brother was more than happy to hand me back the throne. The only thing he wanted was revenge for the brother that took the side of a Roman whore over his own blood." His words stung hard enough for me to take a step forward.

I hadn't forgotten the role he played in the destruction of my family, even if it was unintentional. Kyut stepped forward, but Kole reached over to stop me from advancing.

"All will be revealed in due time. So have a seat and relax," he smiled.

"Fuck you, Ivar!" Kole reached for his axe again.

"Any act of aggression and Rollo won't make it another day. That vampire thing he brought here will meet the sun. Are we clear?" Ivar barked.

Kole looked at me, silently telling me to play nice, even as I was worried he wouldn't be able to.

"We are clear," he responded before finding a seat at a table. "Tell us whatever you need to tell us because by nightfall I have a feeling I will be cleaning your blood off my axe," he turned his head toward me. It was a silent signal if I had ever seen one.

By nightfall the reinforcements would be here. Rollo could take care of himself, but with the sun still up Marcella was defenseless. We just needed to buy some time, and part of me wanted to hear what Ivar and Kyut could possibly have to say.

24 – A Plan Unfolds - Octavia

"Misery is more common than contentment, wouldn't you agree, Queen Octavia?" Ivar made himself comfortable in his chair as he spoke. I locked eyes with him but had no intention of entertaining him. Annoyed beyond reason because the statement was true.

Ever since the ambush, I'd lived in a constant state of misery, up until Kole showed up and changed everything. However, I would not give him the satisfaction of knowing his words rang true.

"Say what you need to say, Ivar. Your voice is torture enough," I retorted.

"I see you still haven't taught the bitch any manners, Kole," Kyut interrupted. I nearly jumped from my chair, but Kole grabbed my arm to keep me still. I wanted to keep my cool for Rollo. Kyut was pushing it.

"How's the leg?" I responded with a smile. "Looks like you have a tiny limp, but I swear it's barely noticeable." Kyut's expression hardened.

"Do you have something to say Ivar, or are we going to trade insults?" Kole asked.

"Where to start I wonder?" He seemed to be in a haughty mood, clearly enjoying having the upper hand at the moment.

"Start at the part where you walked away with your head," Kole drawled.

"Oh yes, that part. After you exacted your glorious mercy upon us and sent us here to waste away, Kyut was more than willing to give me back my throne. He only wanted to repay the brother who turned his back on him. Which was a tragedy, I might add."

"Yeah, I got that part. Get to the part that matters," Kole interrupted.

"The first couple months here I will admit, even though I had my throne, I felt utterly defeated." Ivar dragged along, taking his sweet time to tell this story.

"Aww poor Ivar, his diabolical plan to murder innocent people didn't go right, so he felt depressed," I said sarcastically. "Get over yourself!"

"That is where you are wrong. It was not my plan. It was my father's plan. Which he felt compelled by the Gods to see through. I was merely an obedient son obeying his father's wishes," he turned to Kole. "Same as you, or should I say not the same as you," he scoffed.

"My father never had me turn on my countryman for power," Kole retorted.

"But your father fought in a war at the behest of his Gods and killed hundreds, if not thousands of our countrymen all in the name of power," his statement was meant to silence Kole, but he didn't retreat.

"He fought to defend his home. It was never about eliminating an entire country. It was about having a place to call our own."

"Believe what you like but stop me if I'm wrong. The Gods have been pulling the strings, and we have all been puppets. Overseeing the demise of their own people on both sides. So, in the grand scheme of things, am I still such a horrible person? Did I have any more of a choice than you did? Am I not also guided by fate? Was it not you who keeps reminding me that the Gods allowed me to keep my head?" He waited for an answer but Kole did not give one.

"That's bullshit. You had more than enough chances to choose the same as us," I countered. "You aren't a puppet. You are weak. Too weak to stand up and decide that you were going to be a good person, that's the difference." I could feel the flame rising. "Don't ever try to compare yourselves to us. In the face of the Gods, no one has sacrificed more than we have, all because we stand on what we know is right." I didn't realize I was on my feet until I finished speaking.

"So, you made the right choice when you tore my family apart and killed my father?" Kyut hissed at his brother.

"Of course not!" Kole stuttered. "Odin tricked us."

"So? You could have made a different choice, Kole. You could have done the right thing and stepped down." Kole sat speechless, torturing himself for what Odin tricked him into doing. A wound that would never close, even as he worked towards his father's goal.

"Father believed in a united world, and he would have given his life for it, if the Gods willed it," he claimed, though I could hear doubt hidden behind his words. I wonder if he will ever truly forgive himself for what he had to do in the name of the Gods.

"He didn't have to, but you made sure that he did anyway, because deep down you are more Odin than you would like to admit. They say the All-father has a hunger for power that rivals no other God. They also say no one does revenge quite like him. So, you see brother, we are two sides of the same coin. True decedents of Odin himself, and I promise you before I leave this realm for Valhalla, you both will feel my revenge." His eyes changed to the familiar darkness that I had seen many times in Kole himself.

That could only mean one thing. His powers had finally manifested, and he was going to be a lot harder to deal with than we expected.

"An Odin's oath was made, Kyut. I had no other choice. Breaking it would have ended in the death of all of you. What would you have had me do?" Kole asked.

"The oath never needed to be made. You did all of it to save her!" He pointed at me. "You put her life above everything else, and then you exiled me here, once again showing me exactly where I stand in your life." He had so much anger in his eyes. Ivar shuffled in his chair, enjoying the tension between the brothers. His plan to dismantle the Alexsson household was in motion, and he hasn't even lifted a finger.

"Kyut, I know you are upset, but let us get to the best part of the tale." Our attention went back to Ivar. "News of your exploits in the east made its way back to us. We heard about your battle with the rogue Roman king. Funny how you ended up eliminating him just like my father wanted to. Unfortunately, in true Kole fashion, you made another enemy along the way," he smirked.

"What are you talking about?" Kole asked, even though I believe he already knew.

"You did what you always do because you just can't help yourself, can you? You can't help making a mess everywhere you go and try to hide it under the guise of doing the right thing. It's like a disease, an addiction that you can't shake," Ivar practically spat the words.

"What the fuck are you talking about, Ivar?" Kole was losing his patience. Ivar's eyes changed again in that instant as he stared us both down. A quick flash of color before they returned to normal.

"Would either of you recall making some kind of deal recently?" My stomach dropped. I had a feeling of what to expect, but hearing it made it more of a reality.

"Delphi," I mumbled under my breath.

"You are correct, my queen. Delphi." Ivar confirmed, looking positively gleeful.

"What does she have to do with it?" I asked, terrified of the answer.

"Oh, she has everything to do with it. When Kole made his deal to spare those abominable vampires, he offended the spirit. Instead of stopping there, he went even further. You offered up the essence of the goddess in the moon, knowing that it was not yours to offer," he laughed. "And you disregarded all the warning signs, releasing another curse on this world. All so you could save a bunch of misfit monsters that no one has cared about." His face was serious again. "I have heard she does not take kindly to being outsmarted."

"We've gathered that." Delphi, the infection that just keeps spreading.

"Be proud, my king. You set this in motion. Who else would be chosen by the spirit than the two banished princes' who not only hate you but hate the Gods?" He raised his arms in a motion of victory.

"She is insane, Ivar. Whatever she has given you is for her gain, not yours. If it was up to her, we would all be killing each other," Kole implored.

"Well, at least that would make sense," Kyut interrupted.

"You don't understand, Kyut. There is more to the story that you do not know. I had to make that deal or she…"

"Whatever the reason, save it for the dead in Valhalla," he yelled.

"Don't you worry, Kole. She gave me exactly what I need to not only end you, but to spoil any more plans the Gods have in store for all of us. The spirit told us the Gods used the last stores of their power to get you out of your Midselium prison, so I wouldn't be expecting any help."

Koel Alexander © 2024
Raven & Fire Series

Kole raised up out of his seat, his hand on his axe and his eyes black in response to the threat.

"Kole, what are you doing? What about Rollo?" I asked but Ivar kept talking.

"All I have to do is take you out, and the Gods lose their last two pieces on the board," Ivar explained. I turned to them with my hands on my daggers.

"None of you are leaving here alive," his voice was raspy, almost to the point of a growl, and his eyes turned bright as he hobbled over in pain.

25 – Bruised Ego - Kole

I burrowed into the darkness to use the Odin sight. My eyes opened, making the world completely visible to me. Nothing was hidden. My aura was the same, a dark cloud seeping from the center of my chest. My eyes moved to Octavia, her Roman flame burning bright as the sun. She was such a force, a beacon in the night. Something peculiar caught my eye when I looked deeper. It was so small; I would have barely noticed if I wasn't staring. There was a tiny patch of darkness, but there was no way for me to make out what it could be.

The growl from the throne grew even louder, breaking my concentration and shifting my gaze over to Ivar and Kyut. The same dark cloud I saw in myself was violently seeping out of my brother. He finally managed to do it. His powers had finally manifested, as it did with all children of royal blood. Yet his abilities were a mystery, as of now. But the growl wasn't coming from him. A low rumble came from Ivar. When my eyes landed on him, the realization of his words struck home.

You could hear the bones breaking as he hovelled over in pain. In his center was the swirling green mist. The signature of that maniacal spirit. What had she managed to turn him into? Ivar's screams turned into a howl as he transformed into an animal right before our very eyes.

"It's the curse!" Octavia yelled. That much was clear... but what exactly was he? Odin sight usually gave me a great advantage. It was the way I figured out how we could defeat Marcus, but this was different.

I scoured the beast from head to toe, but I could find nothing. The animal had no weaknesses that I could see. I hated the thought of retreating, but I only had one option to keep us alive until we can figure out how to make sense of this.

Ivar stood behind Kyut, a man no more but a massive beast on all fours in his place. He resembled the wolf from his family's flag. Saliva dripped off his razor-sharp teeth and his dark fur was ragged over his giant ears and piercing eyes.

He turned his attention toward us, snarling as his front row of canine teeth threatened to rip us apart. Octavia and I drew our weapons while taking cautious steps back, making sure we did not take our eyes off the beast.

"Octavia, when I say so, you need to run," I whispered to her.

"We can't run. We need to find Rollo and Marcella," she responded, her daggers tight in her grip.

"I don't know if you can tell, but we are not exactly in the position of power right now," I nodded toward the gigantic wolf stalking us like fresh prey. She scoffed at my notion, her Roman pride urging her to stay and fight, but I know deep down she agrees with me. We kept shifting toward the entrance of the longhouse.

"There is no way out, brother. You can stall all you want, but your time as king will be shorter than you expected," Kyut laughed.

"You think you will gain anything from this? Delphi will dispose of you both once you finish doing her bidding. You traded one puppet for another you idiots." I tried to reason with them to buy us a little more time.

"This puppet allows me to get the one thing that I have wanted since you bought that whore to our shore and destroyed my family," Kyut pointed his axe toward us, ignoring me completely.

Ivar sprung from the throne faster than any animal I had ever seen. We managed to barely dodge him, and he slammed into the empty tables behind us. We scurried to our feet and tried to move back toward the entrance, but Ivar was already lunging for another strike. I wedged the hilt of my axe in his jaw to keep him at bay, but he was so incredibly strong there was no way to hold him off for long.

"Octavia, run!" I yelled, trying to keep his teeth from putting a hole in my arms. Ivar raised his giant paws to try and snap my axe, something I had never seen an animal do before.

"I'm not leaving you!" She was standing directly behind me, looking for an opening to attack the wolf.

"I'm not asking you to leave me. I'm telling you to run." I nodded toward the entrance. She scoffed at me again, but I think she finally picked up the hint.

I used everything I had to push Ivar away as he swiped his claws, anticipating my movements. He had to be just as much man as beast, because he moved with an awareness no animal could have.

Kyut stayed in the background, laughing and enjoying watching us scramble to stay out of Ivar's jaws. I don't know how long I can keep this up. We need to get out of here and regroup.

I waited for Ivar to strike again to give me an opening. I knew that he would be able to anticipate my movements, but this was my only shot. The pain I was about to take would buy me enough time to get us out of here.

Ivar charged me again as expected. When he opened his mouth to try to bite me again, I shifted to my left and punched the beast in the side of the head. Ivar managed to bring down his paw, slicing my arm completely open. The force of the punch sent him back far enough that I could rush back to Octavia, grab her hand and portal out of the longhouse. Kuyt's screams through the darkness sounded out as we managed to escape his grasp.

The portal I opened dropped us in the woods just outside of the city. It was the only spot I could think of quickly. We should be safe for now. I was still having a hard time processing what I just saw. Delphi had used Selene's essence to create a totally different monster than the first time. Now Ivar could run loose and do more damage than he ever could have done before.

I have replayed that day in the arena in my head over and over, trying to figure out if there was a different way to get out of that situation alive. Delphi had us right where she wanted us, and I thought I made the best choice. At least that is what I told myself every night.

The cold air rushed against me. I could feel the blood pouring down my arm, but I was too preoccupied to give it my attention. My brother wants me dead, and the bastard that I was told to spare now has a killer wolf alter ego.

"Are you okay?" Octavia came up from behind me, examining my arm.

"I'm fine," I muttered.

"You are not fine, you're dripping blood everywhere. How bad was the scratch?" I didn't answer, just retreating to my thoughts. I had to figure what we were going to do to get Rollo and Marcella back.

The sun would be setting soon and, although I was excited about having backup, I am unsure what the next move should be. Delphi had played her hand, a monstrous one at that. It had to be some full-circle irony to change Ivar into a giant wolf. The animal on his house sigil, and that specific animal was destined to overthrow Odin himself in the stories that were told to us as children. The animal that drove the All-father deeper and deeper into paranoia, spawning his quest for knowledge and power in the first place. More ironic is that she used Selene's essence to make something murderous from it, and I know when Gio finds out he is not going to take it lightly.

Koel Alexander © 2024
Raven & Fire Series

As powerful as he could be, I just had to remember that he wasn't invincible. Like Gio, since he was tied to the essence of a God, it would be unnatural for him to be absent a weakness. We just had to find out what it is exactly.

"Sit still," Octavia urged me as she tried to clean out the massive cut Ivar left on my arm. I was surely going to repay the favor when I get the chance. "He really got you good. This is going to leave a nasty scar." She used a cloth to wipe away the blood before applying a wrap to it.

"Good. This scar will be the last part of him left in this world," I said coldly.

"We need to find the others. We don't want them rushing into whatever that is we just ran into." She put the finishing touches on my arm.

"Gio should be able to find us with that weird hunter sense he has." Then, like a giant rock dropped on my head, a piece of the puzzle finally became clear to me. "Odin's beard, I am such an idiot!" I exclaimed.

"What are you talking about?" Octavia asked.

"The head of the cursed. It must be him."

"You think Ivar is the head of the cursed that we need to get to the artifact?" she asked surprisingly.

"Does that not explain all of it?" I asked. "Why Odin wanted to spare him. Why, of all places, I exiled him here. Think about it. Now that deal does not seem as farfetched as before. Maybe it was fated to be this way."

I looked into her eyes, hoping she would agree to alleviate some of the guilt I felt about the things I have done.

She sat for a moment, racking her brain and weighing the likelihood of my assumptions.

"I don't like leaning on fate, but I have to admit that it would make the most sense. However, I think you are missing one thing that could be a bigger problem," she said cautiously.

"And what would that be?" I asked.

"Ivar is not the only cursed we know. And based on what Odin made you do before, you need to really examine all the possibilities." Her eyes were intense.

"No, no he wouldn't. Not again, that's not possible. Why would he have me do that?" I muffled my words in disbelief because once again. I needed to be very careful, or I would be on the losing side of yet another deal. Ivar was cursed indeed, but he wasn't the only one. There was Gio, and even worse, there was Kare.

26 – The Curse - Kare

As the sun made its way down, I was counting down the moments till I could be rid of this cave. It has been entirely too awkward ever since Gio berated me about the negative aspects of the vampire's existence. Veronica reveled in my discomfort, which was to be expected. The feud between us simmered, and it was not going away anytime soon it seems. That would have to be put on hold for now, the sound of footsteps catching my attention.

It sounded like two sets of feet, but it could be more. What was certain is that they were headed straight toward us. I shook off my feelings and went into hunter mode. As the second, I directed the others on how we would proceed.

"Everyone stay quiet," I said calmly. "Do not engage until we know what we are facing." Gio was behind me in an instant. A low grow vibrated the cave, waiting to see if we had stumbled on a friend or foe. May the Gods have mercy on them if it was a foe.

The others followed my orders and held as the steps got louder, almost frantic in their intensity. There was no room left as the steps closed in on the openings of the cave. I pushed off with everything I had, grabbing his shirt and lifting him off his feet. My fangs were fully extracted, and a visceral growl left my throat.

The sound of a blade being removed from its sheath came from my left, and through a brief moment of clarity I finally managed to look at the faces of our intruders. One that I had seen my entire life, and in pure Kole fashion, he was smiling as I dangled him off his feet.

"Hello, sister," he chuckled as I held him. "You mind putting me down? This is kind of embarrassing," Octavia stood with her dagger drawn, her palms stretched across that golden hilt.

"Kole, why didn't you say something? I could have killed you." I let him go.

"I didn't think I would be walking into a trap. We have been walking for a while trying to find you guys," he explained, fixing his clothes. Gio appeared at the entrance seconds later.

"It wouldn't be a great campsite if anyone could just walk up here and find it, now, would it?" he said sarcastically.

"We know you know everything about hiding, don't you Gio," Octavia said with a scowl on her face.

"My queen, how I have missed your beautiful Roman charm." Gio gave a half bow with a smirk on his face.

Something caught my attention immediately. It was a strong taste in the air. The smell touched the tip of my tongue and woke me up. It smelled like the only thing that meant more to me than breathing itself. It filled my nostrils, igniting my insides, causing my heart to thump faster in my chest. Gio must have smelled it as well because I felt his hand rest on my shoulder, signaling for me to center myself before I made any movements.

"Kole, are you okay?" My voice broke as I spoke and turned away from him, ignoring the roar coming from my gut. Just like a man, he was oblivious. Even with all that wisdom, how could one remain so clueless I will never know.

"We have a lot to talk about after the run-in I had with your favorite brother and that animal Ivar." He ran his hand through his hair.

"Your arm, Kole. What happened to your arm?" My voice staggered again as the blood started to pour down from the wound that was wrapped.

"Oh shit, the scratches must have opened up again," he pressed his hand to his arm trying to stop the flow. Gio nudged his head toward all the other vampires trying to get my brother's attention. His eyes went wide when he realized. I'm sure he thought I was in way more control, but this was completely unexpected.

"Sorry, Kare, I didn't even realize. Sorry, everyone!" He tried to press down on the wrapping to stop the blood. All I could do was smell the blood. I tried to push past him outside the cave. I just needed some fresh air.

"No worries, my king. She will be fine, I assure you. Let's build a fire and get cleaned up so we can talk. I'm very curious as to what happened up there, considering you both scrambled back here without the traitors." Gio waved to the others to gather some wood.

The fire crackled and singed as we all piled in to hear exactly what took place at the longhouse. The two of them weren't very successful, considering Kole was injured and they hadn't returned with Rollo or Marcella. I hope they were okay, and I hope Kyut hadn't done anything that would further fracture our relationship. His words were almost unforgivable, but he was still my blood. Yet another person I would have to explain my transformation to.

"Are you going to tell us what happened? I am immortal, but we all know I'm very impatient." Gio took a large gulp from his goblet.

"Since you are so impatient Gio, is there anything that you need to tell us?" Octavia spoke directly to him, and I know exactly what she was referring to. The circle was silent. For the first time in a long time, Gio was speechless.

"What is she talking about?" Kole asked, still oblivious to us all.

"It's not important, my love. Just wanted to give Gio a chance to speak if he wanted to before you tell them what happened," Octavia said playfully, waiting to see if Gio would push the issue.

The kiss rushed to my memory, but now was not the time to relive that stolen moment, especially with my brother right in front of me. His mood shifted as he began to recant everything that occurred, starting with the fact that Ivar and my brother Kyut had lost their damn minds.

The city as he described it is rundown and completely unattended, in ruin if you will. A testament to what they have done in their time in charge.

"What do you mean they have lost their minds?" I asked.

"I mean they have completely lost it. They are on some suicide mission from Delphi to overthrow Odin and Mars' plan of a united world," Octavia said.

"Fucking Delphi," Gio growled.

"What's stopping us from just going up there and stopping them both?" I asked. "You're the King, and we have our allies. Let's go up there and clock my stupid brother in the head and find this artifact," I suggested.

"I'm afraid it will not be that simple, Kare," Kole's eyes met mine.

"Why?" I asked.

"The curse," he said lowly. Gio's body went rigid next to me.

"What about the curse?" he asked intently. We hadn't heard anything about the curse since Selene gave us the warning at the wedding. If it had finally come to fruition, the timing could not be worse.

"What did you do?" Gio was on his feet and across to Kole in less than a second.

His breath ragged as he waited for an answer from my brother.

"What about the curse, Kole?! You remember the deal I told you not to make." Gio's fangs curled under his lips as he spoke. Octavia jumped up and pushed him back before stepping in between the two of them.

"You mean the deal that has you here now, living and breathing?" She was face-to-face with him, not backing down. "None of us are absent of the blame for what has happened. Now back off and let him finish. It is and always has been bigger than us." The two of them refused to give an inch, but Kole started to speak to break the tension.

"He's right. I shouldn't have made the deal, but we are here now and there is no going back. Delphi is using my brother and Ivar's vengeance to get what she wants. In doing so, she has transformed Ivar into a giant wolf. The same one on the sigil of his house. She has boosted Kyut's manifested abilities, using the hate in his heart for me." Kole put his head down after he spoke. I did not know what to say, but I had a thousand questions.

"What do you mean he transformed?" Gio spoke.

"I mean he stood in front of me and transformed into the biggest wolf I have ever seen. Stood on all fours, and there is no exaggeration in that statement," Octavia grimaced.

"If this is a curse, then he must have a weakness, same as us. Did anything stick out to you?" Gio pressed.

"No, not at all. The curse came from Selene's essence of the moon, but it was not even nightfall when he turned. If I was looking for a weakness, I think that it would be tied to the moon somehow. He was freakishly fast and brutally strong. It took everything for us to get out of there alive," Kole said.

"What about Marcella and Rollo?" I asked.

"He said that they were still alive, locked up," Kole continued.

"What else did he say?" Gio must have caught his expression.

"He made a comment about seeing what the sun does to her skin," Kole spoke carefully. Gio's eyes popped and went dark.

"I'm going to rip his head off," he growled.

"We need a plan first," Octavia interrupted.

"I have a plan. I'm going to rip his head off. If that beast is part Selene, I must deal with it myself. Delphi can't be allowed to have her be remembered this way."

"While I agree with you, we have no idea how to beat him, and on top of that, the prophecy speaks of needing the cursed head. The only problem is… which cursed head are they speaking of?" Octavia asked. Now, we really did not know what to say.

To find the artifact, stop Delphi and save the world, we needed the cursed head, but who exactly would that be referring to? Now my immortal life did not seem all that long. I knew in my heart though if it needed to be me, I would gladly give up what they needed to get peace. I decided to keep my thoughts to myself.

"Should we be worried?" I asked.

"I won't be trying to use anyone's head but Ivar's, if that's what you mean, sister," Kole smiled.

"Either way, we need a plan," Octavia interjected.

"I have a plan, but I want to make sure you do something for me before I tell you," I spoke.

"Whatever it is, I'm sure I can do it," Kole responded.

"I want to have a chance to talk to Kyut before you all go in there trying to kill him," I interjected. The others let out a long sigh in disappointment before I could finish my statement.

"You are admirable, sister, but trust me that is not the brother that you have once known," Kole said. "He is buried so deep in hatred for all of us. He won't hesitate to hurt any of us."

I wasn't ready to just throw away my blood, and my mother wouldn't want me to either. I needed to fight for the last bit of my family, no matter how much it hurt. It was going to take compassion from them all, but I hoped at least Kole considered it for me.

"Please, Kole let me try. He is our brother," I pleaded. Kole grabbed my hands and pulled me close to him.

"For you sister, I will do anything in this world. If you feel that you can talk to him, I will stay my hand for the time being, but he is nothing to me. If he hurts any of you, I will put him down." He was so serious, more serious than I'd ever seen him before. "Now tell me your plan." It felt good to hear him agree, even though he did not want to.

"My plan is the oldest trick in the book. We just need to distract Kyut and Ivar for long enough to free Rollo and Marcella. Once they have joined the fight, we will be at full strength. Octavia, how would you like to see how big of a wall you can burn down?" She smiled at my question. "I hope you have been practicing because we are going to use you to blow the biggest hole in Ivar's longhouse."

Koel Alexander © 2024
Raven & Fire Series

"The pleasure would be all mine." Her hands began to glow.

27 - Layers Of The Flower - cassia

I sit in the throne room of my father's killer trying to figure out how I got here. I knew this was necessary if I wanted to eventually reign over Alexandria. The only problem is that I long for Cosa. I needed a way to make more trips back home.

The ocean and the tranquil beach give me comfort. The only time that I feel true peace, my parents forever on my mind. I had a lot of mixed feelings toward my mother, but she was still my mother. She wasn't strong enough to endure, or maybe her love was so strong that she was brave enough to take her own life, only the Gods know.

I hope my father is proud of me and what I have accomplished, outside of being a queen. I feel like I am doing exactly what he would have wanted me to do if he were in my shoes.

Floria and I were in Alexandria to clean out any remaining rebels we could find, and the much more important job of securing allies. How could anyone still side with Marcus after learning the truth? It would always rub me the wrong way since my parents were collateral damage.

Floria didn't say much while traveling with me. She just kept to herself, probably fighting her own subconscious. Things between her and Octavia had hit their breaking point back in that cave. Much was said, most of which would be difficult to come back from. She was tossing herself between envy and anger.

I believe that Octavia showing her mercy was a blessing. Many others would not have been so lenient, including myself. That kind of betrayal was usually paid for in blood. Keeping her alive would not have sat well with me. Octavia couldn't bear the sight of her but also didn't want to be her killer, which I assume is the reason she gave her to me.

The hunt for the rebels was quick as my soldiers combed through Alexandria in haste. I ordered them to vet the loyalist properly. I did not want the people to think I was just another cruel tyrant, but anyone who followed Marcus could not remain. I planned on leading Gracia into a time of greatness if the king and queen would allow me to rule here in their place.

Soldiers were falling into the throne room to give me an update. Floria and I sat across from each other sharing a drink in pure and utter silence, which is usually how most of our days go.

"Update from the field, my queen." The soldier stood at attention.

"Go ahead soldier," I waved motioning for him to continue.

"The search for the remaining rebels seems to be coming to a conclusion. Less and less are found hiding in Alexandria every day. We also managed to round up all allies that we could in preparation for what is to come next," he explained, standing at attention.

"That is good to hear." I tried my best to sound enthused.

"My lady, I mean no offense, but what does come next?" he asked cautiously.

"That depends on when we receive word from King Cole and Queen Octavia. I only know that the next test will be bigger than anything we have dealt with before. All we can do is focus on making sure that Alexandria is returned to its former glory." Floria adjusted herself uncomfortably in her seat. The thought of a reunion with her sister probably didn't bring up happy thoughts.

"Floria, I see you flinching at my words. Do you have any objections to what we are trying to achieve here? I know this is your home, and it may be hard to watch someone else pull the strings, but just know that we all have the best intentions for the kingdom." I waited for her to use her words for once.

"How can you have the best intentions for my home if you're not from here?" she questioned.

"A fair assessment, but given your actions, I feel it's fair to say that you gave up the right to make decisions here. Some of the things you did make it seem as if you put yourself above all others," I chastised.

"Don't presume to know me, Princess Cassia."

"Queen," I corrected her.

"Queen... don't presume to know what I had in store for the city, or my intentions. No one can know my intentions but myself. No one knows what I went through while Marcus and his children tormented us all," Floria spat back angrily.

"I won't presume to know your intentions, but I would come down off of that high horse you sit on. You were not the only one to succumb to the vile dealings of Marcus. I am an orphan as well because of his plans. Only difference is I didn't sell my soul for the promise of a throne," I retorted.

"Our lives are not the same and they never will be. You were always in line for the throne. You could never share the same feelings as me. Do you know what it's like to be born underneath the throne knowing that you'll never take it?" Floria asked. "Do you know what it's like to know you won't have it unless something tragic happens to not one but both your siblings? To come so close to gaining the one thing you never thought you could have at the expense of your siblings' deaths, and the guilt that weighs on you with that... only to be ripped from you once again?"

I did not have an answer for her while she spoke these words, and while I still disagree, my heart could feel for the person that sat here and dreamed of something different.

"I'm not here to absolve whatever guilt you have about the past. Right now, we look towards our future. I think this is a great opportunity for you to repay your sister's mercy and show them you can still be of value to your kingdom," I said.

"You heard her when we left the cave. My sister and I mean nothing to each other, and I can only assume that's the way it's going to stay. I won't apologize for it. I'll just move on with my life," she said defensively.

"I heard what you both said, but I'm not asking you to do this for her. I'm asking you to do it for yourself. I don't take pride in taking your place in your home. I want you to be an integral part of Alexandria. Only few people know it like you and your sister."

"What are you saying?" she prodded.

"I'm saying show me what kind of person you can be. Show me the person that is valuable to the kingdom. Show me that the mercy paid to you by your sister was warranted and not wasted." She adjusted herself in her seat again without a word as she continued to take sips from her drink. I guess that meant that our conversation was over for now.

Hopefully, my words will resonate with her and she comes to her senses at some point. In the meantime, I took a walk down to the docks. The water in Alexandria was nothing like the water in Cosa. All these ships coming back and forth took the clarity and purity out of it.

I sat on the edge of the docks and reached out to the waves. The rush of power surged from my chest, shooting down my arm, and I used my hands to sway the water back and forth. My father used to do this to calm himself down before he went into battle. This waiting was killing me. I was given the job to go and rally the troops instead of being one of the ones to fight. It was insulting, but it was the right move.

They all saw what I could do in the arena. My skills are more valuable on the field than they are in politics, but if I planned on ruling Gracia, completing this task would surely boost the odds in my favor. But I needed battle the same way fish needed water. It was a thirst that gnawed at the back of my throat, a muscle that needed to be used. All I had to do was be patient because I was on the cusp of the biggest battle of my life, but I was struggling. What the hell was taking them so long to send word?

I reached out toward the water, flooding even more power to my hands, and the small waves I made started to grow. The water splashed on the dock and began to rock the boats already tied up. People next to me complained and yelped as the water rode higher up the dock, but I did not let go. The sound of the water moving as freely as it pleased calmed me even more.

"You plan on making Alexandria an island next?" I let go of the water and it receded down under the dock. Floria walked up, wrapped in a gold silk robe.

"I guess I got kind of carried away. I can usually play with the waves at home with no problem. There are plenty of beaches there," I chuckled.

"Sounds like you miss home," she said.

"I do," I confirmed quietly.

"I have a question for you." She sat down next to me.

"What is it?" I welcomed the distraction.

"Do you really believe there is a possibility that I can make up for what I have done?"

"I think it won't be easy, but your sister left you alive for a reason."

"What would you have done in her position?" she asked.

"Honestly, I would have taken your head." She was taken aback by my answer. "But I do not have siblings, princess, so maybe I am not the one that should be answering that question."

"I've been through so much since the night Tiberius died and I told myself it was all for Alexandria," she admitted.

"And now it is time for you to show us if you really meant that," I answered. "And I have an idea of how you can do it."

"What did you have in mind?"

"Once Kole and Octavia send us word to join them, I want you to stay behind and watch over Alexandria until I return." She was even more taken aback by my answer.

"I'm not sure that is a great idea," she shook her head.

"And why not?"

"My sister would not like the idea of me sitting on the throne after everything that I have done," she acknowledged, maybe starting to see the errors of her ways.

"Your sister told me to come back here and take care of Alexandria, however I see fit. And this is the best way to use you." She did not look very convinced.

"I'm still not sure about this." She remained apprehensive.

"Listen, with me gone the people are going to need someone to look to. I'm asking you to do this for the good of your home. And look on the bright side… if I die, then it is all yours." I chuckled.

"Why would you trust me with this after everything that I have done?"

"Because I told you what I would do if you betrayed me, and that sentiment still stands," I deadpan.

Floria contemplated for a few minutes, but I knew she would accept. She really didn't have any other choice. I will ask the queen for forgiveness if my decision ends up being the wrong one. On the off chance that Floria decided to slip back into her old ways, I would have no problem killing her for squandering another golden opportunity.

28 – Calm Before The Storm - Rollo

I could feel the rumbling of footsteps above my head as people came and went. They had been holding me underground, and I had lost count of how many days I have been sitting in darkness. The servants bring me food and water occasionally but with no consistency.

Ivar visited me a couple of times to gloat. He liked to lecture me on how stupid I was for following the Gods' plan… blah blah blah. He told me they led me to my death, boasting about how I am expendable. He told me that the death of my family was inevitable because of the decision I made to follow Kole. And the last thing he reminded me of is that if I made any attempt to escape Marcella would be the one to pay for it.

Sometimes I could hear her scream. Gut-wrenching, painful screams that shook me to the core. I couldn't imagine what they were doing to her, but it only served to feed my rage. The only reason I didn't snap his little neck is because I couldn't risk anything happening to her. I should have planned for this. I should have known that this could be a trap. Maybe rushing here wasn't a great idea, but at least I found out what both of them have been doing the last few months. Any time I tried to scheme a plan my mind just went right back to Marcella. She was alive, but in what condition would she be in?

I need to keep my resolve. Whatever the Gods intended for me I know it wasn't to die in some prison. This is not how Norse warriors die. I am meant to go out on the battlefield, my hammer in my hand in a blaze of glory. I repeated it to myself over and over. I just needed to buy myself more time. Kole and Octavia would realize that I am not in Ragnarsson and they will come just as Ivar and Kyut expected.

Their strength would prevail, I had to believe that, but it would be hard for them to believe exactly what I have seen. Ivar transformed into that beast in the middle of the throne room. The ragged wolf from the horror stories we were told as youngsters. The wolf that tormented Odin as his end was prophesied by the fates. Marcella and I barely stood a chance against them, so what would my friends be running into? No, no, I can't think like that. I could have killed him easily. I chuckled to myself.

I heard footsteps approaching, springing me out of the panic attack I was having. Kyut walked in with a smug smile on his face. He would only come down here if he had something to say or gloat about. I wasn't up for conversation at the moment. I was too busy mentally planning my escape, but I decided to indulge. He approached me slowly with his hands folded behind his back. He had the nerve to be wearing the same Norse vest that he used to wear back home in Lundr. The same vest that carried his family's Crest. The Crest he no longer believed in… or was it just the Crest that he swore vengeance to? Either way, it is insulting.

"How are you making out down here, Rollo?" he snarked.

"I think this is a place I can really make my own. Maybe put a chair in the corner, a candle to brighten it up a bit. So many options but I'm in no rush." I smiled.

"The fact that you can still make jokes, even in your situation, is something I've always admired about you. You are dumb as a bag of rocks, but you seem to believe that there is always good in every situation."

"When fate sticks you in a dark dungeon, what else can you do but reflect? You think about what you've done. You think about what you will do. Especially what you will do to the person that is responsible," I insinuated, my smile never leaving my face. Kyut moved closer as the smug look drained off his face.

"I don't think you understand how this works, you muscle-head idiot. You don't come out of this on top. You may come out of it alive, if you're lucky, after you have sworn allegiance to me." I tried to hold it in, but the laughter came bursting out. What fantasy world does he live in? What made him think I would ever pledge any allegiance to him?

"What are you talking about?" I still couldn't help but chuckle.

"Once I deal with my brother and the Roman whore, there would be nothing left but for me to take the throne. I will take our people to the glorious heights we were meant for." He spoke so confidently you'd never know he was delusional.

"And you actually think that Delphi is going to help you get there? And if you do get there, you think she will allow you to remain in power?" I prompted.

"As long as I keep us separate from the Romans that is exactly what she will let me do. I have no love for them anyway, that is no task for me. No one will oppose me," he was so confident in his words.

The spirit had completely warped his brain.

"Kyut, you might be the dumbest person I've ever met in my entire life, and that is saying something. I am a king. I don't bow to anyone, especially not you, but let's save this conversation for when your brother arrives." I opted to end the conversation.

"Interesting you bring that up, Rollo. I saw my brother, and we spoke briefly, right before I sent him running with his tail between his legs. He quickly realized that he could do nothing to save you. He didn't even try to get you out. He ran with his bitch and left you here, Rollo. He's a coward, and I've known he was a coward ever since he didn't have the guts to kill me. When I persecuted him in front of all our people that should have been the end of it. He showed his weakness when he allowed me to live, and I promise you I will not show him the same courtesy once I'm king." The words of his stout revenge didn't shake me, but the fact that Kole was here and I didn't even know was concerning. Why was he here only to retreat?

"You didn't even let me get to the funniest part." Those words caught my attention as he waved the note I had in my pocket before I left. I never got to read it before Thor lifted me away. "He wrote you telling you to wait for him so you could come here together." My face betrayed me because I was in such a hurry I didn't even read it. "And if you would have just had half a brain you wouldn't be here now in a dungeon in chains scrambling for survival," he laughed.

There had to be an explanation, and it was clear that Kyut was going to try to place a wedge between us. It's too bad for him that would never work. I know my best friend and he would never leave me here unless there was a reason. The reason is most likely eight feet tall with four legs, fur, and sharp teeth.

"Your brother let you live because you are his brother. Nothing more. It is not weak to preserve your family, Kyut. Whatever Delphi has promised you has made you lose sight of that. You can't see past your own twisted vengeance, and when the time comes you will have a decision to make. Just remember this if you don't remember anything that I have said… if it comes down to it and Kole can't put you in the dirt, I surely will." Kyut's face twisted with anger as he raised his fists to strike me, but the ground shook, knocking him off balance.

It sounded like someone had just taken down a wall upstairs in the long house. Dirt and rocks tumbled from the ceiling in my cage as the commotion grew. Kyut ran out of the room without a word. I knew like I'd always known that my friend would not leave me down here. He only had to retreat to come up with a plan.

Koel Alexander © 2024
Raven & Fire Series

"Showtime." I reached deep within myself, deeper than I'd ever had to reach before because I was starving and dehydrated.

The power seemed so far away from me, but it was there. It was always there, and it would never leave me. With the distraction from the wreckage upstairs, I should be able to find Marcella and get her out of here.

The lightning inside me flickered like a tiny flame as I urged it to come alive. The element responded as the energy coursed from my chest to my hands. I took one deep breath and with a shockwave, I snapped the shackles off my hands. Now my rescue mission began.

All I could do was run. I had no idea where I was going but she had to be down here somewhere. I had to find her before someone came back to make sure I was still in my cage. The fighting had yet to begin upstairs, so the explosion must have been some kind of distraction.

My heart hammered in my chest as I combed through the tunnels, peeking around every corner hoping to find her. She had just come into my life, and this couldn't be the way that I would lose her. I wouldn't lose her. I pushed harder, rounding the corner until I ran into something almost as solid as a wall, knocking me off course. I stepped back to regain my balance and noticed his slick back hair. He was wearing Roman leather and black trousers. My eyes adjusted as I tried to see through the darkness.

"Gio?" I rubbed my eyes and my head because I ran into him pretty hard. The impact did not seem to affect him much.

"Rollo, I'm looking for Marcella. I can feel that she's close," he spoke calmly, but I could tell he was furious.

"Is that some type of weird vampire thing?" I asked.

"You could call it that if you like, but she is close," he closed his eyes and took off running again.

"Damnit Gio, slow down!" He was gone in a blink of an eye. There was no way I could keep up but I headed in the same direction.

My feet ached from running and my head hurt from all the pounding, but I kept pushing through it. I hit the last roundabout hoping that Gio had run this way.

I heard a faint yelp coming from the end of the tunnel and rushed to the opening. Gio was hovering over as Marcella reached up to him for help. Weak groans of pain followed her feeble movements. When she came into my vision, I was decimated by what I saw. Her perfect skin was dry and separating from all the cuts unable to heal as they usually do. It looked like they spent hours cutting her just to watch her heal before cutting her again. Her arms were also covered in burns and the dirt from the cell floor was matted into her hair.

My anguish turned to rage quickly. I was supposed to protect her, and yet this is the torture she was forced to endure. I was going to mangle them both for what they have done to her. Gio looked back at me and must have seen the storm brewing.

He helped Marcella up off the ground while I ran through all the different ways I was going to pay them back for this. Gio walked her over to me and I looped her arm over my shoulder to help her walk. The scar her father had given her was nothing compared to what I was looking at. Even after these scars healed it would be something she is unlikely to ever forget.

Koel Alexander © 2024
Raven & Fire Series

"Are you okay?" I asked her.

"I'm fine," she forced out the answer.

"She is not fine." Gio interrupted and I could see the anger in his eyes. "These burns on her arms are from letting the sun meet her skin over and over," he pointed at her wounds. "These cuts should have healed but she is starving so they have stayed open and festered." I could practically see steam rising off of him.

"What can I do?" I asked him.

"She needs to feed," he said, and I immediately knelt to offer myself without a second thought. I wanted to help, and I would be a liar if I didn't admit that my body urged for the pleasure I experienced from her bite.

"No!" She groaned out the words. I was taken aback by the rejection.

"You have to eat Marcella." I held out my wrist.

"No!" She slapped my hand away.

"Now is not the time to be stubborn," Gio growled.

"He needs his strength to fight. If I take too much, he won't be able to help anyone else," she said. She had a point, but I couldn't just leave her here.

"Listen, I'll stay with her. Your friends are upstairs, and from what they have told me they will need your help. I'll make sure she gets something to eat. It will feel nice to share a meal again. It's been a while, don't you think?" He smiled at her, and even though she looked like she was on the brink of death she smiled back. "I'm sure one of those guards would be more than happy to lend us his blood."

Someone was going to pay for this. Norse or not, this would not go unpunished. Anyone who took part in her torture would have to answer to me. I reached for my hammer only to realize I didn't have it. I guess I'm going to have to do this the old-fashioned way.

29 – Now It Begins - Octavia

Maybe I might have gone a little overboard with the distraction. The flame was still burning bright as the wall crumbled off the incinerated pillars. It was a fire big enough for even the Gods to see. The smoke blackened the already dark sky, signaling the beginning of our assault.

This should give Gio enough time to find Rollo and Marcella. Kare, Kole, and I are going to try to hold off Ivar and Kyut until the others are freed. With all of us here, we should be able to take them no matter how big of a dog Ivar transforms into.

Kare continued to push for the idea of reasoning with Kyut. She believed that she could somehow get through to him and convince him to abandon this insane crusade. I wasn't optimistic that he was able to be reasoned with. She didn't see the crazed look in his eyes. No one wants to give up on their own blood, but the reality comes crashing in on us eventually. I knew that better than anyone.

We waited as the servants began to scramble out of the giant hole I managed to put in the longhouse before making our way in. Ivar would be expecting us, but the giant fire might have prompted him to call in some reinforcements. The frantic shouts and footsteps heading towards us confirmed our suspicions.

The soldiers came pouring out of the hole in waves looking for whoever was responsible for the fire. Kole grabbed his axe, I already had my daggers drawn and Kare had an arrow notched and ready to fly.

"We take them out quickly, then we make our way inside the throne room. Got it?" Kole screamed over his shoulder.

"Got it!" we shouted in unison.

A Norse warrior rushed Kole, screaming at the top of his lungs, only to be silenced by an arrow before he got too close. Kole and I looked back as Kare had already run to high ground and was firing off arrows faster than we could see. I turned back to Kole and he was smiling. We both were.

"All of that training with Gio must be paying off. I think she has that under control," I said to Kole.

"I would have to agree," he smiled.

Another scream came from behind him as a bigger warrior came rushing us both. Kole dodged quickly, pushing me in the other direction. The sword had just missed us, but the man was pushing for another attack. Kole stepped in front to counter his sword strike, knocking the sword from his hands with a swift parry leaving him defenseless.

The warrior panicked, trying to grab anything he could get a hold of. I wanted to jump in and help, but knew I would just be getting in the way. Kole locked eyes with me quickly and nodded his head, a signal I had become accustomed to at this point. When the warrior tried to grab him, he pushed the man in my direction as hard as he could. He backpedaled, but was too late to avoid my blades in his back. He screamed in agony.

"You could have taken care of him yourself," I sassed, cleaning the blood off my blades.

"Yeah, but you looked like you wanted to help," he smirked. "Let's go."

We pushed inside, quickly shifting from our banter to business. Warriors rushed one after the other as my husband poised to make quick work of them. Anyone that appeared to be an opponent he cut down instantly. No wasted movements, hesitation, or mercy as we made our way through the waves of soldiers to get to the throne room. Behind us we could hear Kare screaming as she fought off a couple of Norse at once. If we weren't careful, she would be overpowered.

"I have to go back and help her," Kole yelled. I nodded telling him to go. I could handle the rest until he gets back.

Fate must be testing me because as soon as he ran off three Norse circled me, breathing heavily and growling for blood. I closed my eyes and reached down to grab the flame. The drums began to pound as I felt the heat flow through my body.

The first soldier on my left ran toward me with his sword overhead. Everything around me slowed down as I tracked his movement. I entered into full battle mode, never feeling freer. I brought one dagger up to block his strike and the other up inside his guard, slitting open his throat.

I spun around as another thought he would take advantage of the opportunity, but he never had a chance. It felt like Mars was on my shoulder guiding me. I dodged his axe and used his momentum to flip him over my shoulder. I pinned my hands on top of him and without thinking I ignited his entire body in flames. The last warrior stood in place, his feet frozen with fear. I could see the flames burning in my eyes through his.

"You're a demon!" he yelled.

There was a time when I would have taken offense but now it felt good to be feared. I looked down at my hands and willed the flames to give me what I need. I picked up my dagger and the fire spread down the hilt, extending past the tip of the blade into the shape of a spear. I didn't wait for him to make another move. I flung the spear directly at his chest and the force pinned him to the wall. He fought to remove the spear, but it burned his hands every time he reached for it. Eventually, he stopped fighting as the flames disappeared and his body fell to the floor.

Kole and Kare came running, both completely covered in blood. My eyes locked on Kare and the drums started to pound louder. The chants for blood became stronger in the presence of what they deemed to be a threat.

"Tav, you okay?" she asked concernedly as her fangs were covered in blood.

"I'm good...." I choked out the words over all the hammering inside my head.

"Calm your mind, my love," Kole reached out to calm me down.

Koel Alexander © 2024
Raven & Fire Series

"Easy for you to say. You don't have a death chant in your head." I closed my eyes and fought against my nature. The spirit of Mars had helped keep me alive, but I needed to separate myself from it. Kare wasn't a threat and I knew that, I just needed to focus. I took a deep breath and focused, willing the voices and drums to lessen. I opened my eyes and watched as the world around me returned to normal. I held off the fury for the time being.

"You good?" Kole questioned.

"Yeah, I'm good. Let's move. We need to buy the others more time." We kept moving toward the throne room.

The longhouse seemed so much bigger when you were fighting waves of reinforcements. We rounded the corner and things started to look familiar. Ivar and Kyut had to be holed up in the throne room. Where else would they be? Cowards, both of them.

"Remember, let me try and talk to him," Kare yelled from behind. I didn't want to say anything, but if Kyut made a move for me I planned on putting him down.

"Kare, I will let you speak, but if he tries to hurt you, I won't hesitate," Kole said.

"As long as you let me try," she pleaded.

"Fine, sister." The house began to rumble again, making the others turn toward me.

"It's not me, I swear," I insisted, raising my hands.

The throne room was just up ahead, and four soldiers stood out front guarding the entrance. They turned when they heard us approach and we readied for another fight. The longhouse rumbled again as the ground beneath us started to crumble.

"Move back!" Kole's arms shielded us, moving us away from the collapsing ground.

A flash of light slammed from underneath and a deep war cry followed. Rollo jolted from underground leaving the entrance in complete rubble as he soared in the air. The three of us looked up in awe as he came plummeting back down. This time it was not a freefall like in the woods. He landed on his feet covered in lightning with a murderous look on his face.

"Rollo!" Kole yelled, excited to see his best friend. Rollo's eyes were completely black, the lightning striking back in forth in his pupils. He turned to the soldiers guarding the gate and raised his hammer in the air. We could hear the thunder rolling in closer and closer. There was nothing that could stop it.

The warriors charged to attack him, but Rollo just yelled and brought his hammer back down. Streaks of lightning rained down on the soldiers, splitting their bodies into pieces before they could even get close.

"Holy shit!" Kare exclaimed. We stared at him in amazement, but he did not even look our way. He turned toward the entrance to the throne room like we weren't even there.

"Wait, Rollo," Kole called to him, but Rollo had not said a word. He just kept walking slowly and purposefully. Kole caught up to him and blocked his path trying to reason with him. "Rollo, it's me Kole... can you hear me?" Again, he said nothing at all. It was like he was talking to a wall. "It's me, brother. Talk to me." Rollo finally looked toward Kole and I could see that he was still in that battle mode.

"I'm going to rip him apart for what he did," Rollo said coldly.

"Who?" Kole asked.

"Ivar." He pushed past Kole again, but Kole would not give up. He stepped in his path once more.

"Rollo, I know you're angry, but we can't kill Ivar. Not yet anyway," Kole emphasized. I don't know what set him off, but the fact that Rollo's expression hardened and his energy shifted made it very clear how he felt.

"You don't know what he did!" Rollo yelled. "He tortured her the entire time I've been here. I had to listen to her being tortured while I lay chained in a fucking cage, all because of him!" There was nothing but pain in his voice.

"I know, Rollo, and he will pay. I promise you that," Kole reassured.

"What if he did the same thing to Kare? Would you preach haste? What if it was Octavia? Would you stay your hand if I asked you to spare him? Would you?!" Rollo was directly in his face, unyielding. Kole remained silent, knowing same as I did he would likely feel exactly like Rollo does in this moment.

"Brother, you know what we are up against. You know what we need to end this once and for all, and he may be the key to ending it. If you kill him, then Delphi wins. No more living free, we will all be forced to segregate... then the torture won't be the worst thing that has ever happened. Marcella would have to go back into hiding and I would never see Kare again." Kole looked him right in the eyes, driving home everything that he said.

Rollo stayed silent but his shoulders relaxed a tad. That meant he knew Kole was right, but he was never going to admit it.

"Let's secure the city, then we can deal with them both. I can't do it alone, Rollo. I need you," he pleaded.

"Fine." They had come to some sort of understanding for the time being. I wasn't sure how long it would hold.

We finally walked into the throne room. The two villains waited in the front like nothing was going on around them at all.

30 – Middle Child - Kole

How could they sit up there like they don't have a care in the world while everything is crashing in on them? Did Delphi bless them with some kind of extreme sense of delusion to prevent them from seeing reality? We had killed half their infantry, maybe more, and they sit there with smirks on their faces.

Kyut was a lost cause in my opinion, but I promised my sister she could try and convince him to leave this fantasy behind him. Ivar doesn't realize how close he was to having his head ripped off by Rollo... and still they find a way to rub it in our faces.

"What a spectacle, my friends You all have been quite busy," Ivar taunted and laughed.

"Ivar, we are going to take the city, that much is clear. Just give up now so we don't have to kill any more of our people." No one can say I haven't tried reasoning with him.

"What do you care of our people?" Kyut interrupted. "You destroyed your own family for a Roman!"

"Our family is not destroyed." Kare came into view from behind me.

"Sister, it is great to see you are well, but please do not let our brother lead you into darkness," he snarled.

"I'm following him because I believe it is right, and if you cared for me or mother then you would stop this. Help us and please come home. Have we not all lost enough already?" She had pain in her voice.

"Home? Where is my home, sister? Last time I checked you sat idle when he sent me off to die up here. Where was all this pleading when he passed judgment on me?"

"That's the thing. I didn't send you to die. I fucking spared you." I couldn't help raising my voice.

"Regardless of the reason, here you are begging for peace because you know you're wrong. You sold your family for a woman, and you sold the world to save a blood-drinking abomination, and now I am going to make you pay for it." He reached to his belt and grabbed his axe. The words struck Kare hard, but she would not back down.

"Do you love me, brother?" she asked genuinely.

"Of course I love you, and I will not harm you. I only need to take care of our brother and his pack of friends. Then you and I can go home and enjoy Lundr as we used to. We can leave this mountain and rule it the way it was always meant to be. You and I watching the boats arrive at the port basking in the sunrise." He had a demented smile on his face, but deep inside he meant what he was saying. He did plan on having a future at home. The only problem is that involved me being dead.

"But I've seen my last sunrise brother," she flashed her fangs, and Kyut jumped back at the revelation with his mouth wide.

"Oh, now this is getting interesting." Ivar leaned up off his throne.

"Will you love me even as I am?" She asked.

Kyuts face twisted in disgust, for once he was speechless. Kare tried to walk toward him, but he backed away.

"No!" He shook his head. "You can't be. You can't be one of them!" He cried out in disbelief.

"I am, brother. Now tell me… do you still love me?" Kyut didn't answer, he just shook his head in defiance. Refusing to accept the truth no matter what she was saying. His eyes landed back on me. Kare was thriving, but I still held some of that guilt for what happened to her. There was no hiding how I felt about the topic.

"Let me guess, you had something to do with this too?" he accused.

"He didn't have a choice, Kyut," Kare tried to explain.

"HE ALWAYS HAS A CHOICE!" Kyut yelled at the top of his lungs. "And he always chooses himself. But no more!" Kyut closed his eyes, and we could feel the power expanding in the room. There was no more negotiating with him at this point. It was time to fight.

"Finally," Ivar delighted.

I remembered that look in his eyes the last time we were here. He tilted over screaming in pain as his bones cracked and shattered before reforming into new ones. His teeth grew long and sharp while fur covered his entire body. The stature of the wolf towered over all of us.

"What in Odin's name?" Kare stepped back. Kuyt's eyes went pitch black and he grabbed his axe, ready to enact his revenge.

"I'm sorry, Kare, but the talking is done," Rollo stood at the ready beside me as heat from Octavia's flames flared on the other side of me.

"I'll take Kyut," she said, her voice low and focused. I nodded my approval and silently wished her luck.

"Rollo, you and I need to find a way to subdue Ivar. Remember, we are not killing him," I stressed.

"Yeah, yeah, we aren't killing him. I get it. That doesn't mean I'm not going to make it hurt," he said.

"I would expect nothing less, brother." We turned to face off against the giant beast.

He pressed off all fours and charged at us with unbelievable speed. We barely dodged his massive claws as he swung to take both our heads off. I opened a portal and dropped out above his head. I could have killed him with an axe throw but I needed him alive, so I would have to settle for knocking him out. Ivar stopped and turned toward me as I was dropping down, anticipating my move. I was freefalling right into his giant teeth, but Rollo threw his hammer and knocked the beast right off his feet.

I hit the ground hard landing directly on my shoulder, which was better than landing into Ivar's mouth. A loud crash came from my left as Kyut and Octavia went tumbling through one of the damaged walls of the longhouse.

"Octavia!" I yelled as the fear for her safety had me frozen. The beast barreled into me and pinned me under his paws. The saliva from his mouth ran down my arms as I tried to keep him from ripping a hole in my neck. "Rollo, a little help here," I shouted.

Rollo tackled Ivar, punching him anywhere he could land a blow. The beast yelped in pain but fought back furiously. It felt like we weren't getting anywhere. Rollo summoned the clouds as the thunder shook the roof above us.

Ivar must have sensed it coming because he didn't wait, he charged Rollo and kicked him with his hind legs before he could bring down the lightning. It was insane that he could move this way. He was so much more than a mindless beast, and we would have to start treating him as such. Not being able to just kill him made it even worse.

"Kole!" Kare yelled from behind me, "I can help."

"No, stay back Kare," I cautioned her.

"Listen to me, Kole. He's still an animal, regardless of the way he fights. You need to treat him as such," she exclaimed.

"I think we gathered that," Rollo retorted back sarcastically as we dodged Ivar's claws again.

"You need to think like a hunter, Would you try to fight a wolf head-on in the wild where he had the advantage, or would you trap it?" She had an excellent point.

"Kare, you're a genius. Now go help the others." She was right. I needed to trap Ivar, not fight him. In the wild, a wolf would be using the terrain to stay alive. I would never be able to fight it head-on, especially if I was trying to take it alive. I needed to immobilize him. Somewhere under the fur and teeth Ivar was most likely smiling. Daring me to try whatever plan I had come up with.

"Rollo, follow my lead." I took off running toward Ivar. We had done this a thousand times together at this point. We didn't have to speak, just follow the flow of battle. We always knew how to play off each other.

I opened a portal and came out right behind Ivar. As I guessed he turned to swing at me with his giant paw. I ducked as Rollo landed a punch right to his snout, stunning him momentarily. We didn't stop there. I opened another portal and threw my axe into the darkness. It opened in front of Rollo, and he caught my axe before trying to drive it down into the beast. Ivar dodged it again as we expected, but while he wasn't looking, I kicked him in the chest.

A painful yelp followed as he slammed against the wall behind him. Ivar was back on his feet in seconds letting out a giant howl that turned into a vicious snarl with a full display of his bone-crushing teeth.

"I think we are finally agitating him, Kole," Rollo joked.

"I think you might be right. No blessing from any God or spirit alike will make you a warrior, Ivar." We both laughed. The wolf shook his head, lost in rage.

The spirit might have given him power, but he was still the same jealous and insecure Ivar under all of that fur. Rollo and I persisted with this plan. I would open a portal and Ivar would try to anticipate the move, but he could only do so many things at once. Rollo would bring down lightning randomly just to keep the beast off balance. Striking him started to become easier the more we overloaded his senses.

Now we just needed to lay the trap and contain him. Rollo and I ran directly toward the beast. He leaned in to bite me but just missed; I barely dodged his teeth. Rollo caught the brunt of the kick from his hind legs. He was trying to recover but Ivar took advantage of the opening and charged.

I opened a portal behind Rollo and he managed to fall through it. He appeared above Ivar and tried to land on him again. Ivar tilted his head upward to catch Rollo, but this time I slid underneath him and kicked his legs out from under him.

The beast fell on its side, and before he could get his legs back underneath him Rollo was on top of him. Ivar was snapping those razor-sharp teeth trying to bite Rollo anywhere he could, but it was of no use. He was pinned down. Rollo charged his fist and punched the wolf directly in the eye. I jumped on the bottom half of the wolf and held his torso down to stop him from getting back up. We just needed to knock him out. Hopefully, he would turn back into a man.

Rollo held Ivar's snout down with his left hand and delivered punch after punch with his right. Each punch letting out more and more lightning, but Ivar was still kicking. Rollo punched and punched until his knuckles started to bleed and slowly Ivar stopped fighting. Fear welled inside me because Rollo kept punching and yelling after every blow.

"Rollo, stop!" He punched again. "Rollo, stop!" He punched again, yelling as the beast lay there unconscious.

"You piece of shit!" he wailed.

"Rollo, STOP!" I raised off Ivar and tackled him to the ground. "He's down. You have to stop. We can't kill him." Rollo pushed me off, anger spilling from him.

"Fuck!" He yelled as the lightning came down and shattered the roof. "He does not get to win!" He yelled directly at me. "He does not get to live!"

"I understand, brother, but for now we need him." It hurt me every time I had to say the words.

"He burned her. He cut her, Kole! He left her in that cell to rot. He deserves everything that I plan on giving him." It killed me to see my friend in so much pain, and nothing would make me happier than to let him finish the job, but we had to stay focused.

The beast's breath was labored, and I prayed to Odin that I stopped Rollo in time. Ivar's body jolted and he began to slowly shift back into a man right before our eyes. He returned to form on the ground, completely nude and barely breathing, not nearly as scary as the beast was.

"Tie him up and make sure the restraints are tight. We can't have him transforming again," I told Rollo.

I heard the crash outside of the longhouse and I realized that Octavia had been fighting Kyut this whole time. Terror welled up in my throat. How could I have forgotten to check on her?

"Rollo, watch him. I have to find Octavia," I ran through the giant hole in the wall.

31 - Family Feud - Octavia

Kyut tackled me through the wall of the longhouse causing us to go tumbling down the hill. Something that he was going to pay for dearly. Our bodies slammed into the dirt below. We both scrambled to our feet more than ready for the rematch. I had my daggers already pulled from their holster.

If this is the type of revenge that unlocked his royal blood ability I doubt he was going to take it easy on me. I could feel the fire warming me up. I could also feel his dark aura pressing against me, fighting for space. It was nothing like Kole's energy. It portrayed a clear message, both frightening and malicious. Kyut stood in front of me with his axe in his hand breathing heavily. His pitch-black eyes flashed a murderous grin toward me.

"You have no idea how long I've been waiting for this," he sneered coldly.

"I wasn't lying about that limp, Kyut. It does look like you are a lot better now," I smiled. The darkness pressed even harder. He was so much more powerful than the last time we fought, and he knew it.

"This whole thing is your fault. You weaved your way into our lives and destroyed everything," he paced as he spoke. "And that wasn't enough for you. You had to turn my sister into one of those monsters," he yelled.

"None of that was my fault. You're looking for someone to blame because you think your life is shit. Do you know how much I've been through? Do you know how much I've given up?" The flames started to cause my hands to glow. "Now look at you. You're a pet for a Roman spirit and you're too dumb to realize it. All for what? So you can do the same thing you accuse your brother of?" Kyut didn't answer me, just charged forward with his axe. If I hadn't been ready he could have seriously hurt me, but I raised my dagger just in time to block it. We exchanged blows, measuring each other's strength.

There were no words or taunting needed. We knew we hated each other and there was no way I would be able to talk him out of this. We had come too far to smooth things out. Being one big happy family was never in the cards for our future. The only other solution was to fight. Kyut was noticeably faster and stronger than before. I was barely keeping up as he pressed me, slashing his axe in every direction.

The howl from the beast inside the longhouse drew my attention for a second and I paid dearly for it. Kyut's punch knocked me off balance, the ringing in my ear instant and constant. With no time to recover, I raised my daggers up immediately to slow down his advantage. My eyes were coming back into focus from the blow, and I could see that grin that I hated so much spread across his face.

The flame erupted inside me and I pushed the heat toward Kyut. He dropped his axe and covered his face giving me a chance to strike. I moved closer and kicked at the leg I knew I had broken before. He saw it coming and moved the leg out of the way effortlessly.

How was he so fast? I aimed straight for his heart with my dagger. He wouldn't expect me to go for a kill shot so soon. Inches away from his chest something stopped me dead in my tracks. My hand was stuck in front of his chest, and it would not budge. I looked up at Kyut confused. I could see his eyes leaking the familiar black smoke, his smile even bigger this time.

"What the fuck?!" I was gripped with surprise.

I dropped my hands to let go of the dagger that was frozen in midair and swiped his legs out from under him. As he was falling to the ground the dagger became free of his control. I caught it and tried to bring it down with all my strength, but Kyut was too quick. He had already rolled back to pick up his axe.

"So, you finally turned into a grown-up," I snarked, rubbing the spot on my face where he punched me. "I could understand if you needed a little help getting there."

"That's not all I've learned, but I won't need half of what Delphi gave me to take you out." Power exploded from him forcing me to take a step back. If I was being honest, a small part of me was worried. The flame simmered under my skin, a reminder that Romans never quit. I slid the flames down the dagger and the spearhead appeared.

"Let's do this," I urged. Kyut and I continued trading blows, neither one of us relenting in our attack. The darkness he wielded was so controlled, nothing like the angry kid I fought before, making it impossible to find an opening where I could take him down. He threw his axe with all his might. The battle hum slowed down, my senses allowing me to just dodge it, but I did not recover fast enough. Kyut was already right on top of me, throwing punches at an incredible speed. I closed my arms over my face to defend myself, but even I knew this was not a good situation for me. If he managed to knock me down again I would be in trouble.

He grabbed my wrist and pried the dagger out of my hand. I was losing the upper hand in this fight. I needed to go on the offensive. I dropped my guard and took a punch to the stomach, but I managed to grab a hold of one of Kyut's wrists before he could pull it back.

The fury inside me wanted to cause him so much pain that the flames bent to my will. Kyut tried to pull his hand away as the smell of his flesh burning sent him into terror. He writhed in pain as I attempted to melt the skin off his bones. I threw my knee into his chest again and again as he clenched, still trying to pull his hand away.

In a last-ditch effort to save his hand he stopped trying to pull it away and elbowed me in the temple. The elbow stunned me long enough for him to get his hand free. The legion in my head continued to march and the call for blood amplified into a roar. Fatigue was creeping in, and I did not know how much longer I could keep this up.

"You bitch!" He cried as he wrapped his skin with a piece of his shirt.

Another loud bang came from the longhouse, and I could hear Kole and Rollo yelling but I could not make out what they were saying. I was starting to worry, distracting me from my cause. What if Ivar had got the best of them? Kyut had grabbed his axe again, his dark eyes trained on me. I needed to get to Kole.

I closed my eyes and grabbed ahold of the flames. This time I was going to rid this world of him for good. Kole would have to forgive me later. Kyut ran toward me again, but this time I stretched my hands out in front of me took a deep breath and just let go. I let go of everything I had pent up inside me. I refused to hold anything back. Forget hurting him, I wanted to wipe him from existence.

The flames came flooding out of my hands, bright and wide. It lit up the sky and burned everything in my path, including Kyut. The flames engulfed him, and I could feel nothing over the painful thumping in my head as I dumped out every ounce of power I had. There would be nothing left of him once I was done and part of me had to thank him. My hatred for him pushed me further than I knew I could go. I wouldn't have unlocked this much power without him.

My energy drained rapidly. I fell to my knees as the flames died out from my hands. My vision began to clear, and I could not believe what I was seeing. After all I had given at that moment, Kyut was still standing before me, his clothes singed and smoking but otherwise unharmed. Black smoke leaked from his eyes as he stood before me.

My body tensed with fear as he staggered slowly toward me. I didn't have any energy left to fight him, but I willed myself back on my feet. He was inches away raising his axe. I tugged deep in my core to bring the flames back up to defend myself but there was nothing left.

Even I couldn't see a way out of this one. I stood with my head held high waiting to meet my death. I lived defiantly, I would die the same. Although I was not ready to die, not when I'd come this far. I was afraid but I would never admit that to anyone but myself, and he would never have that power over me.

He shuffled closer to me with his axe in hand, ready to enact his revenge. I closed my eyes and thought of my husband, his brown skin and that perfect smile and the feeling I would have when I saw him in the next life. I waited for what felt like an eternity for Kyut to strike when a quick breeze hit my face instead. I could hear Kyut grunting.

"Get up off your knees. It's really not a great look for you," I recognized that self-centered voice anywhere.

I opened my eyes and saw Gio standing in front of me chuckling. He was holding Kyut up by his neck, his feet swinging under him like a child trying to get out of Gio's grip.

"I'm never going to live this down, am I?" I relaxed my shoulders as all the pressure of dying washed away.

"Oh, of course not, but since we are on the subject... I assume that my little rescue mission will buy me a little time to speak to your husband," he waited for me to answer, and I knew exactly what he meant.

"My lips are sealed, Gio, for now. Tell Kole when you're ready." We both almost forgot he was holding Kyut.

"Let me go, you animal!" He spit in Gio's face as he fought his grip.

"I have to say that's ironic considering I heard about the giant beast your friend turns into," Gio smiled but he was being serious.

"Delphi told me about you, vampire. She also told me how she used your bitch to turn Ivar in the first place." Gio punched Kyut in the stomach before he finished talking. Blood sprayed out his mouth.

"Be careful what you say next Norse. After what you did to my friend I'm not in a forgiving mood. You're only alive because I feel that you aren't mine to kill," Gio snarled.

"Fuck you!" He screamed as he loaded up for a punch. Gio dodged it easily and ripped into Kyut's neck before tossing him aside like he weighed nothing. I got up to my feet with Gio's help.

A bright green light appeared behind him that caught my attention. The light was coming from Kyut's fist as he crawled away from us.

"What is he doing?" I called out to Gio. "Get to him. Don't let him do whatever it is he is about to do. Anytime the green mist shows up it can't be good." I tried to stand on my own but I was too weak.

"I'll be seeing you both soon." Kyut threw the green mist to the floor and disappeared before Gio could get to him.

"Shit!" I exclaimed.

Koel Alexander © 2024
Raven & Fire Series

"Is everyone okay?" I looked up on the ridge and saw Kole standing there, concern shining through his eyes. He was all scratched up, but he was okay and that was all that mattered, even though Kyut managed to get away.

"Yes, we are fine," I called back. "Where is Ivar?"

"He's unconscious, but we have him. Where's Kyut?" He called back.

"He got away," Gio cringed.

"Got away? How is that possible? We are on the top of a mountain."

"It's a long story," I said. "We are coming back up now."

The longhouse had seen better days. Whatever battle they had in here was much worse than the one I had outside with Kyut. I tried to walk but my entire body throbbed with every step. Between battling Kyut and using all the power I did, I feel completely drained. I can't believe he managed to get away, but thank the Gods Gio showed up when he did. I would be on my way to the underworld if it wasn't for him. Of all the people that could have saved me it was infuriating it was him. It is better to be alive and owe him than to be dead and keep my pride.

I thought back on the fight over and over. I should have been able to take Kyut out easily, but his powers had caught me completely off guard. I should have known his powers would develop eventually as they always do in royal children, and it had to be some God-level irony they mimicked his father's. Yet still, I shouldn't have lost that fight.

We all retreated to the separate rooms in the longhouse. None of them were in pristine condition, but it was enough for the time being. We needed to rest and recover before we decided to go anywhere at this point. I lied in bed for a couple of hours to regain my strength. Sitting still was tough for me, but eventually I was starting to feel more like myself.

Kole brought me food and water, and we just lay in silence enjoying each other's company. It felt like we had been running nonstop since we jumped in the portal, it felt good to just lay here and recharge. Kole ran his fingers through my hair as I made myself comfortable on his chest.

"You scared me. You know that?" He spoke softly.

"I scared you?" I said surprised. "You were the one fighting a giant wolf with teeth longer than my daggers."

"Yeah, maybe you have a point," he agreed.

"What did you do with him anyway?" I asked curiously.

"We chained him in the cells underneath the longhouse. The same ones he was keeping Rollo in."

"Will they be able to hold him? The last thing we need is him getting away as well."

"All the chains are reinforced, and he's being guarded day and night. We should be fine," his hands ran down my arms.

"I'm sorry for letting Kyut get away." The guilt was relentless even though I knew it wasn't my fault.

"I don't care about Kyut. I'm just glad you are okay. If he had hurt you, I don't know how far I would go to pay him back," he said emphatically.

He wrapped his arms around me tightly, possessively. Exactly the way he knew I liked. I looked up at him and thanked the Gods as I often do. His arms overtook me, suffocating any space we might have had between us. When had he gotten so much stronger? Or maybe it has just been a while since I've really looked. His biceps tensed as he held me, and his chest rose and fell slowly as I sat in his arms.

"You have always liked to stare." His smile was ever present on his face, making me feel better as it always did.

"Don't flatter yourself," I returned with a smile.

"Of course not. You do that for me." He laughed before I punched him in the chest.

"You have been prone to violence since becoming my wife. Is this something I should expect from now on?" He continued to jest.

"Is there something else you would expect?" I bit my bottom lip as the words left my mouth.

"I could think of so many things I expect, but I am nothing but a gentleman." His words landed their purpose, so I opened my legs and placed myself on top of him.

The thin fabric between us left nothing up to mystery. He leaned forward as I helped him remove his vest, all so that I could run my hands down his chest. I traced along the many scars he had gained since we met. Some of them he had gotten to save me. This man would walk through the underworld and back just to have me. It sent a rush cascading through me.

I pushed my weight down on him and rocked my hips slowly back and forth. A quick gasp left his lips, responding to my movements as his eyes swirled with desire.

"I don't need the gentleman right now," I rocked my hips a little faster and I felt him grow under me as he pressed against me. "I need the King." He grabbed a handful of my hair and pulled my lips down onto his.

There was nothing gentle about the kiss as I leaned heavily into my purpose. Kole responded exactly as I expected him to. I leaned up and pulled the shirt over my head, the cold air hardening my nipples. His mouth devoured them sending a shock all the way through my body. I grabbed a handful of his hair and pulled him closer as he sucked on them with intent. My head flew back as the sensation provided exactly the escape I needed.

"How am I doing so far?" He asked with that beautiful smirk. Before I could answer, his mouth closed over my other nipple drawing out a sharp moan. The moment completely overtook me, and I wanted every part of him.

I lifted off his lap and dropped to my knees removing his pants for him. He stood at full attention in front of me, enticing me to take what I wanted, showing me that no passion or lust was missing between us. His chest rose and fell quickly with anticipation as I licked my lips, begging him to give me what I craved. I grabbed his thighs as he slid himself past my lips completely filling my mouth.

The motion was automatic as I yearned to please him, sliding back and forth over the length of him, pulling that deep growl from inside him. He thrust back soft at first, then harder as I looked him in the eyes. He was primal as he took me, a king in his own right, but I would be the one who could always break him into pieces. He was mine and I loved being his and only his.

"You drive me crazy, Octavia," he moaned.

That thrilled me to give him more. I twisted my hands and turned my head back and forth, taking him further into bliss. Another deep growl escaped him as he was lifting me off my feet and sitting me down on top of him. I yelped as he thrust himself inside me, shocking me in all of the right places. Our eyes locked as I rocked up and down, deeper and faster. My body vibrated every time he thrust, dragging me to where I needed to be.

"Harder!" I yelled, and he responded. His strength was incredible as he barreled into me over and over until I shattered into pieces all over him.

Even when it seemed like things were wrong this could never be broken. Down to my core, I would forever be connected to Kole and my body would respond accordingly. As I lay on his chest, listening to him breathe slowly, the moment replayed in my head. His touch, his firm hands and his body all over me. If I wasn't careful this could stir me up all over again. Not that he would mind. I laid down and fell asleep to the rhythm of his breathing.

32 - Beautiful Monster - Rollo

Once we secured Ivar in the cells I took off to find Marcella. I couldn't get to her any quicker. I needed her to know that I would have scorched Ivar to pieces if we didn't need him for this stupid prophecy. She looked like she was in so much pain the last time I saw her. I couldn't wipe the images out of my mind. The scars across her perfect face, the burns that bubbled up on her flawless skin. I did nothing to stop any of it. Wrapped in my thoughts, I rounded the corner and ran directly into Gio almost knocking us both over for the second time in less than 24 hours.

"Slow down, Rollo," he drawled.

"Where is she?!" I said anxiously.

"She's in there," Gio pointed to the room behind him. I moved to walk past him, but he held his arm out to stop me. "You might want to give her a minute. She was in pretty bad shape. She needs to feed so she can recover." I heard him but none of the words mattered to me now.

"Gio, move your arm before I break it," I hissed.

"Rollo," Kare spoke softly from behind me, I was so focused I just now registered her presence. "I know you want to see her, and you will, but maybe you don't want to see her like this."

I don't know what they were trying to hide me from. I decided long before this that I would never judge her no matter what.

"I hear you both, but move," I said stronger this time. Kare and Gio slid out of my way as I walked to the door.

"We will check on you both later," Kare said before I walked into the room.

It was pitch black inside which I expected. No reason that she would want any type of light after what Ivar had put her through. I was worried to my core, but the smell snapped me out of my concern. I recognized the smell instantly. There was death here, and lots of it.

It was a mixture of blood and bodies, and some of them had to have been here for some time. In the back of the room, I could hear a low vicious growl and the ripping of flesh. It was very hard to see. I almost tripped over the first body and slipped on the blood that was leaking from its neck. I bent over to see the man's face, but I did not recognize him. He must have been one of Ivar's men. He laid there motionless, his skin pale white, almost like a ghost. More bodies came into view as I moved closer to the growling in the back.

Loud groans of pain came from some of the men who must still be alive. Hunched over in the corner like an animal, I saw her dark hair coated with blood. She didn't even look my way as I got closer.

A soldier was crawling toward my feet, blood gushing from his stomach as he held his insides in the palm of his hands.

"Help me!" he shrieked.

Marcella's head snapped up toward me from the sound of the man pleading for his life. Her eyes were completely absent of life, her mouth painted red with the blood of the bodies splayed around her. Her chest heaved up and down quickly as she swallowed the blood from the man she held in her grasp. We said nothing to each other. I just looked in the eyes of what my beautiful monster was in her primal form. Ruthless, powerful, and unforgiving. Exactly what these traitors deserved.

The man clawed at my feet continuing to beg for help. The smell of blood and sweat coming from the bodies attacked my nose, but I could not take my eyes off her. The scars and burns were healing like it never happened, but it would never erase the memory. She would live with that torture forever, never being able to run from it or let time take it away in death.

I looked down at the pathetic soldier begging for his life and took a step back out of his reach. Marcella grabbed him by his legs in a blur and drove her fangs into his neck, drinking from him slowly and savagely, savoring every last drop. I watched as the hunter exacted the closest thing to revenge that she could get. When she was done, I would hold her, never to judge but only to be by her side for as long as the world would allow me to.

33 – Blood And Lust - Kare

I didn't feel great about leaving Rollo with Marcella in that state. She lost so much blood and it was going to take a lot more for her to recover. I didn't want her to lose control and end up hurting him.

"He will be fine," Gio soothed the concern that must have been written all over my face. When we found her, she was barely conscious and almost burned beyond recognition. I can't believe my own brother would take part in anything that barbaric. Octavia told us all that he got away. No one has any idea how he was able to do that, but Delphi was probably responsible. I was growing tired of even hearing her name at this point.

"Are you hungry?" Gio asked, bringing me back to reality.

"No, I'm okay," I responded.

"Suit yourself," he chuckled. "Nothing better than a celebratory drink after some righteous murder." He sat down on the makeshift bed in the room. Somehow no one noticed that we ended up with a room all to ourselves. I think everyone was distracted with all the other things that have happened. "Even if you are not hungry you are going to need to get some rest," he insisted.

"I will. The sun will be up soon, I can sleep then." Gio shrugged off my comment. "Where are all the other vampires?"

"Down in the cells underneath. Most of them are splitting time watching over our furry prisoner," he grinned.

"It's going to take me some time to wrap my head around that one," I chuckled.

"An immortal gorgeous hunter was easy enough to wrap your head around." His comment was clearly loaded, but I couldn't help but play into it.

"You have a point, but who are you refereeing to when you say gorgeous?"

"My one true love still remains myself, princess," he laughed.

"You're such an ass," I laughed with him.

"So I've been told, amongst other less favorable names," he brought me over a cup of blood even though I did not ask. I honestly was not hungry but when the blood was presented to me there was no way my body would allow me to turn it down.

The blood awakened everything inside me, no matter how much I drank. I felt warm all the way to my core, and that brought all the feelings that I did not need running rampant right now, especially with Gio right next to me.

He made himself comfortable on the other end of the bed, his shirt open as it usually was. I don't know if it is the blood, him or a mixture of the two, but it feels like something is pulling me toward him. I brought my eyes down to the floor trying to situate all these feelings that couldn't have come at a worst time. I couldn't sit, feeling antsy and anxious.

"Your heart is racing," he declared in a low, sultry tone. I turned as he zipped over to stand behind me on my end of the bed.

"I'm fine," I muttered.

"If you say so, but I know that isn't completely true." It felt like he kept moving closer.

"Well, aren't you a know it all," I retorted.

"With most things, yes," he laughed. I was trying my best to ignore him, but he was making it nearly impossible. Why did he have to be some damn charming? It was much easier to hate him when I thought he was just an immortal murderer, but if I'm honest with myself I never really thought of him that way.

I felt his hand run down my arm and my stomach tensed. After having the blood my senses went into overdrive. The sensation completely dismantled my composure. It felt like sparks were sliding up and down my skin.

"Do you think that is a good idea?" I forced the words out.

"You tell me." He whispered in my ear as his hand traced down my thigh, forcing a gasp to slip from my lips. "Seems like a great idea at the moment," he said as he moved closer leaving no space between us, my back plastered to his front.

Koel Alexander © 2024
Raven & Fire Series

He smelled like blood and fresh trees and saying that even just in my head made me question my sanity. Apparently my body had no problem with it.

"If you want me to stop all you have to do is say so," he murmured softly. I nodded my head in agreement with him because I had no words for what I was feeling. It was enticing, exhilarating, and forbidden all at the same time.

Everything that would lead to me doing something that I wanted so badly but would probably have regrets about if anyone found out. Gio's hands never stopped moving; he ran them down my thighs, around the curve of my backside. He caressed my neck and teased me with the tip of his fangs. Moans escaped but still I had no words. I wanted to live in the lustful moments of feeling his strong hands explore every part of me.

"Are you okay, princess?" I had my eyes closed, diving deeper into his touch, but I nodded to answer his question. Then his hands were off me and the anger I felt was instant. Why in the hell would he take his hands off me and deny me what I was feeling just now?

Before I could open my eyes to curse him all the way to Heilhem, One hand found its way around my throat while the other reached under my fabric and cupped my breast. I let out an infectious growl to match his, and my fangs shot out just as quickly.

Gio was still behind me, teasing my neck, grazing his fangs against my throat, and a part of me was begging him to bite me. I wanted it so bad, ached for it even. My back involuntarily arched, pressing my firm behind to his hard bulge. What the hell was happening to me? Gio's hand on my throat loosened and made its way to my other breast. I was on pace to lose myself completely. He worked his hands around my nipples making them erect to a point that I have never experienced. Whatever the other perks of being a vampire were didn't matter because this was the best one. I must have been thinking out loud because Gio spoke to me again.

"You think this is good? I promise more pleasure than you can imagine." I still was having trouble finding the words, but this was an offer too good to pass up. I needed to say something.

"Show me," were the only words I could muster past my moans.

"It would be my pleasure, princess." He spun me around and moved to lower me to the bed, never removing his hands from my body. One hand left my breast and trailed down my stomach slowly to my inner thigh. I shifted up toward his hand anticipating his touch. His hands continued down until he reached my center, then his fingers moved in a deceptive motion.

Moments of undeniable pleasure followed, but then he would move to tease me even more. He hovered over me but never lowered on top of me, making me wonder what his weight would feel like. It was infuriating, but it left me wanting so much more from him I could never stay mad. I reached up and grabbed his arm. His muscles tensed under my grip, but this time I did not let him move his fingers away from me.

I pressed against his fingers, rocking my hips back and forth, taking from him exactly what I wanted. He crawled closer to me, our cheeks almost touching, and growled in my ear as I continued to work his hand in the spot where I needed it most. I was so close, ready to feel that bliss take over me...and then he plunged his fingers inside me. I threw my head back in desperate pleasure.

I grabbed his arm and moved my hip harder now with more purpose. Gio's carnal growl filled my ears, driving my desire to a new height.

"You feel even better than I could have imagined," he said to me. I let go of his arms and reached into his pants. The size caught me completely off guard, but I was too lost to acknowledge how impressed I was. I moved my hands slowly up and down, listening to him crumble under my touch. I wanted him to finish, and I wanted it to be because of me.

"Finish with me," I said to him. He said nothing, just moved his fingers in and out of me, dedicated to his goal as our speed matched.

A perfect rhythm of undeniable need that left us both crashing over the edge at the same time. I didn't know what to feel once my senses dialed down and reality set in. To think I was so worried about the kiss. I had no idea how I was going to explain this. The only thing I know for sure is that I loved every minute of it, and there would be no denying myself that again.

34 – We Still Don't Trust You - kole

We had successfully taken the city back, but it wasn't something to be happy about. Nothing could return this place to its former glory. The vampires were resting, but they wouldn't be much help to us during the day anyway. In the meantime, we could scheme up a plan. It didn't feel right discussing it without the vampires, but with the confusion of the cursed head maybe it was better to have this talk without them.

I do know for certain that I would let this entire world burn before I used my sister to fulfill this stupid prophecy. Odin fooled me once but never again. My family was nonnegotiable, unless maybe it was Kyut's head on the chopping block. He's so far gone that I wouldn't think twice to wipe him out.

Octavia emerged from the bathroom brushing out the tangles in her hair. She looked like she was doing much better after the much-needed rest. Another thing I would have to pay Kyut back for.

"You ready to go?" she asked.

"Yeah, lets go." We made our way back to the throne room to meet up with Rollo. He was sitting at a table when we walked in, already a couple of cups of ale in.

"A little early for the ale, don't you think?" I smirked.

"Kole, if you saw what I did last night you would need one too," he grimaced and took another giant gulp.

"Is Marcella okay?" Octavia asked.

"That depends on your definition of okay." He chuckled. We had no idea how we were supposed to respond to that.

"Is she physically healed? Yes, but the way she got healthy was terrifying and fascinating all at the same time," he admitted.

"I'm sorry, I'm still not following you. What happened last night?"

"No other way to say it other than I watched Marcella drain at least six of Ivar's men of their blood, and when she was done, she curled into a ball and slept like a baby. Still is," he shrugged.

"Okay, maybe I do need a drink." I reached out and grabbed a cup. Octavia just stared at him in pure shock.

"And you're saying now she's just okay," Octavia repeated.

"Yes, she's completely okay, like nothing or no one had ever touched her," he confirmed. We sat in silence for another minute because we were all speechless. There were no words for it, and I couldn't fathom watching it happen right in front of my eyes.

"As fun as all of that sounds we need to talk about our next move and how it could potentially affect all of us," Octavia said.

"We need to find out where we should be looking first," Rollo added. Octavia and I looked at him trying to hint at an idea that we knew he would hate.

"One person knows this place better than us both. He could possibly steer us in the right direction." I looked at Rollo with concern. I had no idea how he was going to react to the idea. His face contorted just as I suspected, a clear sign that he was opposed to our idea.

"No, Kole. Absolutely not," he stood firm.

"I know you don't want to, but we honestly have no idea where to start."

"The all-mighty God of wisdom didn't give you any idea of where we should start looking? What is the point of knowing everything if you don't know anything?" he scoffed. I was speechless because it was the best question any of us have asked in a long time. "How can we even trust what he tells us? Does no one remember that he has tried to wipe us from this life twice now!!?" He stressed.

"No one is saying you're not right but, in all seriousness, we have no idea what we need and where we need to go. Ivar is the only one that grew up here. There must be a hidden path or some kind of secret passageway only someone from here would know," I countered.

"Unless you have a better idea, I agree with Kole." Octavia said softly.

"Of course you agree with Kole. Isn't that how the whole marriage thing works?" Rollo said sarcastically.

"Believe it or not, it's not that simple," Octavia said under her breath.

"Trouble in paradise already," Rollo said in jest.

"Shut up, Rollo. Are you with us or not?" she asked seriously. I expected it would take more convincing on our part but ultimately, he caved.

"Whatever. I'll go with you to talk to the worm," he said with disdain.

"Now promise you won't kill him," I implored.

"Come on Kole, seriously?" he complained. I nodded waiting for what I needed to hear. "Okay, fine. I promise I won't kill him. I swear it. But that doesn't mean I will trust I thing he says, and you shouldn't either." He downed the rest of his cup.

"Understood. Let's see what our old friend has to say."

Rollo walked ahead of us as we made our way through the tunnels to the cells. It was freezing down here. My anger flared thinking about my best friend spending days down here waiting for us to rescue him. Retreating was one of the hardest things I had to do, but I know it was the right choice. It gave us the best chance to succeed, but I would be lying if I said it didn't take a chip at my confidence.

Rollo told me they were keeping Ivar in the largest cell. Guards were posted at every turn preventing any type of escape. I assumed he was being brought food and water, but it wasn't very important to me considering the circumstances. I could care less if he was being treated fairly after all he has done. The stench coming from the cell could be a clear indication of how things were going for him down here. I may need to ask the guards to do something about it for our sake.

The three of us entered the cell. Hanging in the middle of the room was a filthy, half-conscious Ivar. His hands and feet were secured by chains and stretched to four different points in the room. At the ends of the chains metal clamps were hammered deep into the stone wall. Keeping his limbs extended was the only idea we could come up with to prevent him from transforming. The chains were so tight that he would have to rip himself apart in order to shift.

Ivar tilted his head up to us, finally acknowledging that we were in the room. He instinctively tried to move his arms and legs only causing himself more anguish. The three of us just stood quietly as he moaned and groaned in pain. His lips were dry and cracking, he licked them constantly trying to ease some of the pain. Still, none of us were moved by the performance.

"How are you, Ivar? I hope the accommodations are up to your standards," I snarked.

"I'm just hanging out," he forced a smirk, and his dry lips began to bleed.

"I wanted to return all of the hospitality you showed me and Marcella," Rollo hissed from behind me.

"Well, if that's the case then you're doing a terrible job. At least I gave you her screams for entertainment. It gets quite boring down here," he laughed.

Rollo moved to punch him, but I stepped in front of him. He had to know that Ivar was going to be a serpent with his words.

"You deserve so much worse, Ivar. I think we can all agree to that, but we are here to give you a chance to possibly redeem yourself." Rollo went rigid, the thought of redemption likely had to sting.

"And why have I earned such grace from the great King Kole?" he asked sarcastically.

"We are looking for something," Octavia interrupted.

"Well, isn't that incredibly specific," Ivar scoffed.

"It's something ancient, something only a few people would know exists," she explained further.

"Again, could you be more specific, Roman?"

"Is there a hidden place in the mountains that only the royal family would know about? Something that your father would have kept hidden from anyone else?" I asked. Ivar pondered before he answered, almost gauging how much information he would give away.

"My father loved to talk and he kept many secrets. He always considered knowledge as the most powerful weapon you could wield," Ivar spoke slowly.

"Can you get to the damn point," Rollo practically snarled.

"I see your time down here didn't teach you any patience," Ivar countered.

"You still have your head, I'd say I'm exercising my patience just fine," Rollo added.

"You were saying," I intervened, nodding to Ivar. I needed to keep this conversation focused if we were going to get anywhere.

"Sitting in on his meetings was beneficial, but it was the things I learned when I snuck around that was invaluable." Octavia let out a long sigh behind me. It seemed like Ivar was playing with fire the longer he dragged out the story. "When he held meetings with the council there was one subject that was always kept top secret."

"Ivar, by Odin's beard, seriously gets to the point. Do you know or not?" Octavia snapped.

"Temper, temper, Roman. I remember talks about an ancient hidden spot in the mountains trusted only to the King and his heirs to follow. Obviously, you and your meddling have thrown off the passing down of knowledge, seeing as your friend here killed my father. Not to mention you anointed your brother as King," he shrugged.

"So where are all of the council members that he might have shared this information with?" I asked. He smiled again even though I have no idea what could be so funny.

"When you banished me with your brother, most of the council was still alive when we arrived," his evil grin widened.

"So where are they now?" Octavia asked.

"My father always said the more people that know the information, the less valuable it becomes." I froze at his words, realizing what he had done.

"You really are a slimy bastard," I said under my breath.

"I would say that I ensured my survival, and I needed to test out my new transformation on flesh and bone. If you were wondering, it's impossible to get it all out of your teeth."

"You are a piece of shit, Ivar!" Octavia exclaimed.

"Speaking of survival, where is that hard-headed brother of yours? He didn't take the news of your sister being a vampire very well. I hope you didn't kill him."

"He got away, believe it or not. You wouldn't happen to know how he managed to do that?" I asked. Ivar just smiled and said nothing more. "Another piece of knowledge, I assume?"

"You are smarter than you look," he replied.

"So, let me guess... you're not going to tell us where we should start looking unless you get something. What do you want?" I asked regrettably.

"Kole, are you serious!?" Rollo asked.

"Whatever is decided will be discussed between all of us. This isn't something that I will decide without your input, brother," I reassured him. "Now what do you want, Ivar? And before you start, going free is not an option." I would think that was a given, but you never know with this delusional pair.

"Oh, I don't want to go free, Kole. I want to go with you. I won't tell you where you need to go unless you let me take you there." I looked over to the others, questioning the obvious chance of this being an ambush.

"You are such a slimy worm," Octavia looked at him with disgust.

"Slimy worms slip through the surface and survive. The worms will be alive after all of us are gone from this world, your majesty." Ivar's maniacal laugh protruded throughout the hallways as we left the room.

I couldn't tell if this was a victory or a defeat. There was almost a guarantee that he knew way more than he was letting on, but he was the only person left who knew anything. I wouldn't even waste my time discussing it, but I promised the others I would not choose for them.

"So, what are we going to do?" Octavia asked.

"We are going to wait for Gio and the others to wake up, and then we are going to take a vote. Also, we should send a letter back to Cassia to let her know what's happening. She's probably losing her mind waiting on us," my mind paced as I spoke.

"You don't actually believe him, do you?" Rollo asked.

"No, I don't, but I think we are low on options. I see it two ways. One, he leads us there and if he is the cursed head we use him like we intend to. Two, he leads us to an ambush, and you get to kill him anyway as we fight for our lives once again." It was the best I could come up with at the moment, but with Gio and the vampires with us we should be able to counter anything he could throw at us. Kyut was still a problem, but he barely made it out of the fight with Octavia. How much support could he have at this point?

"I don't like our chances, but I can't argue with the result of that second option," Rollo grinned, making me feel slightly less guilty for keeping the man alive who tortured his woman.

"Let's get something to eat and then we can catch everyone else up on our new development." We made our way back out of the tunnels.

35 – Did We Have A Moment? - Cassia

To say my patience was wearing thin was a complete understatement. How long did they expect me to sit around and wait? I was never one to dislike relaxing, but I am going stir-crazy. After getting a taste of battle in Alexandria, having to shut down my battle instincts just to deal with the politics of ruling this country has simply not been enough.

The good news on the other hand is that Alexandria was running as smoothly as ever. It wasn't a popular decision to use Floria at the time, but my instincts were correct. She is a natural. Octavia asked me to use her how I liked, and this was certainly the best way. I was able to travel to Cosa and back without the worry of the country falling into descent.

All of Marcus' rats were dealt with and the real rebuild of this once great kingdom was in progress, even more reason why it should be handed over to my care. Once we win this great battle, I have a very strong feeling that my wish will be easily granted. As much as I enjoyed the thought of taking over Alexandria, coming back home just felt right.

The ocean surrounding the island called to me and restored my resolve. It served as a great way to pass some of the time while the others did whatever they were doing. I stared out at the waves as they slowly rocked back and forth. The clear blue water washed up and down off the sands of the shore, instantly calming my anxiety. My ship was ready and, as much as I enjoyed my beach, it was time to return to my duties.

I arrived back in Alexandria only after a couple of days. Nothing was on fire, so I figured Floria was doing very well. I was greeted by some of my men at the docks as I made my way through the market, making sure I greeted everyone as best as possible.

It was unintentional but I have become somewhat of a famous figure in my short time here. Not that I deserved it, but I did help clean the scum off these streets. After I shook some hands and almost broke my face from smiling, I headed straight to the villa to get some updates on what I had missed in my time away.

Hopefully there was some word about leaving soon to rejoin the others. I had assembled as many allies as possible and everyone was growing a little impatient. The villa was completely repaired, but it was still absent banners, neither Octavia's new banners nor the old Sirius banners hung in the hallways. Red and gold silk drapes donned the halls, but however appealing to the eyes the space lacked a sense of identity. It lacked the powerful name and presence that was here before Marcus tried to wash it away.

I walked into the throne room, but it was empty, only a servant cleaning food and drinks off the tables.

"Hello, where is the princess?" I asked looking around.

"Hello, Queen Cassia. Ms. Sirius is in the garden in the courtyard." Her response caught me by surprise.

Very rarely does a servant mention royal blood without including their title. She must have read the reaction on my face. I was not very good at hiding it.

"I'm sorry, Queen Cassia. I mean no offense, but Ms. Sirius asked that we not call her princess any longer," she bowed her head and continued her duties. I wasn't surprised at the request. Floria was going through a change and she genuinely did not think she deserved to be a person of power and status anymore. It took everything just to convince her to watch over this place once I left. I don't blame her for not being able to bounce right back.

I told my guards to stand down and wait for me in the throne room. I walked over to the courtyard where the garden sits. Upon entering, I paused to take in the sight of Floria, tending to the flowers as if they were her children. The courtyard was like nothing I had ever seen before. The flowers that were once dead now grew large and bright. There was no absence of color and beauty. Tulips, roses, lilies, you name it. They were all growing here.

Floria's head popped up at the sound of my approach and she smiled. Getting her to smile was impossible these days.

Inside the garden is her happy place, the way the beach at home is mine. Her hair hung low on her shoulders, a perfect contrast to the flowers surrounding her. She was in a gold, low-cut dress with her hands covered in dirt. It was quick but I caught myself staring. There was no denying that she was a pretty girl, but now wasn't the time for that at all.

"Good morning, princess," I bowed.

"Why are you bowing to me, Cassia? You are the queen here, and I ask that you not call me princess anymore. I do not consider myself as such." She grinned even though it hurt her to say the words.

"Well, too bad, princess. Your parents were still the king and queen, regardless of what happened," I added a wink at the end and immediately regretted doing it.

"If you say so," she sighed. "I didn't think I would meet another person as stubborn as my sister."

"Conveniently we find ourselves with plenty of time to explore all the ways that I am way more stubborn than your sister. But first, please tell me you if have some word from the others regarding their progress." I tried not to sound pushy.

"Now that you mention it, there was a letter that came from them. I have it here with me. I figured I would wait for you to come back before opening it," she spoke way too calmly for my liking.

"When did the message arrive?" I said anxiously, hoping I didn't miss my window to help.

"Just before you arrived today. Here you can have it." She reached into her pocket with the dirt still smudged in her fingers.

I tried to stop her, but I was too late. All the dirt was smeared on the edge of her dress.

"Damnit! I should have been more careful, I love this dress," she pouted. She brought her hands up to her face to push her hair back. I tried to stop her again, but I was still too late. Dirt smeared all over her cheek. She looked at me and pouted even more. I could not help but laugh at how disoriented she was.

"You think this is funny?" She tried to hide the smile.

"Of course it is," I said through my laughter. I walked over to her, took the letter and wiped the dirt from her cheek. The laughing stopped, and suddenly our gaze locked on each other. I had no idea how we got to this point.

"I think I should go get cleaned up and meet you back in the throne room," she spoke quickly to break whatever moment we were trapped in.

"Okay, no problem. I'll see you in the throne room." I walked out of the garden not knowing what just happened between us.

I made myself comfortable at the wooden table as I waited for Floria to come back. I planned to read the letter together, but I was way too impatient for that. I would just have to fill her in when she showed up. The others had finally reached the north, but I still had some disbelief about the other things that I was reading.

I heard Floria walk in, but I didn't peel my eyes away from the letter. My face must have shown my disbelief. The deeper I got into the letter the more bizarre it got. I just kept rereading it over and over to make sure I was not mistaken. Ivar transformed into a giant wolf. How the hell does someone transform into a giant wolf?

"Is it unbelievable or just unsettling?" Floria stood in the doorway. She had switched the gold dress for a black one. Her hair was not entirely dry from cleaning herself up. I forced my eyes back down to the letter to finish.

"Honestly, it's a little bit of both," I responded.

"Is everyone okay?" she asked instantly.

"From this letter, it seems everyone is in one piece, but I will say the Norse are a weird people." I watched as her shoulders relaxed at the news. A small part of her still cared for her sister. I knew she wasn't completely heartless. Maybe just a little misguided is all. The level of trauma that we have been through would certainly steer most of us off course, which is what made this cause even more important. All of this could not be in vain.

"Would you believe it if I told you that the others fought a man that turned into a wolf?" Her face twisted into a scowl. She must have thought I was teasing her.

"Sometimes I believe that you think I am the most gullible person in the world," she confessed.

"Have a look yourself if you don't believe me." I handed her the letter. "There is some other good news in there as well." She grabbed the letter and took a seat across from me. Even her eyes couldn't believe the part about Ivar turning into a beast.

"Well Cassia, when you're right, you're right. The Norse are a very strange people." She laughed.

The servants brought in trays of food and wine. Fresh baked bread sat in the middle with cheese surrounding the outer rim of the plate. Two casks of wine were sat on opposite ends of the table and a platter of sliced meat to finish off the meal. It was a real spread for a queen. I took a deep breath and reached over to fill my plate. I tried my best to eat like a lady, but it was never my strong suit.

"I assume you are happy with the news from the others," Floria said as she picked at the cheese on the platter.

"Of course I am. It means we are all one step closer to all of this being over. I yearn for a battle, but the thought of peace sounds so relaxing. Once they locate the artifact, I can start moving our forces toward Midselium when the next letter arrives." I picked up my cup of wine.

"It's been so long since I have lived in peace," her head hung low as she muttered. I wanted to cheer her up, but I didn't know what to say. Peace seemed to always be at arm's length. Even when I was partying in ignorance on Cosa, I always knew eventually I would revolt against Marcus to get the truth.

"Titus is dead, princess, and you still have your life. Peace is certainly a possibility."

"Whatever you see in me... I am having a hard time seeing the same," she quavered.

"Like I told you, this is a perfect time for you to earn back the respect of your people. And from what I can see you are doing a great job already." I continued to eat.

"The threat of losing my head helps if you must know," she smiled. I felt kind of guilty for the threat, but if it worked then maybe it was the right thing to do.

"Let's not speak of what will not happen because you are going to do great in my absence. The bottom line is I will be moving to join the others soon, so the time for you to step up is upon us." I raised my cup in a toast to her.

"I will do my best." She raised her cup in return.

"I know you will."

36 - What About My Choice - Octavia

The rest of the day consisted of us killing time before the others joined us. We had so much to discuss, and time was working against us, which at this point was not unusual. Our little dungeon meeting with Ivar went as well as we could have expected. We knew he wouldn't give anything up without wanting something in return.

It is obvious we can't trust him, and he is most likely leading us into an ambush. One that hopefully we could get ourselves out of. Not to mention I am almost certain there are safeguards put in place to guard this artifact. The obstacles just kept stacking against us.

Kole, Rollo and I finished our meal as the sun began to set. I've been experiencing waves of nausea for the last couple of days now. I assumed it was residual from the fight I had with Kyut. I hadn't been pushed to that limit since the wasteland. My body is exhausted, and it is taking longer than usual to recover. Maybe my pride was more bruised than I thought.

We waited for the others in the main room of the longhouse to cast the vote. I was curious which side of the vote would sway the vampires, considering the cursed head portion of the prophecy. Any time I thought the Gods couldn't be any more cruel I remember what they have made all of us do in the name of their cause. How many decisions they have made to set this whirlwind of a life in motion?

Kare and Gio entered first. They moved sort of in sync, something only a woman's eye could see. It was subtle, like all of the vampires' movements were, but something was certainly different. They seemed closer. In what way I couldn't tell just yet, but something was between them… and judging it by what I walked in on not that long ago, I'm guessing it is of an even more intimate nature. My jaw tensed with the urge to tell Kole, but I owed Gio for saving my life. It wasn't my business to tell. They took their seats at the table.

"You two look rested," Kole called out to them both.

"What makes you say that? Do I not look rested all the time?" Kare spoke quickly.

"Um, no. I was just making conversation," Kole laughed, brushing off the outburst. "Gio, will Marcella be joining us?"

Before he could answer Marcella calmly came around the corner. She looked poised and perfect, as she always did. Nothing compared to what Rollo described. Her injuries were certainly a thing of the past, she looked like nothing had ever happened to her.

Rollo jumped out of his seat and ran over to her. They exchanged a whisper as she nodded her head with a smile. It was nice to see that nothing had changed between them despite Rollo witnessing her drain all those soldiers. I glanced her way and nodded; we were in a much better place given we shared a couple of battles together.

Everyone took their seats around the table. It was time to go over all the nonsense. Kole looked my way before standing up to address the room in an attempt to sell the vampires on trusting Ivar to lead us up the mountain.

"Now that we are all here, it's time to talk about what we need to do next." Eyes roamed from one person to the next.

"Is anyone going to say anything, or are you all going to waste your valuable years staring around the room?" Gio slouched back in his seat.

"There is not a very easy way to say this," Kole hesitated while Rollo scoffed under his breath.

"Someone needs to tell us what's going on," Kare spoke up. More silence followed. It was getting very frustrating. My all-powerful husband and king is speechless in front of a group. I thought I would never see the day.

The blowback from this could drive a wedge between us, but what could be worse than Delphi wiping us all out? There was no safety net for us this time around. We need to use what we have to get this done. Kole managed to find his voice.

"As you know, we need to continue our search for the artifact, but we don't know where to start. I have a plan, but I know you guys are not going to like it," he confessed under his breath.

"How will we know if we like it or not if you won't spit it out?" Gio retorted. I hate to admit it, but he has a point.

"We went to go see Ivar this morning," he blurted out. Marcella's body tensed at the mention of the name.

"Hopefully the vermin is dead. Certainly, he isn't worth all this hesitation," Gio muttered.

"Not exactly," Kole said cautiously. Rollo couldn't hide his discontent. The room seemed to shrink with all the tension. "He has agreed to help us find the artifact," Kole said it quickly and waited for the room to erupt. A low growl brewed at the back of Marcella's throat. She was not amused by the news.

"And why would we trust him? I don't think I need to remind you of everything that has transpired here," Gio yelled over the others.

"Trust me, I reminded him," Rollo added.

"As I told Rollo, I am not making this decision for any of you. I wanted to talk amongst ourselves and see if we can agree on what to do next," Kole explained calmly.

Rollo and Marcella could not muster up the strength to hide their hesitance, and no one could blame them after what Ivar put them through. Kare looked toward Gio, and again I could tell there was something different.

"He gives us the best chance to find the artifact in a timely fashion," I interrupted. "I don't trust him at all, but if he gives us a chance to not freeze to death searching in the mountains, I think it's a good move."

"And if it is a trap?" Marcella asked.

"If it's a trap, then we will do what we always do," Kole dropped his hand to his axe.

"As long as I get to kill him slowly, then I will join you," she nodded. Rollo glanced at her and nodded, which I assumed was a yes from him, as well.

"Let's take an official vote. I want to make sure we are all on the same page." Kole was speaking but Gio's laughter interrupted. "Was something I said amusing, Gio?"

"No, young King, it's what you're not saying that tickles my curiosity."

"Speak your mind," I spoke.

"You shared the prophecy with me, but I have been doing some research of my own on how to deal with my little spirit problem. One thing that remains constant in all the prophecies and stories is a certain ingredient to acquire this artifact." He wore a devilish grin that had the others confused, but we knew what he was alluding to.

"Spit it out, Gio! What are you trying to say?" Rollo barked out.

"The part you all have been avoiding since we started on this venture. The prophecy speaks of the cursed head. You remember that, right Kole? The part we haven't spoken about since you reappeared outside the caves." Kole looked at me with worry in his eyes, glancing over at Kare. "Now, up until the events in Alexandria, it was obvious who the cursed was." He took the liberty of waving toward himself. "But now things have changed pretty drastically, don't you think?" He said with that smug look on his face.

"Things have changed, Gio, but the mission remains the same," Kole said sternly.

Koel Alexander © 2024
Raven & Fire Series

"Can someone please explain to me what is going on? Does this have something to do with the parchment you had in your room back at the cave?" Kare asked.

"You want to share anything else you guys talked about that night in your room," I countered. It wasn't a smart move, but I was tired of Gio pointing his fingers.

Everyone in the room at this point was completely confused.

"Okay, what the hell is everyone talking about? Can we get back to the point please?!" Rollo shouted.

My glare burned a hole into Gio's head. If he is going to try to strong-arm us, I am going to push right back. He broke the stare and started pacing around the room, which was a victory for me. It was a small one, but a victory nonetheless.

"My point is that after the deal made by Kole and the transformation of Kare, and now Ivar. Shouldn't we be talking about which head it is referring to?" He emphasized, and if we are being truthful, he was right. "If the head isn't Ivar's, then what would be the next course of action? One thing for sure is that the head would have to be of some significance, which severely trims the options. I am the first of my kind. Kare and Ivar are the first children of royal blood to be cursed. So I assume you would be expecting me to lay down my life for the cause if it isn't Ivar. Or am I to believe you would allow Kare to be that sacrifice? Unfortunately, even though we sit here and vote, none of that has been clear," he remarked. I didn't have to be able to read minds to know that Kole had no intention of letting Kare sacrifice herself because I felt the same way. We just never felt the need to tell her or anyone else. It was out of the question.

"Kole?" Kare asked, waiting for an answer. "You remove my choice from me without even having a conversation." She sounded wounded and her brother's face matched, but it turned to stone just as quickly.

"She won't be giving her life for any of it," he said sternly. "We have done too much to preserve it."

"That is not for you to decide, brother! Regardless of what you think, I am not a little girl anymore!" she screamed.

"I am supposed to protect you no matter what. I will not be risking your life. Why are we even yelling about whether you get to live or die?" He dismissed her words.

"I didn't ask you to! I can take care of myself, and you know that." His shoulders tensed.

"You are my little sister, Kare. It's not an option for you," Kole said shifting the darkness inside him.

"I'm fucking immortal, Kole! You know what that means?" Pain spread across his face. "I will be forced to walk this world alone after all of you are gone. Don't lecture me on protection. My life is no more important than anyone else's sitting in this room," she stormed out of the room not waiting for a response.

The room was quiet again and I could not imagine what was running through Kole's head, but no one said a word. Kare was right, and in the pits of our stomachs we knew that. We would all wither and die and she would still be here.

"So, that got out of hand." I could only sigh in annoyance as Gio started to speak again.

"Do you feel good about yourself?" Kole asked angrily.

"If you think I brought that up for myself, then you are drastically mistaken." It took everything I had not to punch him directly in his smug face.

"I have done my own research on what we should be looking for, and I will only share it once we have reached the artifact," he gave a slight sarcastic bow and turned to leave.

Kole's body hardened. Anger, guilt, and sorrow all mixed and poured off him. He managed to push it all down. It wouldn't serve us any good right now.

"Everyone get some rest. Tomorrow, we head into the mountains." Kole stormed out of the room without another word.

37 – Why Am I So Different? - Kare

I don't understand it. Of all things, why would he remove my choice? I thought we had to come to an understanding. I am not the little girl from Lundr anymore. I am not the little girl that needs to be kept in the dark and protected. For the Gods' sake, I died and came back to life. I wasn't excited about being one of the cursed, but ultimately I knew if it was me then it would be my choice. To be stripped of that from my big brother felt worse than betrayal.

The moon hung high and bright in the sky tonight. It seemed like a giant beacon. I thought about what it meant to Gio, causing, though it did not make much sense, a tinge of jealousy to creep across my bones. The moon represented so much more for him. That moment we shared played in my head over and over. She released him to love again, but would I be the one who would have to contend with her forever? The thought of it all was so heavy. I could feel the pressure crushing my shoulders.

"Even before I spent time with you, I could tell you were strong," a soft voice resounded near me. Marcella walked slowly toward me. She was so naturally beautiful, as if she never had to try hard at all, even with the scar. She sat down next to me and we both glared up at the moon, most likely thinking the same exact thing I was.

"You created some giant shoes for me to fill." I hope she knew that I was being genuine. "Being second isn't all it's cracked up to be." She smiled, chuckling at the thought.

"The others can be kind of a handful."

"You have no idea," I implied.

"Oh, believe me I do. There is a life-sized pain in your ass named Veronica, I assume." She knew the answer already.

"I don't know what I did to make her so angry, but let's just say she is not my biggest fan."

"I heard that you handled yourself quite well. We respect strength, and sometimes the message is delivered... but sometimes others will need a little more persuasion," she confirmed and crossed her arms.

"You're saying that it is not over between us?" I asked.

"I've known her a long time and she has always been a nagging pet, begging for Gio's attention, which ironically makes her even more invisible in his eyes. She will challenge you again, that is for sure," she said rolling her eyes, clearly annoyed by Veronica as much as I am.

"Any advice?"

"Keep your circle small. Trust them, and never underestimate how immortality will turn others into monsters." She spoke softly, but her point was delivered all the same.

"Is that all the advice you got?" I muttered.

"For tonight, yes. Don't rush it, Kare. We have an eternity to talk about miserable things. This has been the most peace I have experienced in decades; I want to enjoy the now while I still have the chance." She lowered her head and smiled.

"Does your peace happen to be Rollo shaped?" I joked. If we weren't technically dead, I could swear that she was blushing.

"Rollo has been something I never thought I would find in this life, and if the Gods will it, I mean to hold on to him for as long as he will have me." Her entire mood lightened when she spoke about him.

I couldn't believe that Rollo would bring about this type of happiness for anyone, but I was so happy to see it. If anyone deserved happiness it was him. I haven't known Marcella long, but why shouldn't she enjoy the same?

"I'm happy for you," I responded. "No one in this world is more loyal, trust me." She smiled again and turned to head back into the cave. "You think we make it out of this thing in one piece?" I called out to her.

"I've lived for a long time, Kare, and fought many battles. Once you get to my age you stop wondering about such things. There is either tomorrow or nothing," she said. "And one more thing," she continued as she walked further away. "Give your brother a break. He is trying. Ruling is so much harder than you think, but I assume you have an idea given you are experiencing some of the hardships." I didn't say anything in response because I was not ready to let him off that easily.

Her ears must have been burning because Veronica came walking out of the cave and was heading straight toward me. My body tensed as she closed the distance. I knew it wasn't over, but I thought I had a little more time before we had any issues.

"What the fuck did you do to me?" Her fangs exposed.

"What are you talking about?" I was surprised by the accusation.

"Don't play stupid with me. During our fight in the cave you did something to me, and I want to know how," she snarled. I replayed the fight trying to pinpoint what Veronica could be talking about. I couldn't think of anything strange about it.

"You think I did something to you because you lost a fight? Please get over yourself, Veronica," I rolled my eyes.

"Bullshit, I don't know how you did it, but you forced me to yield," she pushed me, waking the monster in me. My fangs released themselves on instinct.

"If you mean you yielded so I wouldn't kill you, then yes you are right," I lowered my stance in case she wanted a round two.

"You were controlling me somehow. I would never and I mean never yield to a puppet like you." I tried to make sense of her words. How would I be able to control her?

"I don't know what you're talking about. Maybe you should get some rest since you are talking crazy. I'm the second and you yielded because you wanted to live, simple and plain."

"Fuck you, princess. I knew you weren't right for us and I'm going to make sure everyone knows how much of a freak you are," she turned her heels and marched back into the cave. I stood outside the cave in awe not really understanding what just happened.

"What the fuck?"

I was pushed out of my sleep the next night, the sun setting before I opened my eyes. It was so weird how I could feel the weight of the sun disappearing, almost like my subconscious knew that it was safe. I don't even remember falling asleep, but I somehow must have found my way back into the cave after that weird conversation with Veronica. What I wouldn't give for a bath, even though it didn't particularly do much for me now. The act alone was relaxing, but essentially unnecessary unless I found myself physically dirty.

Gio was sitting in the corner, sifting through multiple parchments. No doubt they were from his room back at Delphi's caves. Whatever he discovered in the pages he decided to horde from the others. I couldn't blame him. I thought we were all past keeping secrets considering everyone was to be considered equal rulers. I walked over to Gio and contemplated laying my hands on his shoulders. After the other night, I was not sure where we stood.

"Are you going to make a habit of spying on me," Gio spoke without looking up.

"I am not spying, I am politely looking over your shoulder to see what you are reading without telling you," I smiled.

"I was not aware you knew Latin," he jested.

"I am not familiar at all, but I could always learn," I shifted closer trying to check the tension between us. His body didn't respond at all. I'm not sure if that is a good or bad thing. Instead of overthinking, I decided to change the topic. "Are we going to be moving soon?"

"Yes. Just double-checking the text. I would hate to be in the mountains and get something wrong."

"Being stranded with me wouldn't be all that bad," I joked.

"Being stranded with you would be a blessing from the Gods," his fangs curled below his lips.

The comment sent a shiver down my spine. That did not help the tension at all. His mood shifted almost immediately, snuffing out the fire he had started deep in my gut.

"It's a shame that your brother didn't feel the need to respect you enough to tell you the full truth about what lies ahead of us. Now I have to be the bad guy, once again," I didn't have a response. I still can't believe Kole would look to minimize me.

"Forget Kole," I hated the words as soon as they came out of my mouth. "Are we any closer to knowing exactly what the prophecy means?" I quickly changed the subject.

"The problem is not really the prophecy but the seriousness of it. It is not foreign for the Gods to come up with a prophecy to deter you from the truth," he explained. "The cursed head could mean that we require an actual head, but it can be exaggerated to keep others away from the artifact altogether." his head twisted in curiosity. "Sometimes you work so hard trying to stop the prophecy that you end up doing exactly what they want."

"So how do we know?"

"We don't," he chuckled. "And I assume that's exactly how they want it. Either way, pack up, grab the others and let's get moving."

"Yes, your majesty," I joked.

38 – I'm Not Very Popular - Kole

The last couple of hours have not been my favorite. Rollo is annoyed with me. Octavia and I are on the mend, but given my history, I was one move away from being out of her favor. Gio thinks I'm dishonest, which is partly true, and worst of all Kare wants nothing to do with me. I've never seen her so hurt and she has never snapped at me like that, but I could not let her sacrifice herself. I was not going to be the one to take away yet another family member. I'm tired of it all, physically and mentally exhausted.

"Holding the world on your shoulders again, my king?" Octavia snuck up behind me.

"You know me so well."

"Don't put too much on yourself. Kare will forgive you, she just needs time. Remember you told me the same thing once," she spoke softly. "I almost killed her maker, and she forgave me."

"That is true," I smirked.

"This will blow over. Let's focus on finishing this so we can finally enjoy our lives." She pressed a kiss against my cheek.

"How did I get so lucky?" I grabbed her tight by the waist.

"Only the Gods know," she smiled.

Rollo appeared in the hallway, the sound of chains dragging along the stone floor reverberating off the walls, likely waking up the entire longhouse. He held Ivar by the collar and dragged him to the opening in the throne room. At least they managed to get him all cleaned up this time. I did not want to have to smell a garbage pile the entire trip into the mountains. Rollo threw Ivar to our feet.

"Feeling cooperative today, Ivar?" I leaned in closer as I spoke.

"As helpful as I can be, your majesty. Something tells me you're going to need me. You have never been as smart as you think you are," he chuckled right before Rollo laid his fist into the side of his head knocking him back to the floor.

"That looked like it hurt, Ivar. Any other jokes you want to tell," I asked. Ivar looked back and forth between me and Rollo and decided it was wise to hold his tongue so that his jaw would remain intact.

"Good decision, boy," Rollo rubbed the top of his head.

"Let's get going, Ivar."

The vampires waited at the top of the hill, a scowl spread across all their faces making it clear that they were still unhappy. It was clear that they stood behind their leader. Kare glanced our way quickly but there was not much exchanged between us. The guilt was like a gut punch.

Rollo passed Ivar over to a member of our company and walked over to Marcella. Her eyes flew to Ivar. The low growl in her throat vibrated as he walked past her. Seeing her abuser certainly didn't spark very good memories. There wasn't enough space for all of this tension. You could feel it in the air, but we needed to put all that behind us to get this done once and for all. I dove deep into the darkness, out of habit now at this point.

Periodically I would check everyone's aura, especially after Delphi managed to infiltrate bodies. I looked over to the vampires and saw the usual cold emptiness surrounding them. I would never get used to the lack of activity happening in their bodies but, to the human eye, you could not tell they were any different. Outside of the fangs of course.

Ivar had the seeping essence of the moon. It felt cold and dark, contained in the green mist from Delphi. Rollo's aura flickered with lightning splintering from his head to his feet. A storm was brewing, ready to be unleashed.

By my side, Octavia burned bright as usual, the fire of Rome igniting every limb. Her aura was entrancing, like watching a fire burn down a forest. My gaze wandered deeper, and again, only if I looked closely, there was a faint hint of a shadow hiding inside of her.

"You okay?" Octavia snapped me out of my focus. I shook my head to regain reality.

"I'm good, my love."

"Are you all ready to go?" Gio called from the top of the hill.

"Lead the way," I responded sternly. It didn't help with the tension, but we all turned and started our march up toward the mountain. I hadn't meant for my response to come off as sarcastic as it replayed in my head.

Koel Alexander © 2024
Raven & Fire Series

39 – Old & Cold - Octavia

Why, why, why did it always have to be so freaking cold? The Gods always hid the most important things in the worst parts of the world. Why didn't the Gods ever hide anything on a stranded island? You could take in some of the amazing weather while you risked your life. It feels like we have been walking for days, no closer to solving this nonsense. The fact that none of us were really speaking to each other made the journey seem even longer.

Kare and Gio snuck words to each other while walking ahead. If there was information to share it didn't look like we would be included. They were taking this way harder than any of us expected. Kare must have known no matter the cost we wouldn't even think of letting her sacrifice herself. It was not something Kole and I were even remotely prepared to do. Even thinking about it rubbed us both the wrong way. Especially since we have all grown so close.

A twinge of anger flared as I watch them snicker and whisper. The fire still rumbled whenever I was surrounded by the vampires, but freeing us from Midseliuem had required Mars to use all his power, and his influence over my emotions lessened severely.

"That must be an extraordinary conversation you are having with yourself," Kole spoke. I hadn't realized it was written all over my face.

"You should talk," I retorted.

"It's an ability we both share. I know you have held village meetings in your head." His shoulders rose and fell as he chuckled to himself.

Ivar's chains clanked ahead of us. Rollo trailed behind him, his hand never far from his hammer.

"How much further, Ivar?" Kole asked.

"Shouldn't be too long now. There is an abandoned structure built into the side of the mountain that should lead us to the tomb. Of course, it would be much quicker if you freed me from these chains," he held up his hands to our faces.

"Not a chance, traitor," Rollo countered. Ivar shrugged his shoulders and kept walking.

Another wave of nausea crept over me. It has been happening more frequently since we started our ascent up the mountain. Ivar's head spun back around towards me, his nostrils flaring awkwardly in my direction.

"What the hell are you looking at, Ivar?" His stare was uncomfortable like he was studying me.

"That is an interesting turn of events," he said under his breath.

"What nonsense are you speaking now?"

Koel Alexander © 2024
Raven & Fire Series

"Just another blight on this world," he spoke slowly before Rollo grabbed him and turned him forward. That was weird and cryptic, but that was Ivar.

The vampires up ahead had come to a stop at the ridge of the path, looking up to the sky. They were really looking at the gigantic mountain that caused us all to just stop and admire it. The forest grew at the base of it and the sculpted cliffside led up to the snow-covered tips. A clean cold breeze flowed through us as we examined the terrain. Kole and I walked to the front to see why we had come to a halt.

Kare and Gio were staring off the edge and still didn't acknowledge us as we came up behind them. Down the ridge, perfectly carved into the mountain, sat a massive stone door. What looked to be Norse runes were carved directly into the face of the door.

"I'm not an expert with runes but I would say that is what we should be looking for." Kole signaled for Rollo to bring Ivar to confirm.

"What does it say?" I asked Kole.

"It's not really words, it's more of a warning," his eyes turned pitch black, clearly tapping into the Odin sight.

"Anything else you can tell us?" Gio asked. Kole tilted his head to the side, I assume still trying to decipher the rune.

"Whatever it means, even the Gods weren't meant to be able to decipher it. I know that the warning is meant to deter anyone or anything from being here under the pane of death." His eyes returned to normal.

"So this is exactly where we need to be," Rollo said from behind us. Ivar nodded in approval.

"Okay, let's head down, and everyone keep your eyes peeled."

"Are you sure you don't want to release me? Whatever we run into, I could be of some help," Ivar attempted to make his case.

"Or you can try to kill us the first chance you get," I countered.

"All things are possible, princess," his evil smile was revolting.

"Shut up and walk," Rollo yelled.

"We will meet you down there," Gio spoke unexpectedly.

"The rest of you stay here and keep watch over the ridge just in case anything tries to sneak up on us," Kare spoke confidently.

Within a split second, they jumped directly up in the air with massive force. I ran to the edge on instinct, my eyes trying to find them in the sky. I watched Gio and Kare soar through the air before falling back down to the ground. A gasp in my throat escaped as they plummeted. There was no fear on their faces as they crashed into the ground right in front of the stone door and looked back up to the ridge where we all stood in shock.

"Listen, Gio is a dick, but that was awesome," Rollo joked.

"Can you do that too?" he asked Marcella. A smile spread across her face highlighting the deep scar on her cheek. She planted a kiss on Rollo's lips and jumped off the ridge, same as the others.

"Thor's beard, I love that woman," he said to himself.

"Whenever you all are done, can we get this over with?" Ivar muttered.

"Don't be in a rush to die, Ivar," Rollo glared at him.

"That wasn't necessarily my plan."

"I pray to the Gods that you have something up your sleeve so I can take your head off myself," Rollo said angrily. Ivar remained silent but his reaction hadn't given me any confidence on what I was dealing with.

"Let's go." Kole opened a portal and we all stepped through.

The stone door was almost three times our height, completely embedded into the mountain. The air was colder in this pocket, but the closer we got the wall gave off a sort of ominous presence. It almost seemed like a living thing pulling at my body. It fanned the flame inside me, willing me forward to what I would assume to be my death. The Gods sure knew how to hide things, but it would have been just as easy to create something that would push you away, not entice you closer.

"Do you feel that?" I asked Kole as my feet started to move toward the door without trying. I felt his arm grab mine, bringing me back to reality quickly.

"No, all I feel is retreat and despair. It feels like I'm not supposed to be here," he repeated.

"Surely you're not afraid of a little mystery, are you?" Ivar said curtly. Kole frowned and moved toward him.

"Why would I be afraid when you're going to be the first one through?" Ivar's face twisted in fear. "If you die at least that's one less thing I'll have to worry about," Kole shrugged.

"Any idea how to open it?" Rollo asked. Ivar looked up to the sky and remained silent. He wasn't in a helping mood.

"Well, Gio seems to be the closest to some answers. If we could put this tension behind us, then we can get this done," Kole said out loud.

Gio was standing in front of the door referring to the parchment he carried all the way here. He still had not said a word to us yet, and honestly, I was starting to get agitated. I get that he is upset, but how was this helpful in any way?

"I can feel the annoyance emanating off you," he spoke plainly as he scaled the marking on the door. I didn't have to guess, I already knew he was talking to me.

"I just think it would be easier if we could figure this out together."

"I bet that it would," he didn't look my way, just kept feeling the stone door. "Unfortunately, I'm not in the mood to work together," he pushed a part in the door. With a slight rumble on the side of the mountain, the giant doors slowly willed themselves open.

"The rest of you stay outside and guard the door. Anything tries to get in, kill it." Kare spoke with an authority to the rest of the vampires.

"I see you found the door no problem. Do you really plan on not telling us what could be inside," Kole stepped in front of Gio.

Koel Alexander © 2024
Raven & Fire Series

"Now why would I purposely lead you into danger and not inform you of the risk? Maybe I should remove your choice. I thought that was something friends didn't do, but I see that you recognize that the thought of it isn't exactly pleasant," he spoke coldly as they shared a long glance.

Kole didn't have much to say in response. We were not as close to a resolution on this as we thought we were.

"With that being said, I honestly do not know what is waiting for us, but it would be foolish for the Gods to leave this here without a certain level of protection."

We stepped through the door into a dark cavern. Water from the melting snow glazed the rocks above our heads. The sounds of the dripping created sort of an eerie setting. I could barely see anything in front of me. The vampires walked with confidence, not worrying about walking into anything dangerous or life-threatening. A perk that I would forever be jealous of. I lifted my hands and willed the flames to the surface. My hand was engulfed just enough so that I can see where I was walking.

"This place is ancient," Kole said.

"That it is, and under the right circumstances this would be amazing," Gio said.

"How about we just do what we have to do and get out of here?" Rollo interrupted.

"Well, Ivar, anything you want to say?" We all looked to him for the help that he was supposed to be giving. Up until this point he had upheld his silence. He was comfortable letting us fumble around the cavern.

"My father never took me here, I told you all that, but since I'm the only here with common sense... wouldn't it be smart to hide something you don't want to be found in the deepest part of the cavern?"

"Whenever you guys are done chatting, let's keep going. We need to find the tomb." Gio took the lead as we ventured deeper into the cavern that seemed almost endless.

How far into the mountain could this possibly go? It was endless, every turn stifled the hope of finding what we were looking for.

"Anyone know how long we should be walking?" Rollo interjected.

None of us responded because who would know the answer to that? Even Ivar was looking around wide-eyed. Just when we thought all hope was gone, the group ahead had finally come to a stop. We had finally reached the empty room in what we assumed was the back of the cavern. We filed in behind each other at the opening trying to make sense of what was before us.

The flame came alive, pulling me toward the center of the room. It was dark but I was sensing something. I took a step down ahead of the others, and when my feet touched the cavern room floor the torches on the wall lit up, one after another illuminating the giant tomb in the center.

"Very clever of them," Gio snorted.

"What do you mean?" I asked.

"This place hides an artifact that can trap a Roman oracle, but the location was only told to a Norse God. To make it even more complicated, only someone of Roman blood can sense the location. The means they have gone to protect this are more than extensive, but I am more worried than before," he said cautiously.

"And why is that?" Kole asked.

"Why does this still feel too easy," he perched his eyebrows.

"I wouldn't say this was easy, we still have no idea how to open this thing," I pointed to the gigantic golden tomb in the center of the room.

40 – Cursed Head - Kole

It felt like a horrible idea to say this was too easy, but I would never say the words out loud. Yes, we located this ancient tomb in a secret room deep inside a mountain without pulling out a weapon. Now we were almost in possession of the artifact. An artifact that was kept from the Gods themselves. He's right. This was the definition of too easy.

The tomb took up most of the space in the room. Power danced along the golden exterior, enough that it pulsated throughout the room.

"You feel that?" I asked the others.

"Yes," they answered in unison.

"I don't feel anything," Gio muttered.

"Probably because you're dead," Rollo joked, but he didn't laugh too hard when Marcella shot him a glare.

"It's powered by the Gods, so no surprise that we can feel it," I answered.

"That's strange because I can feel it too," Kare brushed past all of us towards the tomb.

"Really?" Gio asked.

"Yes, I can feel it. The pull is slight but it's there," she kept walking toward the tomb.

"Fascinating!" Gio said under his breath. Kare's shoulders tensed as her eyes shot back through the doorway.

"Do you see something?" I asked.

"No, but do you guys hear that?" She tilted her head toward the doorway, listening carefully.

"I don't hear anything," Rollo joined in.

"Sounds like footsteps, lots of them," her eyes widened as she turned back toward us.

"Where is Ivar?" Terror welled in my chest.

I had completely forgotten about our prisoner once we found the tomb. The others looked around the room, but we couldn't see anything. All that was here was the tomb.

"He couldn't have gotten far!" I yelled.

"There are more footsteps, much more now," Gio spoke. A low maniacal chuckle came from the entranceway that got all of our attention. I knew it was Ivar, and by the sound of it he was still chained up or a giant wolf would be trying to kill us.

"Show yourself, you mutt," Rollo yelled with his hand on his hammer.

"I have no issue showing myself, you dimwit," Ivar walked back into the room still wearing his chains.

"You're still in chains, what could be so funny?" I asked.

"I wouldn't worry about the chains, my friend. Maybe you should worry about the army that will be flooding this cave any moment now."

"He betrayed us, what a surprise," Marcella said sarcastically.

"I am what I am, vampire. The best part is I can kill you all and take the artifact for myself. Not only will I finally be rid of you, I'll be in control of that spirit. I'll be the most powerful being in this world. A God in my own right," he proclaimed.

"You are the dumbest smart person I've ever met," Gio sighed.

"Only a human can wield the artifact, you idiot, and judging by the fur and the long teeth, you are far from that." Ivar stood silently, but the smile never disappeared.

I want to say the betrayal was surprising, but it was almost expected. The mystery was what kind of army could he have summoned from inside a cage.

"Kyut," I said under my breath. Octavia turned to me as the realization struck us both.

"See, this is why you leave no survivors," Ivar chuckled.

"So, what's the plan?" Octavia asked.

"We need to know how many men Kyut has managed to bring and then we need to address how we are going to open the tomb," I said.

"Jordan!" Kare yelled his name at the top of her lungs, and in seconds he appeared in the cave next to us panting, his fangs covered in blood.

"Odin's beard!" He startled even her.

Koel Alexander © 2024
Raven & Fire Series

"Army outside, led by your super evil brother," Jordan explained, still panting.

"Yes, we know that. How many men?" she questioned.

"I'm not sure, they came from nowhere. We didn't even hear them coming. It was like one moment we were alone, then the next they just appeared," he ranted.

"Jordan! Please relax and tell me how many," she tried to calm him down to get an answer.

"Forty, maybe fifty men."

"Can you hold them off for us?"

"Of course we can, just don't take too long." He was gone in an instant.

"Okay, while they hold them off, can we please try to figure out how to open this thing?" she turned back to us. "Not too obvious or obtuse, but I'm not seeing where a head would go to open this." I walked around the tomb looking for anything.

"Anything in your text suggest what we need to do next, Gio?" I asked.

"Nothing, yet there is a part of a translation that has me a bit confused. I've been trying to sort it out since we arrived."

"Well, spit it out. Maybe we can help," Octavia interrupted. Gio paused and looked at us both with apprehension.

"Seriously, now is not the time to be shy. We are kind of pressed for time," Rollo joined in.

"The cursed head," he repeated.

"Yes, we know that part," Octavia said.

"I'm aware, but the findings in the text never point toward any type of body part being required."

"I'm still not following," Rollo chimed in.

"The prophecy never meant the body part," Kare said under her breath. "The head of the cursed was never an actual head. Gio told me that sometimes prophecies are written in a literal sense to throw you off. What if this is one of those moments?" she questioned.

"You mean what if the head of the cursed is a code word for something else," Octavia asked.

"Not a code word, the same word but a different meaning," I added.

"Exactly. The head doesn't have to be a physical head, it could mean the front, the beginning, or it could mean the leader is the only one who can open it." Gio looked to us all.

"Well, that narrows this down. The only cursed leaders are you, and…" we all turned to the doorway where Ivar stood, but the smile on his face had dwindled to real concern.

"You don't seem to have nearly as much mirth about you now, my old friend. How about you come over here so we can have a little chat?" I walked over to him and grabbed him by his chains. Ivar fought against my grip.

"Maybe we need to think this through a little further before we start removing heads," he said nervously.

"We should kill you for betraying us," Rollo countered. Ivar decided that silence was his best option.

"As much as I agree with Rollo, I think we need to hold off on killing him for now. As you can tell, nothing is clear at the time being. This entire time we thought we would need to sacrifice someone to get the artifact, but thanks to Gio we realize that isn't what the prophecy meant."

"So, this is where you tell me for the second time I'm not allowed to kill him," Rollo growled.

"I think that's what the prophecy wants us to do. This was never supposed to be easy to find. Think about how much had to happen to get us here in the first place." They all looked around toward each other. "We had to meet Gio, Odin had to trick me into taking the throne and sparing Ivar, and the deal had to be made that turned Ivar into a whatever he is. Do you think all of that has led us here to just chop off his head and be done with it? There must be more to it." I explained.

"Okay, I understand all of that, but we are a little short on time now to reflect. What do you suggest we do?" Kare asked.

"I think we do the opposite of what is expected. I think Ivar or Gio has to willingly try to open it and retrieve the artifact."

"And you thought it was too easy before. That seems like the easiest possible outcome," Octavia said.

"Not necessarily," Gio interrupted. "This will only be easy if I am the one to open it. While it is poetic that Delphi would be the orchestrator of her own demise, if it is not me, our fate rests in the willing hands of this dog. I mean that literally and figuratively," he pointed to Ivar. Nothing, and I mean nothing, was ever simple.

"Figure it out. I'm going to help the others," Kare vanished before we could protest.

41 – What a Surprise - Rollo

"So, where should we start?" I asked, ready to be done with this.

"I don't know, but can you please hurry? I can't tell how the vampires are doing out there," Marcella chimed in.

This whole thing was getting frustrating. We spent so much time talking and thinking, my brain is spinning. I was tempted to just go outside with the vampires to get some action. The only thing keeping me here was the mistrust I held for Ivar, and if anyone was going to kill him it would be me or Marcella. If the Gods meant for Gio to open this stupid thing, killing Ivar was exactly what I was going to do.

Gio grabbed the tomb by the side and lifted with what seemed like all his strength. We all held our breath for what I felt was an eternity, but the lid on the tomb never budged once.

"Performance issues, Gio?" I joked.

"Sometimes it's just not your day I guess, Rollo. Hopefully Marcella never has to experience that," his smile spread wider and mine shrunk off my face. I'm not sure I've ever felt myself turning red from embarrassment. Gio continued to struggle trying to lift the cover, but it stood as still as before.

"That went about as expected," Octavia said behind me.

"Who is going to convince the fur ball to open this for us?" Gio asked, brushing the dirt from his hands.

Ivar held up his hands waiting for us to release him. His every breath annoyed me. How much more peaceful would this life be if he just wasn't in the world anymore?

"I assure you all, you won't need to convince me. I am surprised I was the one the prophecy was speaking of, but I had my suspicions. I will open this tomb and take the artifact for myself, as I planned," he smiled.

"And what makes you think we are going to let you live long enough to steal away with it after you open the tomb?" Kole moved forward.

A voice came from around the corner grabbing our attention.

"Because, brother, unless you want me to drive this wood into both of their hearts, you're going to let us get the artifact and make our way out of here untouched." Out of the darkness, Kyut came into view.

He dragged Kare and the other vampire that warned us earlier into view. Something was wrong. The woman holding her was a vampire herself. Had she switched sides?

"Kyut, what the fuck are you doing?" I motioned toward him, my hand hovering over my hammer.

"I wouldn't come any closer, Rollo. One move and they are both gone forever." Kole was fuming, the darkness almost forcing all of us out of the room.

"Kyut, she is the only reason I didn't just kill you the minute I saw you. She wanted to see if there was anything left in your soul, and this is how you repay her! Your fucking blood!" Kole moved closer and the vampire moved the wood closer to her chest.

"She is not my blood anymore! You made sure of that when you let her sacrifice herself for that blood-drinking monster." Kyut pointed to Gio.

Gio's fangs were dripping, waiting to rip something apart as he never took his eye off the girl vampire holding Kare.

"Veronica, what is the meaning of this? She is my second. Release her now!" The command washed over her, but she did nothing. "How is that possible? You must obey your maker." Gio looked surprised.

"Something has changed. Whatever it is, I can't explain, but for once I feel free. I don't feel the weight to obey you anymore. Maybe this is payback for overlooking me for all these years in favor of this Norse pet you wanted so badly." She turned her attention back to Kare. "And if try to get in my head like you did before, princess, you are dead. I promise you. So keep your mouth shut!" Gio looked to Marcella who was just as confused as we all were.

"The pleasantries have been great, but if you could help Ivar with the chains so we can get on our way," Kyut spoke very coyly.

Koel Alexander © 2024
Raven & Fire Series

Ivar looked over toward me and raised his hands again. My eyes shot over to Kole who was still glaring down at his brother, Gio doing the same to Veronica. I always thought Gio controlled all the vampires. How has one managed to escape from under his thumb?

"We don't have all day for you to search that empty brain of yours, Rollo. Release me from the chains," Ivar said impatiently.

Giving him what he wanted just flooded my memory with everything that he has done and taken from us. Even if it meant my death, I would gladly kill him and die in the process. My life would be worth seeing him rot at the gates of Valhalla, never to enter. Unfortunately, my life wasn't the only one in the balance. I couldn't afford to risk all the others.

"Let's go, Rollo," Kyut yelled.

Marcella grabbed the chains and snapped them off in one motion.

"Good girl," Ivar winked.

He walked over to the tomb and began to lift. His arms tensed and his feet sunk deeper into the dirt as he tried to remove the cover of the tomb. For Gio, it never even budged but the cover started to shift under his hands as his claws protruded to scrape the surface.

Kole and Gio remained still. Neither of them cared about what Ivar was doing. They never peeled their eyes off Kare.

"Veronica, listen to me," Kare tried to speak.

"I told you not to speak. I won't allow you to do what you did before. Stay the fuck out of my head or this cave is going to be the last thing you see," she pressed the wood against her chest.

Kole inched forward some more only to be stopped by the sound of the giant tomb cover slamming onto the floor. Mist poured from the opening as Ivar searched for what we should be looking for. None of us even know what the artifact looks like.

"Quickly now, Ivar. I don't have all day," Kyut spoke. I peered over his shoulder as he lifted the golden brace out of the coffin and held it in the palm of his hand.

Koel Alexander © 2024
Raven & Fire Series

42 – I Really Hate Your Brother - Octavia

The artifact glowed intensely in his hand, illuminating the cave almost blinding us all. The power pouring off it all but assured us that it was what we have been looking for. The brace was designed to slip over the wearer's wrist. The straps were gold with Latin inscriptions pressed into the siding.

My Latin wasn't perfect, but it looked like a symbol of confinement. A perfect prison for a rogue spirit. The end of this story was closer than it has ever been, but another obstacle blocked our path as usual. My inability to put Kyut down had us in this mess, and now he was going to get away again.

"Now that we have what we need, let us move on to the next phase of the plan," Ivar walked past us preparing to hand over the brace to Kyut. I didn't have time to react before Kole grabbed his axe and threw it directly at Kyut's head, hoping to end this right here and now. Veronica acted quicker and pushed Kare into the path of the axe. It was going to slam directly into her skull, but Kyut reached out his hands as his eyes went pitch black and stopped the axe right before it hit its intended target.

"Really, brother? Do you think I wasn't expecting you to try and weasel your way out of this with a cheap shot? Now, before you get any other ideas, if you attack me again, I will be forced to defend myself, most likely ruining my concentration. Then your beloved axe will be buried in our sister's skull. Is that what you want?" He smiled. Kare fought against his grip, but he was too strong, even for her.

"Let her go!" Gio growled.

"Guys, it's okay. Do not hurt yourselves for me," Kare forced out the words from under Kyut's grip. "I will be fine, trust me."

"Yes, brother, she will be fine. We will send our regards from Delphi," Kyut turned to walk out of the cavern, but paused and brought his attention back to us. "There is only one problem. I did say I wanted to leave untouched, and since you don't know how to follow instructions, brother, I think you need to learn a little lesson on consequences. You know, cause and effect," Kyut eyes returned to normal. His powers faded and the axe that Kole threw was released and it buried itself directly into Kare's skull.

The sound of her skull smashing under the impact was devastating. Her body fell to the floor and we all froze in disbelief. He had finally lost anything that would make him remotely redeemable. If it is the last thing I do, I am going to rip his heart from his chest.

Koel Alexander © 2024
Raven & Fire Series

The flames erupted from my hands without me even trying and I reached for my daggers to cut out his heart, but I ran into two bodies holding me in place. Kole and Rollo stood before me using all their strength to hold me back.

"Let me go!" I screamed, seeing nothing but red and hearing the war drums pound away inside my head.

"Let me go now!" They both held me and said nothing as I fought their grips. I needed him dead. I needed to feel his life fade from his body by my hand. I was owed that. The Gods owe me that.

"Kole, Rollo, let me go!" I protested again.

"Octavia, stop!" Kole spoke firmly. "Not now, please calm yourself."

"Calm!?" I couldn't believe my ears. "You want me to be calm with this lunatic? No, he is going in the dirt," I tried to get past them again to no avail.

"Look, Octavia," Rollo said.

Kyut was hovering over Kare's body, the wood piercing her skin threatening to puncture her heart and take her away from us forever. I looked up to Kole and tears poured from his eyes. More pain, more anguish, reliving the possibility of losing his sister again. The drums subsided as I realized I was becoming more of a danger than helping.

"That is more like it. She will be much easier to deal with knocked out anyway." He ripped the axe from her head, and she already began to slowly heal.

"Would you like your axe back, brother?" He extended the handle to Kole and was met with a death stare from all of us. "Okay, I guess not. We will be on our way. Needless to say, if we are followed, she and her friend here will die. I appreciate you finding this for me." Kyut crunched something in his hand, same as before, and green mist whisked all of them away from the doorway of the room.

We all stood in disbelief. Not only were we fooled into an ambush, one that we expected, Kyut still managed to gain the upper hand on five of the strongest people to ever walk in this world.

"We need to go, now," Kole grabbed his axe and made his way to the door.

43 – The Keeper - Kole

I was going to rip them both apart, piece by piece. I was going to open a portal to oblivion and drop them off there to never be seen again. I was going to make them both regret the day they ever took a breath in this world. I was seething. I could barely think straight as I moved my way back through the cave. I was going to make the world forget they ever existed in the first place. I was going to…. the cave rumbled slightly under our feet.

"What was that?" Rollo asked. The rumble came again followed by an unnatural sound.

"Do you hear that?" Marcella turned to Gio who had been stuck in his head ever since his vampire pet managed to disobey him.

"Something is coming," he said. "We need to move now!" Adrenaline already pumping, we picked up the pace, running to the exit.

The cave rumbled more as the walls vibrated. Something big was moving and it was going to take the entire thing down.

Octavia was on my heels as the others picked up the pace. We needed to get out of here before whatever is coming for us decided to bury us under a mountain full of rocks.

The ground underneath us began to shake violently. We were tripping over each other trying to get to the entrance of the cave. The moonlight was shining, giving us a pathway to an exit. The rumbling behind us turned into more of a growl, but still there was nothing that I could see. I reached for the darkness to track the aura of whatever was chasing us. Maybe I could make some sense of this, but what I saw just confused me even more. It was a bright golden aura, so massive it was blinding.

"What do you see?" Octavia asked.

"Nothing good," I answered quickly. "It must have woken up once the artifact was taken, but I do not want to stay here and see what it wants with us."

"It's here!" Marcella screamed.

Before my eyes could correct, I was in awe of what I was looking at. A massive beast was squeezing its way out of the entrance. It was horrifying and intriguing all at the same time.

"What the hell is that?!" Gio scanned the beast from head to toe, or should I say from head to tail. The beast had the head of a lion. Sitting on its back I could swear was the head of a goat, though I could be wrong. It has white and gold wings like an eagle, and the tail is the long, black head of a serpent.

"It's a chimera," Octavia said under her breath.

"A chi what?" Rollo questioned, reaching for his hammer.

"I honestly wasn't sure if they existed. We were told about it in bedtime stories. It was a scary story for children." She stared at the beast as he reared its giant head straight up. The lion's mane is a thick golden brown. It stood almost as tall as a building and let out a stream of fire straight into the sky.

"Are you kidding me? This thing breathes fire too?" Rollo yelled.

The beast shook dust and rubble off its fur and spread its wings that were so vast it almost blotted out the moon. We all reached for our weapons, because what else would you do staring this thing in the face?

"The humans seem to be on edge." I thought I was losing my mind, but I think the lion's head spoke to the goat's head.

"Did that thing just?" Rollo asks.

"Yes, I saw it too," Octavia answered.

"And it speaks?"

"Apparently."

"The humans usually are, and I understand the stories tend to embellish a little bit," the goat head spoke back.

I looked over to the others because I needed to make sure this was happening.

"Honestly, why am I even surprised at this point?" Gio stood back.

"From one monster to another, I promise you we mean no harm to you humans, as long as you return what was taken," the lion head spoke.

"Excuse me, sorry Mr. Chimera, but do you have a name?" Rollo asked.

"I've had many names over the years, too many to recount. How about you call me the keeper? I can feel the quiet storm inside you. You are quite powerful. All of you are pulsating power, the blessings have been flowing while we slept." He was speaking to himself again.

I grew uneasy the longer the conversation went on. I needed to get to Kare. I wanted to get to the bottom of this as quickly as possible so we could move on.

"What do you mean return what was taken?" I asked.

"The tomb inside was our responsibility to guard. In hindsight, we didn't expect centuries to go by before someone came looking for it. Time petrified us in the cave, but the power of the artifact awakened us. We can sense though that no one in your party is carrying it." The keeper flapped his wings before tucking them into his side. The serpent head peered over the top.

"We apologize for seeking out the artifact, but Delphi plots to wipe us all out. We need it to save our world," I spoke.

"Your world is such a short-sighted term, dark one. This world you speak of, no matter what transpires, will be here when this is all said and done. The Gods will play their games and the pieces will fall into play once again, but we can sense the good in all of you, so I am here to offer a deal first."

"Fuck me," Rollo said out loud. "Why is it always a deal? Every single time," I looked toward Gio, then back to Octavia.

I was all too familiar with being in this position. One that I was beginning to despise, but this was my destiny. No sense in fighting it now.

Koel Alexander © 2024
Raven & Fire Series

"It is our charge to rip you apart until we get the artifact back," the snake head spoke aggressively.

"We would love your help in getting it back. Having you on our team would guarantee victory. A mangy dog versus a chimera, how could we lose?" Rollo boasted.

"I am unable to leave this place," the keeper took the wind from our sails.

"Wait, if you can't leave, why would we even stay here to help? We could leave right now and you wouldn't be able to stop us," I said.

"You could try, dark one, but I wouldn't," the serpent head spoke again.

I grabbed the darkness and opened a portal back home. The portal opened behind us, but I felt an enormous strain to keep my focus. When I looked into the portal it would not let me lock in a destination, no matter how hard I tried. I heard the keeper spread his wings and let out a roar, and in an instant the darkness was buried and the portal snapped shut.

"What the hell was that?" I questioned myself. I looked over to Rollo and Octavia, and without speaking they willed their powers to the surface. The flames erupted from Octavia's hands but I could see she was straining immensely to keep them lit. Rollo was having the same problem. He usually controlled the element with ease but the lightning was erratic and unpredictable. The chimera roared again, and their powers were doused instantly, same as mine.

"You see, dark one, you will not be going anywhere. Now would you like to hear my deal or are we going to have to kill all of you?" The beast waited for a response.

"Fine," I surrendered.

"It's quite simple, really. You retrieve the artifact for us and bring it back here, and all will be forgiven," the goat head spoke.

"And if we plan to use it to trap a spirit?" Octavia asked.

"Then you bring the body the spirit is trapped in back, and we will place it in the tomb." We exchanged glances, all thinking the same thing. It seemed all too easy.

"What is the catch?" Gio beat me to the question.

"You have one rotation of the moon," the serpent spoke.

"One rotation of the moon," Gio repeated sarcastically.

"And if you let us go and we don't come back?" I asked.

The beast didn't answer, he only looked up and roared once again. A piece of dark stream left me, a bright one left Rollo. Octavia and the vampires stood untouched.

"What the hell was that, man?" Rollo exclaimed.

"I'm answering your question. I now possess a piece of both of your souls. Once you return with the artifact, I will make you whole."

"How am I to fight the biggest fight of my life with part of my soul?" I asked angrily.

"We assure you that it will not affect your strength or abilities. If anything, you should be thanking us. With less of your soul, you may be able to do what you need to do without remorse," the lion head licked his enormous paw.

"But be warned, without this piece of yourself, over time you will become tormented, and the search to complete yourself will drive you mad," the goat head issued the threat as calmly as possible.

"I don't say it often, but I am glad to be dead right now," Gio interrupted.

"Vampire, do not think I will not find a way to seek retribution if you attempt to betray me," the serpent sneered. Gio raised his hands in defeat.

"Now go. Your time begins at first light. May the Gods be with you." We all turned to walk, but Octavia remained.

"Why did you not take a piece of me? Is it some kind of Roman loyalty?" she asked sarcastically.

"Of course not. We would never seek to put you at risk in your current condition," the lion's words confused us all. What condition would he be talking about?

"What do you mean condition?" she asked.

"We would not want to put the little one in danger. Even though it is so early, your body and soul need to remain intact in order to nourish that life inside you." The lion's words froze us all.

"Congratulations, by the way," the serpent's head butted in. We locked eyes, not able to find a single word.

"Holy shit! I'm going to be an uncle," Rollo yelled and hugged us both as we got lost in each other's eyes, still searching for the words, but nothing seemed right. So, we settled on what we always do.

"No matter what." We mouthed the words in unison as Rollo squeezed the air from our bodies.

Koel Alexander © 2024
Raven & Fire Series